PURCHASED POWER

PURCHASED POWER

a novel

DENNIS SHEEHAN

Tate Publishing & *Enterprises*

Purchased Power
Copyright © 2010 by Dennis Sheehan. All rights reserved.

No part of this publication may be reproduced, stored in a retrieval system or transmitted in any way by any means, electronic, mechanical, photocopy, recording or otherwise without the prior permission of the author except as provided by USA copyright law.

This novel is a work of fiction. Any resemblance to real people, incidents, names or descriptions is purley coincidental.

The opinions expressed by the author are not necessarily those of Tate Publishing, LLC.

Published by Tate Publishing & Enterprises, LLC
127 E. Trade Center Terrace | Mustang, Oklahoma 73064 USA
1.888.361.9473 | www.tatepublishing.com

Tate Publishing is committed to excellence in the publishing industry. The company reflects the philosophy established by the founders, based on Psalm 68:11,
"The Lord gave the word and great was the company of those who published it."

Book design copyright © 2010 by Tate Publishing, LLC. All rights reserved.
Cover design by Kandi Evans
Interior design by Chris Webb

Published in the United States of America
ISBN: 978-1-61663-215-1
1. Fiction / Suspense   2. Fiction / Espionage
10.03.31

DEDICATION

This book is dedicated to my wife, Mary Jane, and my children, Dennis, Kevin, Bill and Erin. Their steadfast support enabled me to live the life I have. I thank God every day for the wonderful family I have and the richness our relationship has brought to my life.

PROLOGUE

It has been said that power corrupts. This being true, what was not said is that power is the currency of governments. This is a story of a man who, through no fault of his own, gets caught in the middle of international politics and the corruption it causes. He sees first hand the lengths these people will go to in order to protect their way of life and their hold on power.

Power is based on greed and enabled by human weakness. It is a way of life that has been recorded throughout history; it's built and destroyed empires. Wherever people have wanted to better themselves, there has always been justification for wrongdoing. Power has always been sought and is documented in the Bible, Koran, and goes back as far as the Egyptian hieroglyphics. Since the beginning of time, people have been on a quest for power. The smart, the strong, and the corrupt have gotten it, the weak suffered through its realities.

In the past, power was achieved in many ways: through greed and avarice, military force, or by cunning. Today it's achieved with money and politics.

This story is a look at modern-day power and its effects, as seen through one man's eyes. He sees firsthand how this quest for power corrupts and degrades and how men can be made to do anything in the name of government. He sees how innocent people are thrown to the wolves every day in the name of the common good.

John Moore is an upper middle-class American living the good life in California. A successful businessman, a good friend, and husband, he lived by the rules and enjoyed the fruits of his labor until, at the age of fifty two, he found himself in a situation that forever changed his life. This is a chronicle of those events.

CHAPTER 1

His problems were behind him, but his future was uncertain. John Moore was two days out of Babelthuap Palau; fifty-nine days since he sailed out of San Francisco. He was quickly coming to a crucial juncture in his voyage. He studied his charts, making constant references to his electronic equipment. He figured that he had sailed 5,751 nautical miles and still had 1,739 miles to his destination, Hong Kong. Looking from his charts to the global positing system, he was six degrees north and 134.30 degrees east latitude. He had sailed about 230 miles since yesterday and would be reaching the barrier reef in about an hour. He realized he had only two narrow channels through the reef, and after reviewing the settings on the autopilot, he saw that he should be nearing the larger one.

It was April 6, and John knew he only had thirty days before typhoon season. The southern route would be safer. There were more landfalls, and if the season started early, he could pull into a safe harbor. According to his calculations, this would add five weeks to the trip, even in good weather. *I'm going to sail due west. After all, this entire trip was a risk, so why change course now?*

John Moore was a brilliant boat designer, and he was, one might say, a man's man. John had just turned fifty-two but, being fit and ruggedly good-looking, looked younger. He was socially polished, level headed, and successful.

If that woman didn't do what she had, I would still have my life. What the hell am I doing here? John thought to himself.

John became aware that the water was becoming more turbulent; as he looked up from his chart table, he yelled aloud, "There it is!" The waves were breaking forty feet high along the reef. He climbed up the mast to the lower lookout and peered through his field glasses. It only took a minute to locate the channel. He climbed down to the cockpit, turned off the autopilot, and took the wheel. Steering through the rough channel, he thought the boat handled well, and it brought back memories of his father steering through some rough water. It was a pleasant thought, but John quickly brought his conscious mind back to the situation at hand. As he cleared the reef, his adrenalin rushing, he looked out the vast expanse of water. *The next land I'll hit will be Hong Kong.*

He stayed at the helm for about six hours to make certain he was well clear of the reef. Though he was hungry and tired, he checked all the lines and set the autopilot due west before going below. He rested a few minutes and had a quick dinner of fish and canned vegetables. He then grabbed a beer and went back up on deck.

The seas were calm. A brisk, warm breeze came from the south, and he was making, he thought, about twelve knots. As he drank his beer, he studied the sky; it was almost a deep purple with the stars blinking like neon lights. He located the star formations and could understand how ancient astronomers could depict the constellations as living things. Minutes slipped into hours and eventually sleep.

When he woke, he was still on deck, the sun shinning but the sails hanging lifeless. He had fallen asleep sitting on the bench in the cockpit and both his legs and arms were stiff. He had to stretch and walk a little to get the blood flowing before he could even consider breakfast. After a solid half hour of exercise, he climbed below, made a cup of coffee, grabbed his sextant, and went back up on deck. John was a careful man. Even though he had very sophisticated electronics, he still liked to take his positions manually, just to be safe. He compared his readings with the GPS and decided he could make a steady eight knots for twelve hours under power without getting dangerously low on fuel. After checking the engine oil levels and setting the autopilot, John decided to spend the day cleaning and doing repairs.

Although the sea was as flat as a mirror, it was full of life, and

John enjoyed the quick diversions of flying fish and the occasional whale or dolphin. It made his work and time pass quickly.

Following a light lunch, John decided to take a swim. He rigged the boson's chair and hung off the side. As the boat sailed forward, he dunked himself; the spray was a relief in the afternoon heat. He lowered himself into the wake until he was immersed to his waist with his back riding on the waves. It was so relaxing he almost drifted off to sleep, but suddenly he sensed danger.

"Oh crap!" he screamed as he looked up at the approaching fins. He yanked at the rope, but the pressure of the water was holding him down. The fins were only twenty to thirty feet away. Thinking quickly, he spun himself around to break the pressure, grabbed onto the boat's rail, pulled as hard as he could on the line, and flipped onto the deck. Safe on board, he looked back on at least twenty sharks following the boat. *This is the end of my swimming until I reach Hong Kong.*

That night, John decided to sleep on deck. He loved being at sea, especially when he had the opportunity to relax and study the night sky. It was such a peaceful way to go to sleep.

John awoke to the sound of whales. The sound was a cross between a foghorn and a bass drum. He sat up with a jolt when the spray hit him, he had realized the whale was right next to the boat. He stared into its large eye. The whale was as long as the boat. He was a bit apprehensive but knew he was in no real danger, and besides, John was happy for the company.

"Well, Shamu, do you want a cup of coffee? I'm getting one," he asked rhetorically.

He went down to the galley and returned with a cup of coffee. Back up on deck and realized that he had been sailing under power all day and night. After studying the gauges, he realized he had gone over safe fuel usage.

John went below and shut off the engine, and the boat almost stopped dead. He climbed back up on deck and ran up the sails, but they did not even flutter.

He sat becalmed for the next three days and was dangerously behind schedule; he knew he was now too close to the start of the typhoon season. *At fifty-two years old, how the hell did I get myself in this position?* he mused, but he knew why. It was nothing he had done. He had to get out of San Francisco without leaving a trace. His mind drifted, and he thought of what brought him here.

Peter and I worked our asses off, and the company had become one of the most successful yacht-building companies in the United States. Except for the death of my parents, I've had a great life, until that whore; that unfaithful woman turned it upside down.

Now, at his age, he was about to start life over and was just as apprehensive as that day he walked into the dorm room on his first day of college.

On the day he graduated from Sausalito High School, he heard "John Moore," and as he walked up to the stage, he glanced over to see the proud look on his parents' faces as they admired their son who was graduating with honors.

His father had been especially pleased because John had received a full football scholarship to the University of California Poly Tech. John's father, an architect, was realizing his dream; he had always hoped John would follow in his footsteps.

The Moore's were an upper middle-class family that spent every available moment together pursuing their love of sailing. John remembered his first sailfish, which was a gift from his parents on his sixth birthday. By the time he was ten, he was already an accomplished sailor. At eleven, he was the youngest member of their yacht club ever to win the regatta, which was the club's big annual event.

John's father grew up in Sausalito and had joined the navy at the beginning of the Korean War. His father earned the rank of lieutenant in a year and made captain by the end of his six-year stint. John thought he never remembered his mother complaining about his father being away for almost the first five years of John's life. John remembered that during that time they had moved to the naval depot at San Diego. His mother was always busy volunteering and helping the wives of the men who were in Korea. Shortly after the war, they had moved back to Sausalito and John's father had resumed his career as an architect.

John thought how much he missed his parents. He recalled his father's boat, a thirty-seven-foot sailing yacht called the *Soul Mate*. Every night after dinner they would take her out, often with John at the helm. Although it always made his mother a bit nervous, his father knew John had the skill and intelligence to handle the boat.

Suddenly there was a loud thud and the boat jerked forward. He ran to the bow. He gasped to himself.

"What the hell is that?"

A giant eye was peering up at him. A creature had attached itself to the boat. John could not make out its overall shape, but it seemed to be about seventy feet in length. He ran below to inspect, but there was no damage. He climbed back on deck with his encyclopedia of marine life in hand, and soon identified the animal as a whale shark.

He read that they occasionally attach themselves to boats, apparently to clean parasites from their bodies. Although he did not think he was in too much danger, he went to the gun chest and got his Winchester 30 odd 6, just in case. He watched the creature for several hours but realized that the huge beast was actually pushing the boat forward at an amazing speed, creating a welcomed breeze. After being becalmed for days, it was good to be moving again, albeit a bit frightening.

After some time, John relaxed, and his thoughts drifted back to the summer after high school graduation. His parents had taken the summer off, and the three of them sailed to Mexico. He fondly remembered that as the best summer of his life. As soon as they had returned home from Mexico, John had to leave for college. He remembered packing and loading his stuff into his parent's car and how they all laughed nervously as they pulled up to his dorm. He felt alone when his parents walked out of his dorm room. When they were out of sight, he turned to his new roommate and asked, "What's next?"

Peter Fraus replied glibly, "The rest of your life, stupid."

Peter had an entirely different story. He came from east LA, the product of an abusive, alcoholic father, and his mother, a former prostitute, never seemed to care about him one way or the other. Like John, Peter was at UC Tech on a football scholarship, but unlike John, Peter looked the part, massive and muscular. John and Peter became best friends, almost inseparable on the field and off.

During college, they had been successful, scholastically and athletically. Although professional teams actively recruited them both, they had a different plan—they were going to design and build boats.

Thinking about it now, John reflected, *it was the best thing I ever did.* A cold breeze interrupted his thoughts and as he looked up, he saw the storm. It appeared about three miles away, directly in front of him. He immediately went into action, first making sure that everything was tied down. He then started to lower the jib and mainsail, replacing it with a smaller sail that would be less likely to overturn the boat in heavy winds. He took his present bearings and set a new course, taking into consideration his tack into the storm.

He was happy for the diversion; his adrenalin was already pumping in anticipation. The sky was as black as a raven, and the seas turned from a beautiful turquoise to dark gray. The seas were as bad as he had ever seen. The white caps seemed to be hands coming right out of the sea to pull him down.

As he sailed into the storm, John was on the top of his game. He had thought to turn on the engine so the pumps were working. He was happy that when he had done this, the creature had extracted itself from the boat. He hit the storm and was surfing down the waves and gunning the engine to go up the waves at forty-five degree tack to save on fuel. He was at the wheel for four hours, fighting the storm as if it was a mortal enemy. Suddenly fearful, his mind raced. *What the hell am I going to do when my strength runs out?*

He reached for a length of line and tied off both sides of the wheel. He wrapped the line around his waist and used his body to save some of the strength in his arms. It was working well until a piece of the mast broke off and hit him directly in the head. It knocked him back off his feet, and the rope slid up under his neck, choking him. John knew if he did not get his hands up to the wheel, he was finished.

Desperate, he tried to free himself from the line when a huge wave hit the boat amidships and spun it a full 180 degrees. *This is it*, he figured, thinking he was going to capsize, but the boat righted itself and he was spun out of the ropes that were strangling him. He had to regain control and fast. He spun the wheel, and the boat did another 180-degree turn and he was back on course, at least in the same direction as before. Hours went by, and he fought for his life. Every muscle in his body was burning and seemed to be vibrating. He was nauseous from fatigue, but he couldn't give up. He thought about his wife, and the anger rose in him and strength returned. As if some unseen force came over him, John took his anger out at the storm. It was almost a day and a half later when he sailed into clear weather and he just collapsed on the deck.

When he woke, he looked at his watch and realized he had been asleep for two days. John jumped up quickly and checked his course, turned off the engine, and checked all the rigging. He was surprised to find he was actually dead on course and there was very little damage to the boat. Thankfully, the next few days were uneventful, and he regained his strength and stamina.

The seas were calm, and the temperature was a pleasant seventy-five degrees. It was ten days since he rode out the storm, and boredom and loneliness were shadowing him like a gray veil. He sat on the deck, and his mind drifted back to the day he and Peter graduated college. Peter had no one to go home to and nowhere to go, so John's parents invited him to come home with them. An invitation he gladly accepted. Over the four years of college, he spent as much time with John's parents as he could. He grew to love them as the parents he never really had.

During the first few weeks at John's parent's home in Sausalito, they spent their days planning their proposed enterprise. John smiled, thinking of the day when he and Peter believed their plans were complete and his father simply said, "Where are you going to get the money to do this?" They were that naïve, but they discussed it for days and Peter finally came up with the idea, "We'll go fishing."

Tuna fishing was tough work, much harder than either of them anticipated. Six months out to sea, John remembered telling Peter, "My little comic book mind never realized how hard this would be," and they both laughed, knowing it was true; but in fact, they were doing well. When they weren't pulling in tuna, they were working on their design.

It was two years after they had signed on to the tuna boat when they had the money to build their first yacht.

Their first boat, a forty-two-foot sailboat with all the amenities, was a success. John remembered their excitement when Sailing Yacht magazine featured it. It sold for $175,000, almost three times what it cost them to build.

The next two years were both dynamic and profitable. They had reached five million in sales and were on their way to becoming a real force in the yacht-building market.

John started to think of how that success led up to the first time he had met his wife. It was in Australia at the America's cup race. She was a naval architect and a hell of a yachtsman. She was crewing for Australia's entry in the race. John and Peter's entry, *The American Flyer*, won that year, and at a party after the race, she approached him.

"Hi! I'm Lucy Owens. Congratulations, you sailed a great race."

"Thank you," John replied. "Weren't you crewing on the *Flying Gull*? Who designed that boat?"

"I did," she replied. "And who designed yours?"

John told her he and Peter designed and built her.

"I'm impressed," she said.

They spent the evening chatting about boat design and how he and Peter got into business. *What happened to that girl I met that night?*

Lucy had returned with him to Sausalito right after their two-week honeymoon in the Australian outback. John anguished on the fact that he loved her so much then. How did their marriage go so bad? He thought about what had drawn him to Lucy. She was so beautiful, free, and wild. One of the things he loved about her most was her wild streak, but over the years, the more time he spent at work, the more her wildness was shared with others. He had been aware of her many affairs, but the last one was the straw that broke the proverbial camel's back.

Frank Peterson was twenty years her junior and his employee. John felt himself going into a rage just thinking about it. The blow to his ego was not the core issue; it was the lack of respect she had for him and the betrayal.

John thought back to the day in his office when he picked up the phone and heard his wife's voice, realizing that his young superintendent, Peterson, did not close his extension after his last call. John listened as they plotted to take over his company, Sailcraft Yachts. He remembered how he almost ran into Frank's office but stopped, resisting the urge to beat Peterson to a pulp. Being the type of man he was, John composed himself, did some research, and developed a plan.

He came home a week later and told Lucy he was going to Hong Kong on a business trip. The Asian market seemed to be taking off and several brokers had shown their interest. The next morning, he was packed and ready to go.

The flight was long but uneventful, and he was surprised he was not that tired when he reached his hotel. After checking in and unpacking, he call May Lu, a partner in the Law firm he had contacted, and confirmed their meeting the next morning at nine.

He arrived at the offices of Woo and Lu Solicitors domiciled at 22 Causeway Bay, only two blocks from his hotel, precisely at nine. After the normal pleasantries, they got down to business. It was explained to him that Woo and Lu would set up a Hong Kong Company in his behalf of which Woo and Lu became nominated shareholders and directors. By doing this, the true owners of the company could not be traced. They would also supply a deed of trust, outlining their role as nominees and undated but signed letters of resignation. With these documents, John maintained full and absolute ownership of his stock, but that ownership could not be traced by anyone, private or governmental. He then transferred all of his stock in Sailcraft to the Hong Kong Company. He realized this was wrong, because in his shareholder's agreement with Peter, it stipulated that he would give Peter right of first refusal on any transfer of stock, but that could be worked out after the fact. He had outlined all the details in his letter to Peter with instructions to destroy the letter after he read it.

On his flight back, John realized how much he had liked Hong Kong and was already anxious to return.

He arrived at his home in Sausalito about nine o'clock in the evening and was not surprised Lucy was not home. He took a shower, unpacked, and went to bed. Sleep came easily.

John started to take small amounts of cash from his earnings and had amassed $250,000 in only a few weeks. The last thing was to get the lawyer in Nevada to draw up the uncontestable divorce papers. He thought back on how hard it was to keep all of this to himself during that month-long ordeal. He remembered finding the hidden camera equipment on the Web and how low he felt when he purchased it. When it arrived at his office, it took him three days to open it. He waited for an evening when Lucy told him she was going out, and he clandestinely installed it around the house. A few days later, he told Lucy he was going on a business trip to Zurich, and in truth, it was business.

John arrived in Zurich and took a taxi to the St. Gotthard Hotel. His room was nice and overlooked the Vodka Bar, a nightclub previously called The Bird Watchers Club, he remembered. John had picked the St. Gotthard, as it was only a short walk down the BahnhoffStrasse to Wershaft und Privat Bank, where he had an early morning appointment.

The wake-up call came at precisely 8:00 a.m. He had time to take a shower and dress before his nine-thirty appointment. He arrived at the bank promptly at nine twenty-five, and Peter Tsillman was waiting for him in the foyer. After exchanging pleasantries, Peter escorted him into a small, round room off the lobby. John noticed the room only had one door and was nicely furnished with a couch, two overstuffed high back chairs, a cocktail table, and two original Renoir's hanging on the wall. Peter Tsillman told him that Woo and Lu forwarded all the necessary papers the day before and he would just have to sign a few documents and have them notarized to finalize the transaction. He remembered being startled when the room began to turn and when the door was opposite to where it had been, Peter rose and said, "Let's got to my office and finish the paperwork." John was amazed that the door opened, realizing he was now on the opposite side of the building. After arriving in Peter's private office, he was given a numbered account and received two safety deposit boxes in the name of the Hong

Kong Company, The East Seas Yachts Company Ltd. When the transaction was complete, the banker had asked if there was anything he could do.

John quickly said, "Yes, can I make telephonic transfers?"

In a very businesslike tone, Tsillman replied, "Yes, you simply call this phone number and ask for special handling. The person who will answer will identify themselves and ask for some information. Give them your account number and a password."

John decided on "blue skies but stormy seas" as his password, and Tsillman entered it into his record. Because it was a Hong Kong Company, it was a private numbered account with complete anonymity; a privilege not afforded any longer to American citizens. John fondly remembered his few days in Zurich; although he had been there before, he never had time to investigate the city and its surroundings.

He remembered coming home after that week in Switzerland and walking into the house to find Lucy out, as usual, and feeling relieved she wasn't there. The following Sunday, he had got up at about 9:00 a.m., dressed, and picked up his tennis bag and headed for the front door. As he passed Lucy on the way out, he handed her the envelope with the divorce papers and the tapes from the hidden cameras and simply said, "See ya" as he exited.

John drove to the office and left the letter for Peter. It explained everything, including some emergency numbers to call if he had to, but went on to say he wouldn't get any messages for at least three months. Leaving the office, John felt certain Peter would understand. He drove directly to the marina, got on board his boat, *The Good Life*, with a quarter of a million dollars in his tennis bag, and sailed west out of San Francisco harbor. *That was almost four months ago.*

He was now questioning whether he had been right in just leaving Peter a letter instead of talking to him. *Peter would understand. It was better this way. I'll contact him when I get to Hong Kong.* He also took into consideration the fact that if the telephone records were subpoenaed, it could be explained that Peter was simply talking to his new Hong Kong partners.

John's thoughts were interrupted by a sound coming from

the bow. He peered up out of the cockpit and saw fishing boats. They were typical Chinese junks. He was almost in Hong Kong waters. John was nearing the end of his journey and entering the beginning of a new life. It was a little unsettling. Several months ago, if someone had told him he would be in this situation, he wouldn't have believed it. He shook the thought from his head and enjoyed the view, trying to forget what got him here.

CHAPTER 2
Washington DC, the White House

"Mr. President, your nine o'clock has arrived."

"Very well, show him in and turn off the recorders."

The president was ill at ease having this man here at the White House, but he had no alternative. The man he was about to meet, Ascot Chen, was known as an important business man, and this meeting was arranged by the man in Memphis who was responsible for his presidency.

"Mr. Chen, please, come in and sit down. It's a pleasure to finally meet you."

Ascot Chen gave the president a warm but respectful greeting and sat down on the couch opposite the president's desk.

"Mr. President," he began, "it is so gracious of you to see me." I am representing certain groups who wish to donate a rather large sum of money to your personal campaign fund. I am aware of the laws concerning such matters, and I assure you it will all be done through our US companies so there will be no political fall out."

"Well, sir, how much are we talking about, and what do your people want for it?"

"We are thinking of starting with $200 million," Chen replied, "and we will only hope that you will consider proposals from some of our members. It will be mostly business but some political, and very infrequently, a personal favor."

"Well that sounds just great," the president stated. "I'll be only happy to help where I can. That is a considerable amount of money, and I can assure you that I will look closely at any such proposals. Now is there anything else I can do for you?

Would you and the missus like to stay a night in the Lincoln bedroom? I can arrange that lickety split."

"No thank you, Mr. President. I will be leaving the States tonight and don't think I'll be back for some time. I have a representative here who is a friend of your secretary of commerce; whatever requests we have will come through him. Mr. President, it is such an honor to meet you, and I thank you for the time you have spent with me."

"It was my pleasure," the president said as he walked Chen to the door. The president stared at the man leaving his office and wondered to himself how bad this was going to be.

"Mr. President, your nine ten appointment is waiting."

"Yes, yes. Show them in." His mind eased into the next topic, but he still felt that uneasy feeling that he knew so well. *It's only politics.*

CHAPTER 3
Hong Kong, The Beginning

The azure-colored sea shone brightly against the green islands of Hong Kong. The view in front of him was breathtaking, puffs of low-lying clouds hovering over mainland China as a backdrop to the busiest harbor in the world.

He left San Francisco harbor almost 115 days ago, and during that time he spent his days alone, surrounded by the vast Pacific, wondering persistently if he had done the right thing.

His thoughts were abruptly interrupted by the sound of a loud whistle. He had sailed into the shipping channel of Aberdeen, the Eastern port city of Hong Kong. Following normal protocols, he called the harbormaster on the radio, who instructed him to pull in to the Aberdeen Yacht Club for custom's inspection and immigration formalities. The customs official explained that as a US citizen, John could stay in Hong Kong for thirty days on a tourist visa. John knew this was good for him. Not wanting to be found, if there was a cursory check by a private detective, a tourist visa would not reveal his location; tourist visas were not generally registered.

John temporarily forgot his problems. It took several hours to get through the government formalities. When he was finished, John stood on the wharf of the Aberdeen Yacht Club and was amazed at the amount of activity out in the harbor. Intermingled with ocean freight vessels were several different types of junks and thousands of smaller sampans. It appeared as if these boats were almost fused together in some sort of maritime kaleidoscope.

Aberdeen was more of a typhoon shelter than a port, but

there was no doubt it bustled with activity. There were fishing boats tied to one another, ten and fifteen deep from the shore. The fishermen and their families seemed to live on these boats year round, and there was an unspoken protocol, he noticed, about the inhabitants walking from their boat across all the others to get to shore. Amazingly, in the center of the all this activity, there were two large floating restaurants. John could see the names of these restaurants in huge, neon signs, The Jumbo and The Royal. Locals and tourists took small junks and sampans out to these restaurants. Judging from the constant flow of these boats loaded with customers, John surmised, *they must be good.*

With the formalities completed, his next task was to find a berth that could accommodate his boat. He asked the customs official and was told he could try the Aberdeen Yacht Club or sail around to the other side of Hong Kong and berth at the Victoria Yacht Club, which was between Hong Kong Central and Causeway Bay.

He was directed to the office of the Aberdeen Club, where it was explained to him that he could not be a member of the Aberdeen Yacht Club, as he wasn't a resident of Hong Kong but they would accommodate him on a month-to-month basis. After going over pricing and regulations, he agreed and was given a tour of the club, told where he could eat, and shown which areas were for members and their guests only. He was assigned berth 49 and given a set of club rules and a complete history of the club that he could read at his leisure.

Berth 49 was an inside berth, and as he tied up, his attention was drawn to the beautiful Chinese junk that was tied up in berth 48, while berth 50 was empty. When all of his lines were properly secured, he step off and started to take a closer look at the junk. It was the first one he had ever seen close up, and unbeknown to him; this one would change his life forever.

The Aberdeen Yacht Club was a total surprise to him. As he walked up the gangway from his boat, he stopped to look around the harbor. The amount of activity amazed him. All around were the Chinese fishermen with their pants rolled up over their knees and tattered T-shirts and bare feet accomplishing a whole array of daily chores, from washing clothes, preparing food, to repairing nets, all as the children chased their pets around the boats.

Aberdeen was not the cleanest place he had ever been. There were broken boats, which must have been caught in the typhoons so common in this area, strewn along the shore. The unkempt repair yards and piles of unused and discarded steel of all shapes and sizes seemed unusual neighbors for this very prestigious yacht club. It was now low tide, and a very distinct odor, not at all pleasant, filled the air. It seemed to come from the human waste from all these fishing boats. All of these new and unfamiliar sights and fragrances were swimming around his head as he walked into the Aberdeen Yacht Club for dinner.

He wasn't sure if it was disbelief or bewilderment as he entered the guest's dinning room for the first time. Everyone was formally dressed, dinner jackets for the men and ball gowns for the women. As the soft sound of the string orchestra wafted through his ears, he was politely told he was inappropriately dressed and could not eat in the club but one of the floor boys could take him to the pier where he could get a water taxi to The Jumbo, which allowed casual attire. The stark reality of these two worlds, so different, coexisting in such close proximity, was hard for him to believe. His first day in Hong Kong was so eventful and exotic that he temporarily forgot his troubles.

He had a fantastic dinner on The Jumbo, with steamed scallops in ginger and fried clams in black bean sauce. He also had Peipa Ha, which were a type of shrimp, each one over a pound, purple and white in color and simply delicious. He had a couple of Mou Tais, a Chinese liquor of 145 proof, which was enough to give him the first good night's sleep in what seemed like years.

The next morning, John went to the club office and asked if they could arrange for a car and driver, which they did in a matter of minutes. The driver wore a heavy cloth, gray liveried uniform complete with driver's cap and white gloves, even though it was ninety-eight degrees with ninety-nine percent humidity.

His name was Chong Lee, and he told John he knew everything about Hong Kong. As they drove along, Chong gave him a history of the island country as well as the locations of the two racetracks, several of the best massage parlors, the best nightclubs, and the best places to buy clothes.

The first stop was the Aberdeen market, a shopping village just outside of Aberdeen proper. It was a maze of small streets with shops and open-air stalls. John was surprised at the number of shops and restaurants in this little shopping village, and it was noticeable how many of the people shopping there were not tourists. After picking up a couple of designer shirts and several of pairs of shorts, John asked Chong if he wanted to have some lunch. Chong said yes but not there. When they got to the car, Chong produced a map of Hong Kong and the New Territories, handed it to John, and proceeded to give him the entire history of Hong Kong.

Chong explained, "Hong Kong is an island country, but the largest portion of land area is actually on the Chinese mainland. The area directly across the harbor from the island of Hong Kong is Kowloon, and beyond that area is the New Territories, which end about fifty miles from the harbor at the Chinese border. Hong Kong was a self-ruled British colony for ninety-nine years. The British had leased it from the Chinese, and the lease was up in 1997. It is now self-ruled under the sovereignty of China. The British and Chinese sign something called the Hong Kong Accords in 1997, which provides that Hong Kong will stay self-ruling for another fifty years and then will revert completely back to China. The population is about eight million people, six million living on the island."

Chong pointed to the map. "Here we are now, in Aberdeen. The yacht club is here. We are going to go north to Repulse Bay. It is about five miles from here. If we stay on this road going north, we will hit the tunnel, which will bring us to the other side of the island. The tunnel will let us out in Happy Valley."

John was glad Chong did this. It gave him a better perspective on where he was. They got back into the car and drove a few miles along the coast to Repulse Bay, a posh residential area with high-end shops and multi-million dollar homes. This duality of crowded streets with shopping stalls and villages with boat people all coexisting with this high-end material opulence was still a little bewildering to John.

As they walk into Spices, a very nicely appointed restaurant, John realized that although this had the look of an old Colonial British establishment, it was actually rather new and nicely appointed with belted ceiling fans and cane chairs and white-uniformed waiters.

An American, in fact, owned it. John found this out while ordering. A pleasant-looking man with an American accent approached him and said, "Hi, my name is Mike Severson. I'm the owner here. Are you from the States?"

John looked surprised by the question. "I heard the American accent." Mike sat down and the three men talked for several hours.

When they were about to leave John told Mike it had been a pleasure. "I can't remember when I enjoyed a meal so much."

"Well then, don't be a stranger. You're welcome anytime." Mike shook Chong's hand and John noticed that Mike had passed some money to Chong.

Once outside John asked, "Did he give you a tip?"

"Tip, what Tip? No one gave me a tip." John gave him a strange look. "Ok, he gives me a tip when I bring in a new tourist." To break the awkwardness of the moment, Chong asked, "Did you notice that the staff calls him Shiverhand?"

"Yes I did. Is Severson hard for you to say in English?"

Chong laughed. "No, it's a joke, Shiverhand means itchy ass in Chinese. Mike has been here a long time but has never learned Chinese. The staff always has a good laugh fooling him. We always do this to Gwuy Lo, which means foreign devil."

Chong went into stories about the original colonization of Hong Kong by the British and how the locals of the day called the owners of the trading houses Tai Pans, which actually meant bathroom attendant, and how the foreigners thought being called Tai Pan was a privilege. As they drove around Repulse Bay, Chong pointed out various high-rise buildings and told John how expensive rents were and the surprising cost of an apartment upwards of three million dollars.

As they left Repulse Bay, Chong turned into the tunnel, and when they came out on the other side it was as if they had driven into another world. This was the Hong Kong that John had seen in movies and read about, a major metropolitan city. The tunnel exited into Happy Valley, and the famous Happy Valley racetrack was in front of them. John thought it was incredible, a huge racetrack surround by apartment complexes and commercial buildings right in the center of the city. Traffic was almost at a standstill, so Chong had plenty of time to fill John in on the history and operation of the track. After more history and sightseeing, John realized it was near 9:00 p.m. and asked to be driven back to Aberdeen.

John had gained respect for Chong during the day, not only for his knowledge of the area but his politeness and pleasant manner. "Could you drive me tomorrow?" he asked. "I have a ten o'clock appointment with my solicitors, Woo and Lu."

Chong agreed. "They have office in the Attenborough Tower in central, they are very fine solicitors."

They arrived at Attenborough Tower at ten minutes to ten, which gave John enough time to find the offices of Woo and Lu and be precisely on time. After he went over the paperwork with Florence Lu, a very attractive woman of about thirty who was May's daughter, John asked if he could use a phone for an intercontinental call. He was given a small office for privacy. He stared at the phone for over ten minutes. He wanted to be certain he would have everything straight in his mind when he talked to Peter; after all, it was four months since he disappeared.

John picked up the phone. He noticed his hand was shaking while he dialed the number. "Hello, Peter?"

"John? You son of a bitch, where are you? You leave without saying a word and now just call out of the blue?"

"Did you get the letter I left for you?"

"Yeah, I got it and I understand you had to get out of Dodge while you were sorting this out, but four months?"

"Peter, I'm sorry, but it was the only thing I could do at the time."

"Where are you?"

"It's best you don't know. If she has you deposed you won't have to lie. You have a new partner, a Hong Kong company called The East Seas Yachts Company, Ltd."

Peter screamed, "What, you sold your shares! You can't do that, it's in our agreement, I have right of first refusal."

"Calm down, Peter. I don't want to go over this over the phone but I am just protecting my assets. I need you to go along with me on this one."

There was a long pause. "John, you know I'll back you one hundred percent. I have your back and I know you have mine."

"Man, you don't know how happy I am to hear that. Once this divorce is final I'll explain everything. Have you talked to Lucy?"

"Yeah, and I told her if she tried to do anything with the company I would leave and she would have nothing. I fired the boyfriend."

"Thanks, Peter; I am sorry all this has happened."

"I am to. You didn't deserve this. You take care of yourself and don't worry. If you need anything just call."

"Peter, you're a good friend, if you need to contact me call Lucy Lu at Woo&Lu Solicitors in Hong Kong." John gave him the phone number and hung up. He sat there for a minute and let out a sigh of relief. *I knew I could count on him.*

Over the next several days, Chong brought John shopping and to a tailor. John was certain Chong would get a commission, but he didn't mind. He was actually happy that he would make a buck; he really wasn't charging much for his services as a chauffeur. By the end of the week, John was totally fitted out with a new wardrobe, including several dinner jackets. Chong was a great help and John offered him a full time position, which he accepted. John thought there was more to this guy than met the eye.

Chong was now John's driver, advisor, translator, and teacher. John had a good ear for language, and in a matter of a few weeks he was becoming conversational in Cantonese. This really impressed Chong, who boasted to his friends that this foreigner was already speaking their language and their employers who had been in Hong Kong for years only spoke English.

It had been three weeks since John arrived in Hong Kong, and he realized he was going to have a visa problem. Chong told him not to worry.

"You only have to leave for a day and can come back in under another thirty-day tourist visa. I'll arrange it for you."

That afternoon, Chong brought John to a friend of his that worked in the China travel office, and for 150 Hong Kong dollars, about twenty US, he got a visa to China.

CHAPTER 4
Finding Home

Over the next few weeks, Chong taught John Cantonese four to five hours per day and he proved to be a very able student. His knowledge of basic Cantonese was impeccable. John would spend the rest of the time exploring the island. He was growing to love this place so different from the world he came from. He was cordial to the other guests and members of the Aberdeen Yacht Club, but he realized if he really wanted to learn this place, he was better spending his time with Chong.

He spent his evenings walking around the Chinese sections of Hong Kong, meeting the local people, and practicing the language. He was completely immersing himself in Chinese culture, knowing that there was not much he could learn from his fellow expatriates. He was an accomplished enough businessman to know that to be successful in Asia he had to learn the culture and nuance. John was not quite certain yet if the market here was going to be worthwhile, but from his travels around Hong Kong so far, he had learned two things: first, there was a lot of money here, and second, the Hong Kong residents liked to play hard. Both of these things were major forces in the marketing and sale of upscale boats.

As clear as these things were to John, Chong was an enigma. He seemed to be well educated and extremely knowledgeable in many areas. Everywhere they went, Chong seemed to be well known, and in a few instances, it appeared he was feared.

"Chong, you seemed to be well known everywhere we go. How do you know so many people?"

Chong laughed. "I get around, boss. Oh! Look over there, that is the poultry market but they tell tourists it is a pet center."

"Chong, seriously, how did you become so well known?"

"Hong Kong is a small place, boss."

It was obvious that Chong did not want to talk about himself, but John persisted. "Where did you work before the Yacht Club?"

"Here and there." Chong got quiet and John decided to let it go for the moment.

After a few months here, John was getting the hang of the place and started to develop a routine. It gave him a sense of belonging but also gave him more time to think. He was starting to think more and more about his wife and what she had done to him. He needed a diversion.

It was Friday night, and John decided to get out and have some fun. "Chong, where can I go to see some nightlife?"

"You can go to Volvo on the Kowloon side. Volvo is very, very big. They drive you to your table in a Rolls Royce." "Really? What kind of entertainment do they have?"

"Oh! Boss, many, many girls. Very beautiful, very young. You can do hom sop."

"What's hom sop?" Chong made a gesture with his hands that John recognized immediately. "No, Chong, I have had enough to do with women for a while."

Chong looked disappointed. "You can go to Joe Banana's, on Lockhart Road. All the gwuy lows like it there."

He arrived at Joe Bananas at ten, and the place was jumping. After he had a drink, he decided it was a little too loud and the crowd was a little too young for him, so he thought he would try some of the clubs down the street. John found himself alone at the end of Luard Road, staring at a spectacular view of Kowloon across the harbor.

John was enjoying the view when an elderly Chinese woman tugged at his arm and pointed across the harbor. "Kowloon means nine dragons," she said. "It is called that because it was built on nine hills coming down from Lion's Head Peak. The hills slowly descend into the harbor and resemble dragons slithering into the sea." Then she smiled and walked away.

John, somewhat bewildered at the unsolicited geography

lesson, shrugged and walked on. He was getting used to the elderly Chinese people who would yell at you or offer advice, or as in this instance, unsolicited information.

Chong had already told John that Kowloon was the shopping and nightclub district of Hong Kong. The famous Peninsula Hotel was located in the center of Kowloon and was probably the most luxurious hotel in the world. Most of the hotels located in Kowloon were rated five stars. The nightclubs were just as luxurious. There are literally thousands of bars and clubs in Kowloon, some with exotic name like Hot Lips and The Bottoms Up. The expat community usually prefers the Hong Kong side, and there, Luard Road was a center of activity. There were bars everywhere, some on the street level, others upstairs, all adjacent to one another, and all seemed to be busy.

John was enjoying the scene of neon lights and throngs of people. He stopped at a noodle shop and had a bite to eat, and he started to think about Lucy again. As his anger rose, he felt more like another beer. He went into one of the bars just a few doors down. He was consumed by the music and the interaction between the bar girls and the other customers. He had forgotten about Lucy for the moment and was starting to feel good. Two hours and ten beers later, John left the bar.

At the corner of Luard and Locart Roads, he walked past a group of drunken Philippine sailors. He recognized some of them from the bar, especially the one with the snake tattooed on his face. As he walked through the center of the group, one of them pushed him, and he pushed back.

John was not generally a mean drunk, but with the frustrations he was battling tonight, he suddenly found little patience for these locals.

The man came at him. John deflected his punch and threw him to the ground. John stood there for a second and said, "I don't want any trouble."

He didn't even see the other man coming at him from his right side. His fist connected with John's jaw with a tremendous crack. John tried to stabilize himself, but he was hit by the third guy and could feel himself going down. Everything seemed to be in slow motion. He hit the ground just as one of them kicked him in the face. Two of them were on top of him punching him in the head while the others were kicking him all over his body. John did the best he could to protect his face, but all of a sudden he was getting numb, and everything went gray. He woke up lying in the gutter, bloody and sore. He tried to get up but stumbled, and as he fell back to the ground he felt a hand grab his arm.

She told him her name was Elsie. As she helped him into the cab, he asked why she was helping him, and she laughed. "Someone has to. You can't take care of yourself."

He woke up in Elsie's flat in Jordan, a section of Kowloon where foreigners were rarely seen. He looked out the small window, only to see the window of the flat next door about three feet away. It was a typical government flat, one room painted in a light green where you could see the wall through all the stains. Elsie was sleeping, and he did not want to disturb her. John remembered she stayed up most of the night and early morning tending to his wounds, none of which were serious, but it hurt just the same. Although he was rather strong and athletic for his age, he was having a hard time getting around this morning. He left Elsie a note of thanks and a hundred dollars US and quietly left.

He went to the corner outside of Elsie's flat and hailed a cab. Forty-five minutes later, he pulled up in front of the Aberdeen Yacht Club and asked the driver to get as close to his boat as possible, as he didn't want anyone to see him like this. As he climbed onto the boat, Chong came up from the cabin and leaped onto the deck, helping him below.

"What happened, boss?" Chong asked. "Who did this to you? Were you robbed?"

"Just a little scrape, Chong. Nothing a hot shower won't fix."

"Sit down and let me have a look." John's face was bruised, and his nose appeared to be a little crooked. Chong tapped it.

"What the hell, Chong?"

"As I suspected, you have a broken nose, sir. Have your shower. I know what to do."

He came out of the shower, and Chong told him to sit in

the chair by the galley and carefully put a spoon on one side of his nose. With one swift motion, he heard a crack, and the pain in his nose subsided. Chong held up a mirror, and to his amazement, his nose was straight again and free of pain.

"Where did you learn that?" asked John.

"On television," said Chong.

But John knew better. He was too good at it.

John slept for the rest of that day and through the night. He was awakened by Chong, who stood over him with a cup of tea and some Chinese herbs.

"Take these; they will make you feel better."

Chong brought him his meals, and with each one he had to drink a jar of Brands' essence of chicken, a disgusting black liquid, which Chong assured him he needed. The next few days were comprised of marathon language lessons. John didn't leave the cabin.

It was Saturday morning, a week after his beating, when Chong came and told John to get dressed. They were going out to get some exercise.

The walking path at the peak, the highest point in Hong Kong, was cool and lined on both sides with lush greenery. They soon reached the old artillery bunker left there as a memento of World War II. Chong entered the bunker area, and they were in a large room with a dirt and grass floor.

Chong put his parcel down and turned toward John and said, "Attack me."

"What?"

"Attack me. If you are going to roam around by yourself, I better teach you how to take care of yourself."

This began John's training in the martial arts. Each day, Chong would drive to the peak and John would jog around the path. It was about four miles long, and he would end up at the old bunker. This became the favorite part of John's day. The scenery along the path was breathtaking, and it was always about ten degrees cooler here than in the city below. He would spend hours learning the ancient art of self-defense.

He once asked Chong where he learned the martial arts and was simply told, "I grew up here. Everyone knows how to protect themselves."

"Seriously, Chong," John said. "You are not only my employee and teacher, you're the only friend I have out here, and I'd like to know something about you."

Chong looked into the distance for a long while, at what John didn't know. "You're right, John, we are friends. It's time for me to be honest with my friend." Chong sat on a bench and offered John the seat next to him.

"Many years ago, I was a detective in the triad investigation division of the Hong Kong police. The triads are Chinese-organized crime families, which were started centuries ago. Their tentacles cover all of Asia and extended around the world. They control the entire drug trafficking in Asia as well as gambling, prostitution, slavery, and murder. They are the most ruthless criminals in the world."

John leaned forward and absorbed the information. He expected the rough past, but he was glad to hear Chong was one of the good guys.

"While working undercover, I traced a large drug operation back to a high-level British inspector. That's when I got too close. Long story short, I was framed for a silly crime and thrown off the police force."

This explained a lot to John, who told Chong he would never discuss it again.

CHAPTER 5
Finding Friends

It was a Thursday morning. John and Chong had just gotten back from the peak. Today's workout had been extremely hard, and John wanted a hot shower to relieve some of the stiffness.

Chong was preparing a snack before they began the language lesson when they heard a woman's voice.

"Hello aboard the Good Life, permission to come aboard."

John came up from below, sweaty and disheveled, not in the mood to receive visitors, but stopped dead in his tracks when he saw her. She was obviously British, a beautiful woman of about thirty. She was well dressed in a Laura Ashley frock, string of pearls, and striking blue, almost purple, eyes. John said hello and told her to come aboard.

"Hello, I'm Rebecca Dreed, your neighbor," she said as she pointed to the Chinese junk in the next berth. "I'm sorry I haven't been over earlier to welcome you to our little community here, but I've been out of the country on business. I'm a solicitor and the head of the flying squad here in Hong Kong."

"Hello, my name is John—"

"I know," she interrupted. "You're from San Francisco in the States. I had you checked out a few weeks ago. Sorry, just routine."

"What is the flying squad?" John asked curiously.

"We seek out and arrest the manufacturers of gray market goods ... knock offs, I think you call them in America."

Chong came up from below carrying a tray with three bottles of beer and snacks. John noticed a blink of recognition in Rebecca's eyes. "Chong, this is Rebecca Dreed. She—"

"Yes, I know missy Dreed."

"Yes, we know each other. Hello, Chong."

"Nee Hau," Chong said as he went back down below.

"Oh, well, John, I just came over to invite you to have dinner with my boyfriend, Ian, and myself Friday evening. Come aboard around seven."

"I have been curious, Rebecca, The Dream of the Red Chamber is an odd name for a boat. How did you come up with that?"

She laughed. "The Dream of the Red Chamber is the title of a famous Chinese book containing over two thousand characters. I went through two hundred characters to get it." They both laughed and then Rebecca said, "Sorry, John, I have to dash, see you Friday."

John stood on the deck and sipped his beer watching Rebecca walk over to her boat. John smiled to himself. *A very attractive lady.* John heard Chong coming back up on deck. "Chong, you didn't seem to like her much. You two have a problem?"

Chong looked over at her boat. "No, boss, no problem." Chong walked to the bow and John heard him say under his breath, "Damn British Inspectors."

John dropped the subject and went below to take a shower. While showering, he realized he had come out clean when Rebecca had him checked out, which gave him a peaceful and reassured feeling.

John stood next to the junk. *The Dream of the Red Chamber … quite a name for a boat*, he thought. He was about to announce himself when he heard footsteps behind him. As he turned, he saw Rebecca coming down the berth carrying groceries. He took some of the parcels from her, and she apologized for being late but said she was delayed getting away from work. He helped her below with the packages and stopped in amazement. The inside of the junk was magnificent with hand carved teak and mahogany walls with inlaid countertops and silk pillows thrown about it. It was beautiful.

Rebecca saw his expression and said, "It's not much, but its home," and laughed that delightful laugh he remembered from yesterday. She quickly started to unpack the groceries and stopped to pour John a glass of wine and asked him to make himself comfortable.

"When I have dinner organized, I'll give you a tour."

As a yacht designer and builder, John was anxious to see the rest of this, but he politely said, "No rush."

As he relaxed with his wine, Rebecca explained that she had gone shopping in Marks and Spencer Food Store in the Edinburgh Tower, the only place in Hong Kong to get real food. John watched her move around the galley and listened to her talk, but his mind drifted back to thoughts of Lucy and how she used to be when they had first met.

"Coming aboard," a man's voice yelled out, and John heard heavy footsteps across the deck. As he came down the ladder, John thought to himself, *this guy is big*. Ian came in and nodded hello to John and went over and kissed Rebecca. Rebecca formally introduced them.

"Captain Ian Grant, Royal Marine and Commanding Officer of Tamara Naval Base, Hong Kong Admiralty, may I present John Moore, boat builder."

John could immediately see Ian was a man's man. He stood over six feet tall, was solidly built, and although very pleasant, there was a hint of a dangerous, dark side. John decided he liked him.

The three of them sat around the dinner table and talked about their lives and backgrounds, never getting too personal but giving each other an idea of themselves, at least enough to perk each other's interest to want to know more. After dinner, John was given a full tour of the junk and they went up on deck and finished off a bottle of Port. It was after 2:00 a.m. when John said goodnight.

Chong woke John up at 8:00 a.m. and told him to dress for a workout. While taking a shower, John realized he had too much to drink the night before and this workout was going to be tough. He got dressed, and after a cup of coffee and as much stalling as John could get away with, they got into the car and drove toward Hong Kong Central District. John wasn't as sharp this morning as he usually was, and Chong laughed.

"You had gin and tonic and wine and port last night, didn't you?"

"Yes," replied John. "How did you know?"

"You went to dinner with those British people. They always have gin, wine, and port," and he laughed again.

John didn't see the humor in it. They turned onto Cottonwood Drive. Chong made a turn and went in the opposite direction they normally went. As they drove through the Harbor Tunnel, John asked, "Where are we going?"

Chong said they were going to Shatin.

"You won't be any good fighting today, so we will rent bikes and take the ride from Shatin to Taipo."

The bike path from Shatin to Taipo was thirty kilometers each way. The bike path was built along the coast of the new territories behind Bai yu Mon. It started in Shatin not far from the temple of ten thousand Buddha's and went to Taipo, once a fishing village but now a city of high-rise government apartments. The heat of the day and quick pace Chong was setting sweated the toxins from his body, and by noon, John was feeling good. They stopped halfway at a barge/restaurant and had some POCO energy drink to replace some electrolytes, and fried pickled octopus for stamina.

They got back to Shatin about five, and John asked Chong if they could stop and visit the temple. When they arrived, John was surprised to find that inside the temple gate the Fung Shui were lined up and busy telling people's fortunes and predicting their futures. Incenses were burned everywhere, and people were burning bits of gold and silver paper at the shrines.

Chong explained that this represented wealth and the people burning it were sending it to their ancestors. Donations of food were being offered to the monks in return for prayers; fruit, whole cooked pig, and other delicacies that John didn't even recognize. The temple structures were beautiful. They had green tiled roofs with dragoons running along the eves, which were turned up slightly, showing the red color of the ceiling below. The large wooden doors with high sills he had to step over gave an ominous appearance.

The inside of the temple was smoky from all the incense

burning and people were kowtowing to various Buddhist statues. There was a long hall with statues of ferocious looking warriors, all deified as the various Buddahshivas. The walls were painted red with green and gold trim, all the statues being gold. Huge wooden columns, each about two feet in diameter, held up the ancient roof.

Although he didn't count them, John was certain there were ten thousand statues of Buddha. They stayed for about an hour, and Chong asked if John was hungry.

"There is a restaurant nearby that specializes in tofu and pigeon, very famous and very good."

"John, is that you?" the voice said. John turned to see an old school friend, Chuck Burns. "Chuck, what the hell are you doing here?"

"This is my parish."

"What?" John asked bewildered.

"Yeah, I know, but the wildest of boys make the best men. I'm a priest, Mary Knoll."

"Well, I'll be dammed," John said.

"I hope not," his friend replied.

"Listen, why don't you come to dinner with us?" John asked.

"I have an appointment, but here is my telephone number and address. Come over eight o'clock any Wednesday night. Me and a few of the local boys have a card game, not big money, but its fun."

When they got back to the Aberdeen Yacht Club, it was about eight thirty. John met Rebecca walking up the berth. She was wearing an evening dress and said, "Hello. Get dressed; there is a ball tonight at the club. I'm a member, and you're my guest. I'll leave a card for you at the desk."

"Okay, I'll meet you there in about forty-five minutes," said John.

John arrived just at the completion of "God Save the Queen" and the festivities started. Rebecca introduced him around, and the eclectic group of people he met was impressive. Newspaper writers, bankers, government employees, ambassadors, counsel generals, police inspectors, and businessmen, but he was surprised at the obvious lack of Chinese people.

"The Chinese have gotten into the Jockey Club and The Hong Kong club," said Rebecca, "but the Aberdeen Yacht Club and the Cricket Club are still off limits." John didn't quite get this colonial attitude, but he was a guest and decided it was best to say nothing.

Toward the end of the evening, John heard someone calling Rebecca's name and heard Rebecca say under her breath, "Here comes the dragon lady."

John looked up and saw Wendy Frost hurrying over to them. She had an expensive gown that, although impeccably tailored, didn't seem to fit. It was offset by her dyed red hair that was a shade of red that didn't have a name. She was not totally unattractive but had an overbite that could open cans. Rebecca introduced them, and Wendy stuck out her hand. "Wendy Frost here, secretary to the governor."

John politely shook her hand, and she actually batted her eyes. He bit his tongue not to laugh. She turned to Rebecca and said, "Darling, you are coming to the governor's ball on the twelfth, aren't you? I will not take no for an answer. Ian will not be able to take you, the governor has him going to Beijing to renegotiate some term of the Accords, and it's so tedious. Anyway, Ian has to go for some reason, so you have to find an escort."

Rebecca turned and asked if John was available. He said yes, and Wendy asked his address and was told, "Here, at the yacht club."

"Splendid, I will send you an invitation on Monday."

The next day John took the Hydrofoil over to Macao and gambled for the next few days. When he returned, he quickly got back into his regimen of martial arts and language, and Chong was happy with his progress.

The evening of the twelfth came quickly, and as he walked up the berth with Rebecca on his arm, he thought to himself, *Life has really changed for the better.* The ball was a success in more ways than one. John had made ten appointments for people to see his boat, and by the week's end he sold it and three others.

He called Peter with the good news and asked him to make arrangements to ship four boats over because he sold three in addition to the *Good Life*. He was also happy with the fact his profit was twice what it would have been if they were sold in the states.

Peter was equally exited and told him he hired a new, young designer who had some great ideas. John was pleased and told Peter to ship him the fourth boat with the new design. Asia was going to be a great market for them. John asked about Lucy, and nothing had changed, although John's lawyer had called and said he was near a resolution with her lawyer. It was smart of him to leave.

CHAPTER 6
Rome, Italy 1976

It was around nine o'clock in the morning when Sergio received the call. Sergio Ruffino was a mid-level official with total control of one aspect of his government's business—he was in charge of all the export of pasta and foodstuffs from Italy. Sergio was now on his way to meet a very important person, Ascot Chen, but why he wanted to meet in the park was beyond his comprehension. He had met Mr. Chen at a dinner for the installation of the new director of the police department which controlled all the police activity in Italy. Mr. Chen knew all of the top-level officials, and they all reacted to him as if he were a very important man. Sergio entered the park with some apprehension. *What does this man want of me?* Deep in thought, he heard his name called out, and then he saw Ascot Chen sitting on a bench feeding the pigeons with some breadcrumbs.

"Sergio, how nice of you to come on such short notice," Ascot showed a warm and generous smile. After exchanging their hellos, Sergio asked, "What did you want to see me about?"

Ascot looked at him with a serious, almost frightening, stare. "I have been thinking of you since the dinner for the director of police. After our discussion, I thought you were much too bright to be wasted in the position you now hold. I want to help you in your career. I am not without influence."

Sergio sat in disbelief. *This man is right; my talents are being wasted. I am a lot more than a puffed-up clerk.* "How can you help?"

"I have an idea. As you know I represent several multi-national corporations. I would like to propose that we purchase, through these various companies, the entire national production of food products with seven percent price increases per year." Chen handed him a portfolio. "Here is a written proposal I want you to give it to the minister of commerce as your own."

Sergio was shaken and in momentary disbelief. "Thank you, but how can I repay you?"

"Don't worry about that now. I have some connections with the press and will make certain you get the credit for this personally."

"Mr. Chen, I don't know what to say."

"Good. Don't say anything. We will require an additional two percent in export credits, but it will cost the government nothing due to the reduction in sales and marketing expense. It is all outlined in the proposal."

Chen glanced at him and knew he had Sergio right where he wanted him.

"Oh yes, there is one more thing. You will receive the equivalent of USD $250,000 per year in cash in this account."

He explained that a man on the way up needs resources. When he handed the bank book over to Sergio, he thought the man would pass out.

Sergio said, "Why are you doing this for me?"

Ascot studied the man and was certain that his ego and greed would allow him to accept the answer.

"You impressed me greatly at the dinner, and I have been thinking about it ever since. Some of your government's ministers are, allow me to be blunt, stupid. After our conversation that evening, I thought to myself that if there were more people like Sergio who made the decisions, Italy would be a lot better off. After all, we are entering into a global economy and these old bureaucrats are slowing everything down. We need bright, young people with vision, and I believe you are one. My group will assist your rise through the ranks and, if need be, will offer any needed assistance along the way."

Sergio was now wide eyed and listening intently to every word.

"You will speed through the ranks, and with our help, in five years or so you will be the Minister of Commerce."

Sergio thanked him profusely, and Chen told him, "As I said, just follow our lead and you will be there."

Sergio had no idea he had just sold his soul to the devil.

CHAPTER 7
Jakarta, Indonesia

In the plain but elegantly appointed office, YK Chen sat across his desk from General Ma and realized that this was going to be a very profitable meeting. The general was like most of the Chinese generals, moon faced with that look which was both stupid and strong at the same time. He wore the physical badge of the uneducated peasant warrior, but his looks were deceiving, and Chen knew it.

"General, could I interest you in some tea or something to eat perhaps?"

Y.K. was trying to be as polite as possible, but the general replied gruffly, "No, let's get to business. As you know, we have discovered the exact locations of the secret nuclear sub base the Americans have set up for the Taiwanese, and the last ship we purchased for scrap through an Italian dealer from Russia actually had nuclear weapons still aboard when they were delivered to Dalien. That means that the Russians have lost control and anything is for sale to anyone with the money. These facts, coupled with our border disputes with India, who has ballistic missile capability, leaves PRC in a vulnerable position. We have nuclear capability but no way to deliver it. We have our silkworms, but they only have short-range effect. We need missile guidance systems equal to or better than the United States. Can you deliver the technology?"

Studying the general, Chen replied, "General, what you ask is a very difficult proposition; the COCOM Treaty is still in effect."

The general peered at him and in an almost threatening voice said, "Mr. Chen, what will it cost?"

Y.K. thought for a moment and replied.

"Six hundred million US dollars up front and a safe haven within the borders of PRC for our drug trafficking with guaranteed safe passage in and out of your borders. We will guarantee no sale of drugs in the PRC, but we wish to have free trade in Hong Kong and Macao. After we have delivered, we will also want one hundred fifty electronic and computer contracts and half of the US cotton quota at a fixed price of fifty cents per dozen of all finished clothing for twenty years, the sole distributorship of all latex products going into the PRC, as well."

The general thought for a moment and said, "That's acceptable, as long as you agree to pay the normal tax for your enterprises within PRC. When can you deliver?"

"I will have to contact our US office, and I will have a firm answer by the end of the month," replied Chen as he stared directly into the general's eyes.

The general studied him and said, "Okay, but no later."

"Well, General, if that is all?" Y.K. escorted him to the door. As the general left his office, Chen got on the phone and ordered his deputy, Ascot Chen, to personally escort the general to Liddo's private airport, and he was further instructed to make sure that there were no flight plans filed and no record of his flights in or out of Jakarta.

YK Chen was a genius, and probably the most powerful man in the world. He was the chairman of the Liddo Group, a holding company that controlled businesses from oil to agriculture, from silk garments to steel. They had holdings in every type of business imaginable and either owned or controlled the media in almost every country in the world. All of these legitimate businesses were financed and backed by drugs, gambling, and power broking. Liddo had government officials, police, judges, and even heads of state on the payroll. They used this power quietly, effectively, and wisely, using money to get what they wanted and their power over officials and the media to keep it quite. YK Chen was the shadow emperor, a man with no equal, no bounds, and no rules. He ran his empire with vision, strength, and the ultimate power of endless wealth.

YK Chen called the Liddo office in Memphis, Tennessee, which had been set up as a legitimate business in chicken trading, but it's real purpose was to launder drug money from Liddo's drug sales in the US. Liddo was smart enough not to distribute drugs in the US, it left that to the Columbians and the Haitians, but it acted as the major supplier, financier, and launderer. Each day, more money was transferred through banks in Memphis than the entire yearly state product of Tennessee. The Liddo Group did this legally.

"Hello, Jen Pao. This is YK. Is your scrambler on?"

"Yes, we have a safe line," was the answer.

Jen Pao was the CEO of Liddo USA, and after hearing what was being asked of him, he said, "It will be difficult, I don't know if the secretary of commerce can pull this one off. I think we are going to have to go all the way to the president."

"Can it be done?" asked YK.

"I think so, let me have a meeting with our political experts here and I'll be back to you with a definitive plan in a week. Ascot Chen had a meeting with the president several months ago, and we made a significant contribution that should make it somewhat easier."

"Very well, don't let me down," ordered YK Chen.

"Good-bye," replied Pao, and as he hung up the phone, a plan started to formulate in his head. He called in his right hand, Jim Lowery, senior VP and chief counsel for the Liddo Group USA.

"Jim, set up a meeting with our inner council and get Manheim and the governor in on this one. Let the governor know this isn't going to be public, and make sure no one sees him coming here. We are going to arrange for missile guidance technology to be sold to the Chinese."

CHAPTER 8
Hong Kong

Over the weeks after the governor's ball, John, Rebecca, and Ian were becoming friends. Ian was able to check out scuba gear from Tamar, and they would sail over to the Philippines and go diving on the weekends. Chong always made himself scarce when they were around so it was just the three of them.

John had become Rebecca's escort when Ian wasn't available and quickly became known as part of the upper social scene of Hong Kong. He did not mind this, as it was good for business, but when his picture wound up in the *Hong Kong Tattler*, he decided to be a little less carefree.

It was almost five months to the day he ordered the four boats and decided he would call Peter in San Francisco to make the final arrangements for their receipt. They were being shipped on the K lines ship Maura and John would have to be at the Port of Hong Kong berth 5 by 3:00 p.m. on the coming Monday to supervise the offloading of the boats.

He had arranged with Peter to have Sailcraft sell them to the Hong Kong Company, The East Seas Yachts Company Ltd. at cost. Hong Kong only had an 18 percent flat tax, and the profits would be wired to Zurich for distribution. Peter realized he was lucky to have a partner he could trust without question. The boats arrived in good order, and only a few minor repairs had to be made before delivery. With Chong's help, he had his new boat registered as *The Hong Kong Lady* and sailed her around the island to Aberdeen. The new design was great. Peter was right in every respect, and she handled like a dream. The cabin space was laid out better, there was a lot more room, and it was much more comfortable. He tied up around seven o'clock and was anxious to show his new boat to Rebecca. He announced himself coming aboard and found Rebecca below crying.

"What's wrong?"

Ian had been transferred home to England and had broken it off with her. She was really down, and this wasn't the time to show her the boat. He asked if there was anything he could do, and she replied no, so after excusing himself, he left.

He was unpacking and heard a knock. It was Rebecca. He looked at the clock, and it was after midnight.

"Do you have any gin?" she asked.

"Sure, come on in."

Rebecca remarked on how nice the new craft was, but John knew she was just being polite. He felt bad for her. The pain was visible. John suggested they go up on deck to get out of the mess he had made while unpacking and brought a bottle of gin and two glasses.

John poured the drinks and handed one to Rebecca. "If I'm not being too personal how did you meet Ian?" He noticed a tear in her eye. "Rebecca, if you would rather not talk about it…"

"No, I'm sorry. I'm a bit emotional these days. When I first arrived in Hong Kong I was invited to a Military Ball at Tamar. As soon as I walked in I saw him. He was dressed smartly in his uniform and looked bigger than life. He was the most beautiful man I had ever seen."

John stood and looked out over the harbor. *Why the hell did I ask her that?*

"Ian saw me watching him from across the room and came over and asked me to dance, and before it was over I had said to myself I will never let him go."

Rebecca started to cry and John put his arm around her to offer some comfort. *What the hell did I get myself into?*

"That's it, let it out." He held her for a few minutes and she had seemed to recover a bit. "Feeling better?"

"John, you are a nice man." She went on to tell him about the four years she spent with Ian, and John could see the pain in her.

"Rebecca, everyone goes through this sometime in their life. You'll get over it but will never forget it."

John got up and made two more drinks. "My wife was unfaithful to me, and when I found out it was like someone reached into my chest and pulled my heart out. It has taken a long time for me to be able to think about it without going into a rage."

Rebecca looked into his eyes and saw the hurt was still there. She kissed him on the forehead. They were both quiet for a long while.

As the sun came up, they sat there with his arm around her and her head on his shoulder, two lonely people consoling each other for their losses. When Chong came on board at 8:30 a.m., he found them sitting with the glasses still in their hands asleep. He woke them up, and Rebecca jolted. She was late for work and said good-bye.

John looked up at Chong and said, "Don't say anything."

Chong just laughed and went below.

Rebecca and John became inseparable, seeing each other almost every day. John would listen to her attentively as she told him about her daily adventures in the flying squad, but he declined to spend too much time with her friends. He wasn't sure if it was the age difference or he just wanted to be alone with her, but at any rate, besides her and Chong, he was happy to be by himself.

John used his time alone to explore Hong Kong and its people. His Cantonese, now very good, allowed him the luxury of getting around on his own, which was enabling him to gain his own perspective on the place.

One afternoon, to John's surprise, Chong invited him to meet his family. It was the first time in all these months Chong even mentioned he had a family. John was honored, as it wasn't normal in this society for a foreigner to be invited to a Chinese home.

As Chong's wife greeted him, John was looking around. *This is a ghetto.* It was government housing, and the flat was small with a communal kitchen in the hallway outside the apartment. Chong saw the look on John's face and explained.

"Chinese people do not like big houses."

Chong Yen was a small, attractive woman who seemed shy and quite. Chong told him that was only for his benefit. She yelled at Chong often and was considered the boss in this house, and then Chong laughed. The two boys were eight and ten, respectively, and his daughter, Chong Ah Man, was twelve and as pretty as her mother. Ah Man spoke English and attended the Christian School of Knowledge and Light in mid levels. Chong Yen was very proud they could afford to send her to a private school.

As the day went on, several of Chong's relatives, all who seemed to be policemen came in. They ate and laughed and played "Marjon" loudly, and John's perception had changed. *Chong is lucky to have all this.* John had a pleasant day and told Chong he would take a taxi home.

When he arrived at his boat, an alarm went off in his head. The door to the galley was unbolted, and he knew he closed it before he left. He opened the hatch and carefully crept down the ladder.

"I didn't think you would ever ask, so I'm making the first move," Rebecca said. She was lying naked in his bed. John froze. He didn't know what to do. He started to say something, and she said, "Just be quiet and come here."

They spent the rest of the night fulfilling each other's needs and filling the void each of them had felt for so long.

They had breakfast together, and she kissed him good-bye and went off to get ready for work. John was already showered and shaved when Chong arrived. Chong looked around and said, "The British lady was here last night?"

"How the hell did you know that?" John asked.

Chong just laughed and got ready for the day's lesson. During their lunch break, John asked Chong again how he knew Rebecca was there last night.

"Psychic," replied Chong laughing. By the end of the day, it was gnawing at John and he asked again, "How did you know?"

Chong laughed and finally admitted it was no trick, she left her bra on the chair in his galley, and it was too big for a Chinese woman. They both had a laugh.

For the next few days, John familiarized himself with all the new features built into the *Hong Kong Lady*. She was a beauty—fifty-eight feet with a fourteen-foot beam and a new hull design that made her both fast and stable. The inside cabin was roomy with a parlor equipped with satellite TV, CD Player, and stereo and a full galley equipped with a propane stove, a sink, and plenty of cabinets and counter space, and an added feature, a wet bar. The master bed room suite had a king size bed, shower, and something new. At the press of a button, the bed folded into the wall and revealed a hidden Jacuzzi, which could be used while in port, and if left full, it was extra ballast at sea.

Peter was right, the new kid was good. There was a guest room, crew's quarters, and built in storage space everywhere. The boat was powered by sail and twin Volvo diesels, with a back up pumping system that would get you through the worst weather. John took Chong out for several trial sailings and taught him the finer points of sailing and navigating. Chong turned out to be an excellent crewmember.

John was anxious to really put her through her paces and asked Chong and Rebecca if they would like to sail to Singapore the following weekend. They agreed, and plans were made. Over the next few days, John got busy plotting his course and applying for the necessary papers.

John was anxious when the day finally came. They were all aboard, and John explained what was expected of each of them as a crew. Several hours out of Hong Kong, they came into a little weather, and John was happy to see what she could really do. She sailed like a dream.

Just off of Hainan Island, eighty miles south of the China coast, a stainless steel guideline snapped. It was not critical, but repairs had to be made. John called ahead for permission to enter the port without proper documents and was granted permission by the Chinese authorities.

They sailed in under power at the direction and scrutiny of the Chinese port authority. The shipyard was small, but the necessary repairs were done efficiently, and they were underway within hours. John explained to both Chong and Rebecca that breakdowns were normal and the reason you wanted to make as many and as rough trials as possible when you first put a new boat in the water.

They all remarked on how beautiful Hianan Do was and agreed to make a trip back soon. The next two days sailing were uneventful but totally enjoyable. They arrived in Singapore in the morning, and it was several hours of formalities and arranging for a berth before they were ready to go ashore.

Chong told John he had relatives there and asked if he could leave for a few hours to visit them.

"Sure," John replied. "Rebecca and I will go over to Raffles for a drink. I have heard so much about it, I'm really anxious to see it."

Raffles was an old colonial hotel famous for the drink that originated there, the Singapore Sling. It was a beautiful building with a colonnade façade of British styling circa 1800.

Inside, they found the bar, a large open room with fans slowly turning just below the ceiling. The bar was at least 100 feet long and made out of teak and hand carved in an oriental style. Looking at Rebecca with certain admiration, John said, "I can't believe it; this is exactly how I pictured it." They sat at a table, and John ordered.

As they sipped their Singapore Slings, Rebecca gave John a full history of the place. John did not say a word but listened as intently as a child listened to a fairy tale. After two drinks each, they decided to spend the rest of the day sightseeing. Singapore was an interesting mix of Chinese, British, and Malaysian cultures. The downtown area was much like any modern city, crowded streets, skyscrapers, and traffic. John thought the distinctive point was that it was so very clean, almost antiseptic.

John's thoughts turned to Lucy, and this upset him. Trying to change his mood, John grabbed Rebecca around the waist and hugged her and said, "Isn't there anywhere we can have some fun here?"

"If you mean something different, we can go to Bongi Street," she replied.

When they arrived on Bongi Street, John remarked on how beautiful the women were, and Rebecca laughed.

"What's so funny?" John asked.

Rebecca said, "You're so naïve, all of these *women* are female impersonators." She laughed again.

"They are not," John said as he felt his face turn bright red.

"Yes, this is Bongi Street, famous for the transvestites."

"Let's get the hell out of here," John said as he pulled her away.

Rebecca laughed and laughed. She thought it was hysterical that a man as smart as John could be so dumb. They wandered around and found themselves on Snake Street. John was fascinated by the activity there.

He said, "Let's try one of these restaurants?"

Rebecca looked at him quizzically but said okay, and they went into a small café called the Magic Sear. Sear means *snake* in Chinese. As they sat down, a man came to the table with two glasses of wine and then produced a box with a handle on the top. John almost jumped up from the table as the man opened it and pulled out a three-foot long poisonous snake. He milked the venom into the glasses of wine and told them to drink. John looked at him in sheer horror. Rebecca said, "No thank you, we're not used to it, we might get sick."

The man nodded and walked away, looking at them strangely. One could almost read his mind. The man was thinking, *If they don't want snake, what are they doing here? Crazy foreigners.*

Rebecca looked over at John and again began to laugh. They decided to leave and paid the waiter a tip for his patience.

They got back to the boat around five, and Chong was waiting for them. He told them his cousin had just opened a restaurant and they were invited for dinner.

After the snake, John was a little hesitant but didn't want to offend Chong. He asked Rebecca if she was hungry, and she replied, "I could eat." They took a cab to the Malaysian section of Singapore, and John was getting a little anxious about the kind of food they might find. Rebecca looked at him and smiled a kind, knowing smile and said, "Don't worry, love. If it looks too exotic, I'll make an excuse."

John leaned over and kissed her on the cheek and said, "Bless you."

Chong announced they had arrived, and as they got out of the taxi, John and Rebecca both convulsed in laughter. The name of the restaurant was Wild Bill's Tex Mex Saloon. Once inside, they told Chong where they had been that day and why they were a little apprehensive, and they all had a good laugh.

Chong's cousin, Alfred Chong, could not have been more hospitable. He brought out tray after tray of food and pitchers of Margaritas. Chong got up and sang karaoke, and both Rebecca and John were impressed with his performance. They stayed late into the morning hours and were all feeling good when they got back to the boat. The next day, they set sail for Hong Kong.

Upon their return from Singapore, Rebecca told John she wouldn't be seeing him for a week or so, as she was working on something big and would be leaving Hong Kong. She had not wanted to tell him while they were on their mini holiday. She left the next morning before John woke. The days passed, and John missed her but carried on working on the boat and continued his lessons with Chong.

CHAPTER 9
Bonn, Germany

The ceremony was very impressive. Helmut Klieg was being installed as the director of the BND, the Bundesnachrichtendienst, the intelligence service of the Federal Republic of Germany. It was one of the most powerful positions in the German government, and Helmut knew in his heart he deserved the post. He had done an exemplary job as president of the Bunserat. He was, of course, the main framer of basic law article 50.

Standing on the dais, in front of a large crowd, all he could think was, *Even though I've worked hard all my life, that one mistake. What will they want of me now?*

It was almost five years since the day Ascot Chen came to his home and produced those vile videos. In these last five years, the Liddo Group has used his influence to gain their strong hold in Germany. He reflected on that day when Chen had visited his office and asked for concessions on several businesses. He remembered telling Chen it would not be possible under any circumstance, but then Chen showed up at his home and produced the video.

To the public and even his close friends, Helmut was a conservative and moral man, but his deepest secret was exposed on that video. *How did they get those pictures?* He asked himself over and over again. He knew deep in his heart that despite the fact that Germany was liberal and what a man did in his private life was private, if those tapes had come to light, he would have never been in the position he held today.

The video showed him wearing lace bra and panties with a

matching garter belt and nylons, being whipped by a vinyl-clad dominatrix, while his boyfriend, Claus, danced naked to the eerie sounds of "Bolero."

As he walked away from the podium, just finishing his acceptance speech, that nagging question filled his mind, *what will they ask of me now?*

CHAPTER 10
Finding Himself

During the week of Rebecca's absence, Chong told John he had taught him everything he could in the martial arts. Chong realized it seemed to come naturally to John, but he taught him everything he knew. Chong suggested that if he wanted to go to the next level, he would introduce him to Phoenix Leung, a woman who was a well-known master in many forms of the martial arts. John agreed, and Chong brought him to meet Phoenix Leung.

John was surprised as they entered the rear yard of the temple on Lantau Island. Several people were training in the martial arts, some with weapons. He and Chong sat at a table off to the side, and a mature but striking woman served them tea. They watched for over an hour and were served toast, fruit, and more tea. When the exercises were stopped, all of the participants left quickly.

It was coming on to dusk, and the temple yard took on an entirely different appearance. The woman who had been serving them sat down and asked Chong if John was his student and introduced herself as Phoenix Leung. She was about sixty years old. Her face appeared young, and her shape was that of a much younger woman. She spoke a dialect John did not understand. It was Hakka. The Hakka dialect was only spoken in one small area in Canton. Chong explained to John that the Hakka people were interesting. For centuries, the Hakka women had done all the physical labor and the men had done the household chores.

Phoenix asked John to stand, and she rolled up the sleeves

of her tunic, exposing arms that were slender but muscular. She stood facing him and ordered him to attack her.

He was hesitant, but after several seconds, he lunged forward and quickly found himself hitting the ground hard.

"Again," she said in perfect English, and again he found himself on the ground. John was embarrassed, being thrown around by this little woman of no more than ninety pounds. After an hour of getting beaten, John was embarrassed and demoralized. Phoenix stopped and started to walk away; when she was near the door, she turned and said, "Be here tomorrow at 4:00 p.m.," as she disappeared into the temple.

John looked at Chong and said, "What the hell was that?"

CHAPTER 11
Rome Italy, the Present

After the ceremony, Sergio was greeting the long line of people who were now on their way into the reception. He nodded and smiled politely, but his mind was elsewhere. He never really believed he would be the Minister of Commerce of Italy. It had taken more than the five years Ascot Chen had predicted, but he was here just the same. He thought to himself that he had paid a great price for this. He had given up his integrity, his self-esteem, and his morality was gone forever, but he kept justifying his actions by thinking when he got to this level he would be beyond their reach and would be able to do good things, of course he was wrong. They put him here, and he would be theirs forever.

As the line of well-wishers went by, he became more and more bored, until someone said, "I knew you would make it."

Sergio looked up into the face of Ascot Chen. Ascot leaned close, as if he were congratulating him, but whispered, "Sergio, I must see you tomorrow. Be at the park at 7:00 a.m. sharp."

Sergio was almost physically ill.

CHAPTER 12
Memphis Tennessee, USA

They were all assembled in the bubble room at Liddo's office in Memphis. The room had already been swept for bugs, and the scrambling devices had been activated. In attendance were Jim Lowery, Mike Manheim, the governor, Whipple Strong, the ex - presidential lawyer and advisor, and Helen Basey, a Whitehouse intern and Liddo plant.

Jen Pao brought the meeting to order.

"We have an interesting proposal in front of us, and we will all have an active part in seeing it implemented. Certain parties in China wish to purchase a guidance system from the US. We have already located a company that is willing to sell it, but we have to arrange for the technology transfer. Any ideas?"

The governor started by saying, "It won't be easy. We will have to call in a lot of favors on this one. We will have to start with the secretary of commerce; does anyone have anything on him? No? Then we will have to have pressure put on him from above."

"What about the attorney general. Will she give us a hard time?" asked Strong.

The governor replied abruptly, "No, she's taken care of. If the administration says jump, she says how high."

Strong interjected, "Yes, but it might be a good idea to bring her into the loop so she can start to develop a plausible defense for the deal."

Manheim said, "I can control that through the media. It's going to take some money, but the real problem will be transferring it. Jim, who is that Chinese guy we used before to get access to the Whitehouse?"

Lowery replied, "Johnny Trong, and he's a good friend of the secretary of commerce. He'll be perfect."

Jen Pao ordered, "Have him set up a preliminary meeting at the White House with the president, the secretary of commerce, and the CEO of the company selling the technology. Governor, you get to the president and see what he wants, but gently remind him we put him there. Let's not have the McAllen law firm handle this one. Get a firm out of New York, and make sure they are Republican. Get Johnny Trong to use that guy Gua, the restaurant owner, again to start fund raising, and we'll launder the money through the Buddhist temples, Chinese restaurants, and laundries again. Let the vice president take the credit for the money going to the DNC. Mike, we'll use you to offer the president a sixty million dollar media gig when he gets out of office, a million to the library and three million in contributions to his legal defense fund. Offer the secretary of commerce a contract for a million a year for three years when he leaves office. Use one of our subsidiaries in any location he wants. Okay, we all know what we have to do; we'll reconvene on Tuesday of next week. Helen, would you stay for a minute. I want to talk to you."

CHAPTER 13
Lantau Island

John was getting tired of taking the ferry back and forth to Lantau, so he rented an apartment on the beach there. It was a three-bedroom flat over a restaurant and was close to the temple. Chong arranged for a massage girl to come every day. After every workout with Phoenix, Chong would remark on how well John took a beating and would laugh uncontrollably. John was never amused.

During the week, Rebecca was busy in Hong Kong but spent the weekends with him. Rebecca was not allowed to watch John's training sessions but was amazed at the injuries he was receiving from a little woman. Months went by, and John only left Lantau three times for visa renewals, although next month he would have to be back in Hong Kong, yachting season would be starting.

A week before John was to return to Hong Kong, Phoenix arranged for a match between John and two of her other students. John was a bit nervous going up against two accomplished fighters, but once the match began; his natural instincts and competitiveness gave him the edge to insure a win.

Although John was still a beginner, Phoenix was happy with the results she saw in this short time but told John to be careful, not to let his ego get hold of him. Phoenix agreed to see him for two days every two weeks to continue his lessons. John didn't understand a word when she said something to Chong in Hakka. He asked Chong what she said, and he replied, "Nothing." Chong did not want him to be overconfident. She had actually said John had become her best student, and for a foreigner his age, she never saw one better.

When John returned to Hong Kong, his first stop was to the tailor. He didn't realize he had lost so much weight. He was in the best shape of his life; he felt great and was down three suit sizes. That night, on his boat, he realized how at home he felt here. It was at the same time troubling and comforting.

The next morning, Chong dropped him off at the Hong Kong Club for a meeting with some potential buyers at eleven o'clock and told him he would be back outside at 1:00. When John got back in the car, he was excited. He told Chong the buyers gave him an order for twelve yachts and asked for a distributorship for China.

With business booming in the PRC, there was a class of neuveux riche with plenty of disposable income. It was a virgin market, and he already had a lock on it. John was pleased.

As they drove along Cannaught Street, John saw Rebecca walking and called out to her. She didn't turn around or respond at all, and Chong noticed the undercover cops following her.

"Leave her alone," Chong said. "She's working."

That night, John apologized to Rebecca. She told him not to worry, "But if you see me on the street, please ignore me and never call my name in public."

They spent a pleasant evening together, and Rebecca told him the police inspector's ball was in a week's time and asked if he was willing to go.

"Of course," he replied, "if any of my dinner jackets are back from the tailor's."

A few days later, John was coming home, but as he started to walk down the berth, he saw several Chinese men pushing Rebecca around. He yelled and started to run toward them. They looked up at him and slowly started to walk further down the berth where their speedboat was waiting. John started to run after them, but Rebecca stopped him.

"They are triad," she explained. "It's part of the job."

"They know where you live," he said.

"Hong Kong is a small place, love," replied Rebecca. "I'll call headquarters and have some guards posted."

She explained that they were coming down hard on the triads

manufacturing businesses, and although they roughed her up a little, it was just to frighten her. They weren't crazy enough to hurt a British policewoman.

From what Chong had told him, John wasn't too sure of that.

"Why don't you stay with me for a couple of nights, just to be safe?"

Rebecca thought for a moment and said, "Let me get a few things, and I'll be over in a flash."

After a few glasses of gin, Rebecca was visibly calm. They sat on the deck enjoying a pleasant evening. Rebecca rested her head on John's shoulder and fell asleep in her chair. John carried her down the ladder way and put her to bed. John was just about falling into sleep when the explosion knocked both of them to the floor. The force of the blast blew all the glass out of the portholes, and furniture flew across the cabin. They could feel the intense heat of a raging fire. John bolted up and told her to stay down until he investigated.

The *Dream of the Red Chamber* was ablaze. John grabbed the wash down hose from the berth and opened it full blast. He first soaked his boat to try to prevent any more damage and then tried to extinguish the flames coming from the *Dream*. Rebecca came up on deck and screamed. Everything she owned in life was aboard that boat. John yelled to her to get another hose, but she was in shock, standing there just staring at her whole life going up in flames.

By 5 a.m., the fire was out and the police were all over the pier. Rebecca was talking to a group of British inspectors who gruffly told John to go back to his boat. One of the British cops took John by the arm and started to walk him over to his boat.

"Sir, we will contact you shortly," he said in a very official manner. He tried to go back and talk to Rebecca but was pushed toward his boat by a couple of cops. He didn't resist at all. He surveyed the damage to *The Lady* and saw that from the intense heat, all of the fiberglass on the port side would have to be replaced. Rebecca came over to him.

"John, I can't tell you how sorry I am for all of this."

He told her not to worry about anything. "It's not your fault."

She told him she was being taken into protective custody

and she would contact him as soon as she could.

Later that day, he made arrangements to have the *Lady* taken into dry dock for repairs. He told Chong he was going to Macao until the boat was ready. Chong wanted to go with him, but John said, "No thanks, I need to be alone."

John checked into the Oriental Hotel and Casino, which was in walking distance from the hydrofoil landing. He spent the next few days gambling and exploring the hidden treasures of Macao. While playing Roulette one night, he was alone at the table when a man sat beside him. After losing several large bets, he heard the man say "Merdre," which led John to believe the man was French. John was losing as well and excused himself, leaving the table. He went down the long circular stairway to the bar and sat down for a drink. The man who had been playing next to him asked if he could join him.

"My luck is terrible tonight," the man said. He introduced himself as Andre Pauud. Andre told John he was working on an oilrig in the French section of the South China Sea oil leases. He explained that the Chinese government offered offshore leases for oil exploration; the French firm, Alliance, had won the bid for the largest lease. The Americans weren't competitors. They lost interest after the Arco disaster in the early eighties, forty-nine men were killed, and since then, the American companies mostly did consulting and supplied the Chinese with equipment.

John found the conversation interesting and invited Andre to have dinner with him at Pinocchio's. Andre admitted, during dinner, he was a little apprehensive when the taxi drove into the empty lot and John told the driver to stop.

John laughed and told him, "I had the same feeling the first time I came here." They talked, ate, and drank for several hours. After a great dinner, they returned to the hotel. Andre asked John to come to his room, he had something private to discuss with him. John was hesitant, but Andre seemed like a nice enough guy. Andre's room was identical to John's. After

Andre made him a drink, John asked, "What's the mystery?" Andre appeared embarrassed and told John he had a business proposition for him.

"The tables were really bad to me tonight, and I'm afraid I lost everything I had." Andre produced two large 28 mm south sea pearls and asked John if he would like to buy them. Andre explained that they were cultured pearls. The Chinese had a pearl farm on Hainan Island, and that was why they were so perfect and exactly the same size. John, although dubious, asked, "How much?" and was surprised when he was told only $800 US each.

"They look like they would be worth a lot more than that," John replied.

Andre looked even more uncomfortable and said, "No, my friend, that is what I paid for them, and if you take them, you would be helping me out of a spot. I think that is what you Americans call it, is it not?"

John bought them and told Andre that he had been to Hainan Island a short time ago. *Hainan is getting more interesting. I have to go back soon.*

They went back to the casino and split up; John went back to the roulette table and Andre to the Champ de Fair table. About two hours later, John was on his way back to his room when Andre came over to him and said, "Mon ami, you have been good luck for me. I have won about $40,000 USD; please, let me buy you a drink."

John agreed, and they talked and drank until last call.

Before saying goodnight, they made plans to have lunch the following day.

At lunch, Andre asked John if he would like to go into the pearl business with him.

John was uncommitted, but he did want to go back to Hainan Island, so he agreed to meet Andre there in two weeks and at least take a look.

It was almost a week after he had lunch with Andre when

John got a call from Chong, who told him the boat was back at the club.

"Great," John replied. "I'll be back in a couple of hours."

John was happy to be going home. He thought, *Home that does not seem as strange as it would have a few months ago.*

Upon his arrival at the Hydrofoil Terminal in Hong Kong, John saw Chong was waiting for him with another man—a Brit. John knew he was a cop just by looking at him.

Nigel Palfrey was the type of guy a movie company would cast as a cop. Tall and broad, brutish, and smug, he fit the profile exactly. He told John that Rebecca was sent back to England for her own safety.

"The boys in the foreign office wanted to talk to her before she would be back in Hong Kong."

John wasn't too happy with this news, but at least she was safe. Palfrey refused a ride with them and left on foot toward the Western District of Hong Kong. Chong remarked that he was probably going to shake down a few restaurant owners before he went back to headquarters. John brushed off the remark, as he knew there was no love lost between Chong and the British inspectors of the Hong Kong police force.

On their way back to Aberdeen, John told Chong about Andre and showed him the pearls.

"Where can I have these put into a setting?" John asked.

Chong thought for a moment and suggested, "The Golden Mile Jewelry Shop in Hutchinson House."

It was on the way back, and he could park in the lot in the Furama Hotel across the street.

Tony Wai, the owner of the shop, had a long time reputation for being fair and honest. His shop was in the Hilton Hotel for twenty years before Li Kai Shing decided to tear it down to build an office building for the Chinese government.

Tony was a nice guy who spoke English very well and was surprised that John spoke to him in flawless Cantonese. Tony brought out some pictures of finished pieces to get an idea of John's taste, and when he was satisfied, he told John he would design something very nice for him. John got a call in three days from Tony Wai telling him the necklace was ready. When John arrived at Tony's shop, he saw the necklace in the display case in the front window. It was a twenty-four inch strand of 9 mm pearls with the two South Sea pearls at the bottom separated from the other pearls by two jade carvings and connected together by a gold cylindrical clasp with 9 carrots of diamond chips.

Rebecca is really going to like this, John thought.

Tony placed the necklace in a velvet pouch and handed John the bill. John was delighted with the price, saying it was more than fair, and asked Tony if he would be available to go to Hainan with him as an expert consultant.

Tony did not want to sail there but agreed to a plane ticket and further agreed to spend one night. Tony was obviously well versed in jewelry and pearls and would be an important part of John's decision-making process in going forward with this deal.

John had spoken to Andre by phone, and arrangements were made. John would leave Hong Kong the following day, and it would be two days sailing. He told Andre he should arrive at Alliance's pier on Hainan Do about 3:00 p.m. the day after tomorrow, and asked if Andre would make arrangements for him to tie up there.

John had gone back to Chong's friend at China travel, and in a matter of hours, had a visa for the trip. Hainan Island was in the People's Republic of China.

John had still not heard from Rebecca and was becoming concerned, but Chong told him that she was safe in England.

"Don't worry, boss. You'll hear from her soon."

The sail over to Hainan Island was uneventful, and Andre was waiting for them at the Alliance Pier, as arranged. They tied up and met the oil company's port captain, and after the normal formalities, they drove to Hainan's only airport to meet Tony Wai. The airport was on the other side of the island, about a two-hour drive. They passed through fishing villages and pineapple and coffee plantations, all which were interspersed with rice paddies. John was enjoying the drive when, about five miles before they reached the airport, they drove along the most beautiful stretch of beach John had ever seen. White and pink sand beach lined with various types of palm trees on one side and the blue green waters of the South China Sea on the other. The occasional junks sailing by with their odd shaped sails made it a truly exotic sight. John wished Rebecca were there to share this.

They picked Tony up at the airport and drove directly to the Ministry of Animal Byproducts office on the island. They were greeted by a delegation of about twenty people. The manager, Mr. Li, started to introduce everyone, and John smiled.

May I present Mr. Wu, Mr. Pu, Mr. Lu, Mr. Tu, Mr. Gu, and so on? John smiled, not because it seemed funny the names were so similar, but because he knew he would never remember which was which.

Mr. Li asked if John would mind going to the pearl farm immediately, as they had another engagement that day elsewhere on the island. John agreed. Chong went with the Chinese, who got into two vans, and Andre followed in his car with John and Tony Wai.

Tony told them that he had escaped from China during the Cultural Revolution. Both his parents were killed by the communists, and at age twelve, he made his way through the military guards at the shore of the Pearl River near Quangdong. He made it down river at night and hid during the day. He made it through the border crossing at Macao hiding in the back of a truck delivering fish to the Portuguese colony. Once in Macao, he had called an aunt in Hong Kong, and she wired him enough money to take the slow ferry from Macao. He was briefly put in a refugee camp and then let out on his own. A man who owned Ying Tai Tailors took a liking to him and gave him a job delivering clothes. During the next few years, Tony learned the tailoring trade and worked there for the next twenty years.

He learned English and became quite successful selling to the American and British tourists. Over the years, he saved his money, and when the shop next to Ying Tai, which was located in the Hilton, became available, he talked to his boss and asked if he would be interested in being his partner in a jewelry shop. His boss was surprised at how much money Tony had saved over the years. Tony didn't drink and gamble as much as the other salesmen. His boss and mentor put up some money, and Tony used his own to open the shop. He continued to be frugal and built up his inventory year after year until it had become one of the best jewelry shops in Hong Kong. He had eventually bought out his boss, and the shop was all his. With his reputation for quality and honesty, he was very successful.

It was a three-hour drive to the pearl beds. After they were given a tour, it had been agreed that they would all meet at the hotel for dinner and discuss preliminaries. After dinner, they had discussions late into the evening, and all agreed to visit the beds again in the morning.

John was quiet during the drive. He listened to Tony and Andre swap stories, and he realized how unworldly he was. He had made these new friends, and he liked them both. Andre was surprised that John was an accomplished businessman and was able to hold the negotiations in fluent Cantonese. Tony translated for Andre. The Chinese told them that they could harvest twenty-five to twenty-eight mm pearls of good quality every ten months and that their system of production was state of the art.

That night, they worked out a kind of future deal, where they could buy the whole crop at a reduced rate at time of seeding, but the risk of return would be on John and Andre's side. They showed them records of the last two years, and the harvest rate was about 92 percent of seeded oysters. After prices were set and it was established that insurance could be gotten from the People's Insurance Company for destruction by weather or force majeure, a deal in principle was agreed to. A letter of intent was already drafted while they were at the oyster bed site and would be given to them before they left that day. It was further agreed that someone from the ministry would take Tony back to the airport after lunch. His flight was at five o'clock, getting him back to Hong Kong by six.

The morning went great, and Tony assured John and Andre that they had a good deal. Tony told them that even he was surprised at the technology the Chinese had. It was far superior to even the Japanese technology. They asked Tony if he would be interest in being a partner. Tony said, "No, but I'll be a good customer."

They said good-bye, and John thanked Tony for all his help

and asked him to send him a bill for his consulting services.

John and Chong stayed for two more days going over details with Andre. This looked as if it was going to be a profitable sideline.

When they returned to Hong Kong, John immediately called Nigel Palfrey, but there was still no word from Rebecca. John asked Chong if some of his relatives on the force could nose around and see if they could find a way for him to contact her. It took three days before Chong had the information. Rebecca could be reached at a telephone number with a city code from the midlands in England. John called the number, and a woman answered and asked only, "Where did you get this number?"

He heard Rebecca's voice asking for the phone. Rebecca sounded stressed, but she told him she was fine and she missed him. She couldn't tell him anything about what was going on but would be back in Hong Kong in the next few weeks, but she wouldn't be able to talk to him until she arrived.

John was upset after the call, and the next day he asked Chong what he heard from his relatives.

Chong told him, "There was no information, but they were holding an investigation to find out how you got the number."

"I hope I didn't get anyone into trouble," John said.

"No," replied Chong, "the British couldn't find an elephant in the middle of central."

Chong laughed, but John could see in his eyes that Chong was more than a little nervous.

CHAPTER 14
Memphis

Jen Pao had asked Helen to stay after the meeting to quiz her about her relationship with Mike Manheim. Jen Pao had first introduced the two of them with the understanding that she told him everything that she could find out about Manheim. Helen was the most mercenary woman Jen Pao had ever met and would be ideal for his purposes. One hundred thousand dollars per year above her already generous salary was put into her account for this service. Jen Pao knew that the only person standing between him and the total control over the North American arm of Liddo was Manheim, and he wanted to know every move Manheim made. Eventually, he would make a mistake and it would all belong to Jen Pao.

Michael Manheim was a brutish man, but his rough way and size only masked a brilliant mind. He was one of the most ruthless and feared men associated with the Liddo group in America. He was not directly connected with Liddo, but that was only for propriety. He was the top man of Liddo in North America, but only a few even within Liddo were privileged to that fact.

During the Vietnam conflict, mad dog Manheim, as he was known, or dog to his few friends, was an officer in the USMC Force Recon unit working with the Montangards and Vietnam Special Forces on the Laos and Cambodian borders. It was there that he made his first contacts with the Liddo group. He was supplying arms to the drug lords in the golden triangle in return for their cooperation with US troops working on the borders. He was lured in by the promise of money and all it entailed. He started by smuggling drugs into the US on private planes used by US intelligence for purposes they would never admit to. It was perfect. Arms in and dope out, all making him a very wealthy man. He proved himself to be smart and fearless, and the Liddo group needed an American to head up their US operations. Manheim was an orphan and never had a job except for the military; he was a loner and did not make many friends. He was a great organizer and problem solver and could be expendable with no repercussions. He was just what they were looking for. By the time the war was over, he had amassed over fifty million dollars in several overseas banks. He moved to Memphis, where Liddo had already set up their operations and began his rise as an entrepreneur.

At Liddo's direction, he began to buy radio stations, all funded by Liddo. He then went to television and finally print media. By the mid 1980s, he ostensibly controlled, openly or covertly, almost all of the media in the US. It was done through a maze of corporations and front companies, all controlled by but never leading back to Manheim. Although he had no visible control, he ruled with an iron fist, and anyone who did not do what he wanted was fired or simply died. Manheim's use of the media made governors and presidents, and he wielded this power with the agility and precision of a world-class orchestra conductor. He never took money for this, but he used this power to control some of the highest-levels of government in the US, and recently the highest level, the most powerful position in the world, the President of the United States, and Manheim was in control. He was now truly a man with no limits or boundaries. The real genius of this was that he was totally unknown.

CHAPTER 15
The reunion

John was waiting anxiously at the arrival hall of Kai Tek airport. It had been almost two months since he'd seen Rebecca. Her plane's arrival was announced, and John, normally in control of himself, was ready to jump out of his skin with anticipation. It was a full half hour before she came through the double set of doors from immigration. As she walked down the ramp into the arrival hall, John walked beside her ten feet away, a fence keeping them apart for another fifty feet. When she reached the end of the fence, John grabbed her and pulled her toward him. Someone from behind grabbed him around the neck, and as he was pulled away from her, undercover police surrounded him.

"Don't touch him," Rebecca screamed.

They backed off, and Nigel Palfrey came forward. "Sorry, Miss Dreed. Orders are that you are not to see anyone until you report to headquarters."

"Just give me a minute, will you?" she replied. She took a step toward John and took his hands in hers, telling him she would call him as soon as she could. As she pulled her hands away, he felt the note and palmed it before the constabulary could see it. Rebecca was whisked away, and Chong told him they better leave.

Their car was on level three of the car park, and as they walked to the car, John noticed Palfrey leaning up against it.

"What the hell do you want?" asked John.

"I just want to tell you that Miss Dreed will be kept safe, and it will be easier for all parties concerned if you don't contact her until this business is finished with."

"What business?"

"I'm not at liberty to say, but believe me, I'm on your side with Miss Dreed. She's good people, she is. I'll try to let you know from time to time how she's doing." With that, he walked away.

Chong remarked, "Don't trust him," and John was inclined to agree.

On the drive back to Aberdeen, John opened the note:

> John, if you are reading this, it means they have picked me up at the airport. Don't worry. I'm safe. I want you to contact Imelda Browne at the Helena May, 35 Garden Road, Hong Kong. It's a women's residence across the street from the American consulate. Imelda is my oldest and dearest friend, and the only person besides you I trust. She works for MI5, and I will have free contact with her. She will keep you informed of my whereabouts, and she will try to arrange a private meeting for us. I miss you.
> Love, Rebecca.

John was beside himself and asked Chong, "What is this MI5 she mentioned?"

Chong explained that MI5 was similar to the American FBI, and that MI6, the foreign office, was like the CIA.

"Foreign office," John said. "That's who she was with in England."

Chong said, "Wow! She's got herself into some serious mess. Those boys don't fool around. If they are involved, it's probably best you stay away for a while."

John didn't sleep very well that night. He woke up to find Chong walking around with headphones and carrying some kind of equipment, slowly waving what appeared to be a microphone in front of him.

"What are you doing?"

Chong motioned for him to be quite and continued while John went in to take a shower. After his shower, he went into the galley and poured himself a cup of coffee and went up on deck. Chong came up and motioned him aft and told him he was sweeping for bugs. John laughed and then looked into Chong's hand and saw two small electronic devices. John stopped laughing and told Chong he wanted to go to Hong Kong Central. John felt sick. He was more angry than frightened, but this was totally new ground for him. Why were they bugging him? What did Rebecca get into that could be this sensitive? If they started to investigate him, would Lucy be able to find him? All of these thoughts were spinning around in his head when they approached the Helena May.

Chong passed it and kept going up the road toward the peak. He pulled into the Japanese school to turn around and stopped. He turned to John and said, "If they are bugging your boat, they probably have someone watching you. Write a note to the woman you want to talk to and tell her to meet you in Chatter Square on Sunday about 10:00 a.m. All the Philippine Amahs will be there, and you can get lost in the crowd. When we go back down, I'll park in front of the Helena May and you go across to the American consulate. If you are being watched, it will look normal. I'll get the note to the woman. I know her by sight."

"You know everyone," John laughed.

Chong told him he had never met her but she was famous in MI5 and the police department for having the largest breasts in Hong Kong. As John crossed the street to the consulate, he noticed Chong get out of the car and bend over, as if he were picking something up from the street. Chong looked up and down the street and then knocked on the door of the Helena May. A matronly woman answered the door, and Chong asked her if there was anyone there with the name Missy Browne. The woman replied yes but explained that she was out. Chong told her that when he parked here to drop off his boss he noticed this letter on the ground and he picked it up, it was addressed to Missy Browne. The woman assured Chong it would be given to Miss Browne immediately upon her return.

It was 10:10 a.m. Sunday, and Chong pointed her out in the throng of people in Chatter Square. John noticed Chong was right, they were the biggest breasts in Hong Kong. John turned and walked away. Chong approached her and slipped her the note. It simply said, "Meet me at the address below in one hour," and was unsigned.

Chong had made arrangements for them to meet at his sister's flat in North Point. Chong's relatives were scattered along the route they had prearranged to look out for any MI5 boys or British cops that might be following them. If any were spotted, his sister would put a statue of a gold dragoon in the window to call off the meeting. When John arrived, the window was empty, so he went in. Chong waited for Imelda. He didn't see anyone suspicious, so he escorted her in. Once inside, she was introduced to John. Imelda Browne had a pleasant face but an enormous chest, *It must be a 58DD*, John thought, and then he caught himself and looked back into her face. She laughed and told him not to worry, she was used to it. John felt a little embarrassed, but Imelda's warm personality soon had him comfortable.

"How's Rebecca?" he asked.

"She's fine, but she is in a dangerous situation. I can't give you the details, but she has uncovered a crime ring, which will implicate many government officials of several governments, and she is being used as bait. She told me to tell you to get out of Hong Kong for a while. She is afraid someone might come after you to get to her."

John was feeling the onslaught of his first anxiety attack. Imelda noticed his apprehension. "Keep a stiff upper lip. You have to be strong for her; I will meet you at the Meridian Hotel in Phuket three weeks from today. In the mean time, if I need to get a hold of you for any reason, I'll contact Chong."

Imelda left on her own, John and Chong waited a good hour before they walked out to the street.

John plotted his course and figured sailing time to Phuket was about nine days so he would have time to stop at Hainan Island on the way. The next day, he arranged for visas for both Thailand and China. He sailed out of Hong Kong harbor Wednesday morning after Chong had swept the entire boat for bugs. That night, he pulled alongside the Alliance pier and John was glad to see Andre. John needed a friendly face about now. Andre was affable. He was always ready to tell a joke or a story. He was a rough looking guy but had an ease and charm about him that was calming.

Andre and John went to dinner in a restaurant out on the water, kind of a bamboo shack built on stilts. There were two young boys fishing out of the back door and seeming to catch a lot of small fish. John wondered if that was dinner. Andre laughed and said, "You can't get fresher than that."

While they were eating, two Americans came in, and John was surprised to see them. There were only two tables, so they sat down at the empty one about two feet from John and Andre. As John and Andre spoke, one of the men asked if he was American. When John replied yes, the man introduced himself as Charlie Wilcox. "And this is Fred Medford."

"Are you guys in the oil business?" one of them asked.

John told them Andre was but he was only visiting. John asked them the same question, and Charlie, the more vocal one, told him, "No, we're mining rare earth."

John asked, "What the hell is that?"

They went on to tell him, "It's a strategic element, very rare, and used in the manufacture of weapons and computer screens. There are only three places in the world you can find it Australia, the United States, and here. This is the largest vein in the world; it cuts across this island and goes through China to Vietnam and into Laos. You can see it from the satellite pictures of the earth. This vein is long but only about four inches wide. Andre asked, "Its four inches wide, and you could see it in satellite photos?"

"Yes," Fred replied. Nothing will grow for about three meters on either side. This vein was discovered during the Vietnam War. When the soldiers got close to it, their weapons wouldn't fire."

"You're kidding?" John went on to say. He didn't believe them, and Charlie pulled out a small lead box from his pocket.

"Give me your watch," he said to John. "Here, place it on the table."

John placed his watch on the table, expecting some trick, but Charlie wasn't kidding. As soon as he opened the little lead box, John's watch stopped. John looked inside the box, and there was a small stone about the size of a pinhead. John sat there in total disbelief of what he had just seen. When Charlie resealed the box, John's watch started to work. They all laughed, and Andre asked, "How do you mine that stuff?"

"By hand," was the reply. "You can't get equipment to work around this."

They talked for several hours telling stories of their individual adventures in Asia and all agreed it was quite a place. On the way back to the hotel, Andre turned to John and said, "Tomorrow I'll show you my mine."

John looked at him quizzically but didn't say anything. Andre called for John about 7:00 a.m., and they had a light breakfast of conge, a rice gruel and yochow, and deep-fried dough that was twisted and pulled like a cruller.

During breakfast, Andre told John they were going swimming, so he wore shorts and a T-shirt. Andre had a small boat and motor in a private marina on the opposite side of the island from Alliance. He had scuba gear and diving buoys already on board. They started to sail due south, and about two miles out from shore, they pulled alongside of what John thought was an oilrig. Andre explained to John that his company started to operate this rig and eight others at the same time, but instead of oil, they hit large thermo faults about 2,000 feet down and got nothing but steam.

"I came up with the idea of building generators on the top of the rigs and using the steam to generate electricity, which my company now sells to the Chinese government. I'm going to show you what neither the company nor the Chinese are aware of."

After they were suited up in their scuba gear, Andre handed John a large scrapper and a canvass diving bucket and told John to watch him and then do the same. They dove down, and Andre swam to one of the legs of the rig. He put the bag against it and started to scrape off sediment until the bag was full. John followed the procedure, and when both bags were full, Andre gave John the universal scuba signal to surface. Andre put his bag on the diving platform behind the boat and climbed up the small ladder. He took John's bag from him and gave him a hand getting up. John went to lift the bags into the boat and almost fell with the weight.

"What is this stuff?"

Andre smiled and said, "Be patient, mon ami."

When the got back to the marina, they carried the bags ashore and loaded them into Andre's car. A short distance away, he pulled into a yard behind a small metal building. Andre unlocked the door, and inside, John saw a long cylindrical tube about ten feet long. Andre started a stand-alone diesel generator and motioned for John to bring the bags over. He opened the cylinder and dumped the bags in. He then turned on a water valve and flipped a switch. The cylinder started to spin at an enormous speed, and dirty water was rushing out of one end, and then John heard metal falling into a series of metal boxes along the side of the cylinder. As John watched, Andre explained this was a centrifuge and it was cleaning and separating the material they scrapped off the legs of the rig. After several minutes, the machine quieted down and Andre turned it off. He walked John over to the side, where the metal boxes were, and told John to open them all. In each box, there was a pile of minerals. As John looked closer, his eyes showed surprise.

"That's right, mon ami," Andre said. "This one is gold. This is silver, copper, tin, magnesium, and so on."

John was going into information overload. *The guys last night with rocks that stop a clock and now this?* He started to feel he was losing all reality. Andre looked at his face and burst into laughter. Andre explained that when the steam is pulled up from below, it heats the water around it, and with the spinning of the generators, it causes the whole rig to become electromagnetic.

"The super heating of the water at the base of the rig separates the minerals in the water, and they are collected by the legs of the rig, acting as magnets. God made this for me and no one else," Andre said. "I need a partner to transport it for me to the refineries in Hong Kong or Singapore. Are you interested?"

In the last several months, Andre had accumulated several kilos of each material and told John there was no problem with customs in HK or Singapore but he doubted the Chinese would be very happy.

They both laughed. John told Andre he didn't know anyone in the business that he could bring it to and maybe he should find a professional.

"What about Tony Wai?" Andre asked. "He makes jewelry; he might buy it from you."

John agreed and thought to himself he was now in the pearl and precious metals smuggling business. *Man, has his life changed!*

He told Andre that he would stop back on his way from Phuket to Hong Kong and to have the ten-kilo box ready for him then. For the next week, he just wanted to lie on the beach and relax. With all that had happened in the last month, he needed a break.

He sailed to Phuket and tied up in a small marina in the lagoon adjacent to the Meridian Hotel. He was a day early, so he would have a chance to look around before Imelda showed up.

CHAPTER 16
Rome, Italy

Sergio was at the park at 7:00 a.m. as instructed. Ascot greeted him with, "Good morning, Minister." Sergio shuttered to think what was going to be asked of him.

"Good morning, Ascot. It is so good to see you," he said lying. "What can I do for you?"

"Ah! Sergio, always right to business. Take some time to smell the roses, as they say."

Sergio repeated, "What can I do for you?"

"All right, right to work. You are going to start off in your new position with a bang. Here are several contracts you will sign for barter deals with five different companies, all from Asia with the exception of one from America. The contracts are for different commodities from Italy, in exchange for rice from Asia and wheat from America, all fairly standard. You will also appoint these men into top customs positions. All of the imports will be shipped in bond into our warehouses, and it will be agreed to have all customs formalities done on these sites."

Sergio turned red, "No! I won't do it. I know what you are doing. I helped you too many times bring drugs into Italy. This will give you carte blanch. I won't do it."

"Sergio, this is not the right time for you to be exposed. How will you explain the second salary? I believe it's now $22,000,000 you have put away. How you are going to explain that to the public. Sergio, my friend, you are not the type of man that does well in prison, and if you resign, you will be killed. I'm sorry, my friend, but we must protect our investment."

With that, Ascot Chen got up and walked away. Three days

later, it was announced that the new minister of commerce had signed several contracts worth well over eighteen billion dollars, which would stimulate the slow Italian economy.

CHAPTER 17
Bonn, Germany

Helmut Klieg was enjoying the morning in his new office at the BND. When he became director, he had hit the ground running and by all accounts was going to be remembered as the best head of the BND in history. He was born for this job. His credentials were impeccable, and he was a quick study. In a few short months, he had already formulated a protocol for the intelligence operations in both Eastern Europe and Russia. He had handled several major problems with Iran and Iraq and had put to bed what could have been a serious problem for Germany in Tursjakastan. He really enjoyed this position, and he was good at it.

Studying the morning's briefings, he did not see anything urgent, but it appeared there could be some trouble brewing in Austria and Germany with the Nazis and skinheads again. He had foreseen these problems with the influx of Eastern Europeans into Germany and Austria over the past several months. They were starting to impact the economy and the labor force. When the east became part of the European Union, the Eastern Europeans simply could no longer afford to live there, and at least one member of the family had to come to Western Europe to make enough money to allow their families to survive.

The German and Austrian firms took advantage of cheaper labor without taking into consideration these people grew up in a socialist society and had no work ethic at all. Even though they were only being paid about half of what German and Austrian workers were paid, they didn't do even half as much work. The western workers were feeling it, not only in the fact they had to produce more but jobs were becoming scarcer and the unions were starting to complain and the membership in both the skinheads and Nazi movement were rising quickly. Nazi graffiti was all too prevalent, and the young people were starting to attack foreigners again.

Helmut thought about the problem and knew he had some of his best people infiltrate these organizations and his intel was good, but he wondered if he should be doing more. The buzzer on his desk rang.

"Mr. Klieg, there is a gentleman here to see you. He says he is a friend... Ascot Chen."

His stomach knotted, and he actually felt faint. *What is he going to want from me*, he thought, knowing that whatever it was it was not going to be good.

"Ah! Yes send him in."

As Ascot walked through the door, Helmut felt a wave of nausea come over him.

"Helmut," Ascot said in a friendly, if not jovial voice.

"Please come in," Helmut said and closed the door behind him.

When he was assured no one could hear him, he said, "What do you want from me?"

"Now, now, Helmut, is that the way to talk to a friend?" Ascot asked, jeering at him. "I was in town and thought I would drop by and say hello." Helmut knew this was a lie. Ascot Chen never visited anyone without a reason.

Ascot continued, "I'm only going to be in Bonn until tomorrow and wondered if we could have dinner tonight? There is a nice quaint little restaurant in the old Hotel Bonn. Do you know it?"

"Ah, yes, I do," Helmut replied.

"Good, I'll meet you there at eight thirty then. Good-bye, I'll see you tonight."

When the door closed, Helmut was physically and violently ill. *This could be the end to my career.* He started to shake and cancelled all his appointments for the rest of the day. He sat there thinking. *How did he get into the building?* Then he realized he was not the only *friend* Ascot had in the government.

CHAPTER 18
Phuket Thailand

The Meridian hotel was beautiful. It was built around an open-air lobby, which led to two large pools, which separated the hotel from the beach. Between the pools was a bar, and from the top of the bar flowed a waterfall that cascaded into the two pools on either side. The building was designed so every room had a view of the ocean. It terraced downward like steps so every room had an open balcony. The rooms were appointed in modern oriental and all had king-size beds. The beach was dotted with blue and white striped hooded chairs and small groves of palm trees. Under the shade of the palm trees, women were giving massages to guests.

The clientele was mostly European, Italian and French, and the women were mostly topless. Along the water's edge, there were rental sailboats and water cycles, basically a motorcycle on pontoons, which would travel through the water at about seventy miles per hour, the concierge told John.

The hotel had all of the normal resort amenities, nightclub, bars, health club, and restaurants. John had surveyed the hotel grounds and thought he would go and explore the rest of Phuket. He asked the concierge if there was a town nearby and was told the nearest town was Patpong. He checked out a motorcycle from the guests' service desk and proceeded down the road to Patpong. The landscape was hilly, and there were tiered rice patties on the side of every hill, and people were working the patties with their water buffaloes. The vegetation was lush and various shades of green, giving the area a storybook quality. About ten miles from the hotel, he saw a sign. "Patpong two kilometers."

Before he got his first look at Patpong, he could already hear the music. It was that deafening bass sound that was so popular in Asian disco. He pulled into the first street he could turn into. There were outdoor stalls one after the other with a bar and several bar girls in each one. The music was sickening loud, and the girls were ridiculously forward. John thought he must have come into the wrong end of town but soon realized this was it. Not being his style, he turned the bike around and went back to the hotel.

He had dinner in his room and went down to the beach for a swim. After 6:00 p.m., the pools were closed, as the pool area doubled as a restaurant. He walked along the beach and went in for a swim and then back to his room for the night. A comfortable bed and the sea breeze allowed him a good night's sleep. He woke up at eight in the morning and had breakfast. About 10:00 a.m., he rode the courtesy car to the airport to meet Imelda. She came off the plane and recognized him immediately. John took her one bag and escorted her to the van and back to the hotel. While she was checked in, she told John she would change into her swim costume and meet him on the beach. He arranged for two chairs to be set up a bit away from everyone else. It was almost an hour before she came down to the beach.

John called to one of the waiters who constantly strolled the beach, and he ordered two piña coladas. Imelda seemed pleased. She began to tell him that Rebecca was well and working hard at closing this case, but it had gone much deeper than anyone had realized. Imelda continued to say that Rebecca couldn't trust anyone and was in a very dangerous situation, but as long as she remained the center of attraction, so to speak, she was safe. John asked, "How did all this happen?"

Imelda collected her thoughts. "Evidently, while running down the knock-off artists, Rebecca came across a drug operation that was run by the Green Bamboo triad. The Green Bamboo went back centuries. It was started in Shanghai and moved with the Kuomintang to Formosa after WWII. Chaing Kai Shek was a member, which should give you an idea how powerful they are. During the Vietnam War, they made deals with the American CIA and became even more powerful. The CIA needed their help to stop the NVA activity along the Laos and Cambodian borders and also needed intelligence about the VC movements in South Vietnam. In return, they supplied the Green Bamboo with weapons and military training and helped support the drug armies of the golden triangle.

Rebecca uncovered one of their operations and found proof implicating Hong Kong, Chinese, British, German, American, and other government officials. She found a series of computer discs, which had the pay-off schedules for government officials, police, and newsmen around the world. It goes a lot deeper than even the Green Bamboo. They are now using Rebecca to flush out the ringleaders and the fronts for government officials. No one else could have operated on the scale of this magnitude without plenty of government protection."

"This is like a movie script. I can't believe this is happening."

"Believe it, my dear, it is."

Imelda went on to say she couldn't tell him any more other than he should be careful.

John said, "I have to get her out of there. She's going to be killed."

"That would be some trick, with four government agencies protecting her and half of the Asian underworld trying to get her." John thought he was having a bad dream. Imelda told John "Rebecca is my oldest and closest friend and if there was anything you could do, I would help, but in the mean time, why don't you try to relax and clear your head. If we are going to do anything, we'll have to be clear headed and well rested." John agreed and stayed quiet for the rest of the afternoon.

They had agreed to meet in the lobby at 8:00 p.m. and went to the poolside restaurant for dinner. Imelda remarked, "It is so lovely here."

The hotel had placed tables around the poolside and lit candles floated in the pools along with a local folk band seated in several canoes that floated in the center of the pools. The soft music and cascading waterfall made for a very romantic ambiance. John thought, *I wish I could be here with Rebecca.*

The food was superb, the service impeccable and the company

was pleasant. John liked Imelda. She was down to earth but well educated and interesting to talk to. Her personality was bubbly, and she seemed generous to a fault. She was definitely someone John wanted on his side. Under other circumstances, this would have been an enjoyable evening, but John felt guilty having a good time while Rebecca was going through hell. After dinner, John excused himself, saying to Imelda, "I'm going to turn in early." He walked Imelda to her room and said goodnight.

John stayed awake most of the night, trying to come up with a plan to help Rebecca. He awoke sitting in the chair in front of the balcony door. He realized he must have fallen asleep about two hours ago. He got up, showered, and brushed his teeth, thinking the entire time he had not thought of anything that would work to help Rebecca. This was over his head. He was out of his realm, and he knew it. He was just about to go to breakfast when Imelda knocked on his door and said, "Darling, you're not doing anyone any good cooped up in your room. Get out in the sun and relax. Listen, dear, take it easy. I'm starting to develop a plan in concept, and by tomorrow, I'll have it formulated enough to discuss it with you. In the mean time, relax. If I do come up with a workable plan, I'll need you, and you'll have to have your wits about you."

CHAPTER 19
Washington DC

The president picked up his private cell phone and listened to the voice on the other end.

"Mr. President?"

"Well, I'll be. Mike, how are you?"

"I'm fine. I just wanted to invite you down to play some golf this weekend."

"Well, I don't know. I'm pretty busy here in DC."

"I've already talked to the first lady and explained it to her, and she is amenable."

"Well, in that case, I'll see you this weekend," replied the president.

When he hung up, he had a concerned look on his face but immediately started to smile at the people around him. The president knew that this was a command performance and it couldn't be good. That night, he went to his quarters and asked his wife if she knew what is was all about, but she just smirked and said, "Attorney and client privilege. I've already ordered Air Force One to be ready 3:00 p.m. on Friday."

He just stared at her as she left the room.

CHAPTER 20
Memphis, Tennessee, Friday 4:30 p.m.

"Mike. Hey, buddy, how are you?" asked the president.

"I'm fine, but get rid of the reporters and tell the secret service people that they are not allowed in the house. I'll see you there in one hour, okay?"

The president looked uneasy but replied, "It's done."

The first lady rode with the president to Manheim's house but did not get out. She asked that the two best secret service men, O'Hare and Brume, stay with her; she did not play golf and wanted to visit her mother. When the president entered the house, he looked back and the first lady was gone. The secret service positioned themselves around the house, but none went in. The president thought this was one of the reasons she took O'Hare and Brume. They would have never gone for this. He stood alone in the large foyer for seconds when Mike Manheim came in.

"Well, powder my ass and call me a biscuit," he said as he walked up and hugged the president. "Well, look at you, the President of the United States. A long way from Tennessee, hey bubba?"

"Mike, you look great."

"Come on in, son. Let's have a drink. I've arranged for us to tee off at 6:00 a.m., is that too early?"

"No, that's just fine," he answered. "Mike, I haven't thanked you for all you have done for me, and I want you to know I appreciate it."

"I know that, Mr. President. No thanks required."

From the way Manheim said *Mr. President*, he knew Mike

was not showing respect. It was more like ownership, and he did not like it.

"Hey, where is that beautiful wife of yours. She has to be the smartest woman I have ever met."

The president replied, "She wanted to visit her mother while we were here."

"Sure, I can understand that. You never get too important to visit your folks."

"Mike, let's get to it. Why am I here? What do you want?"

"Mr. President, I'm hurt. I just wanted you to get some rest and a round of golf, nothing more. We're going to have a nice dinner, then get some rest, and play golf in the morning. The governor and a few of your old buddies are coming over tomorrow to see you, and that's that."

After a round of golf, they were on the way back to the house when it occurred to the president that there was not one newsperson or reporter anywhere to be seen. This was a first since he had become president, and he marveled at the power Mike had over the media. When they got back to the house, the governor was there and the president was truly happy to see him.

"Let me get you boys some drinks. The cigars are in the humidor," Mike said as he was leaving the room.

The governor looked up and said, "Mr. President, I need your help."

"What is it?" he asked his old friend.

"One of my constituents needs some export licenses for China."

The president looked at him and said, "Well, that's no problem. I'll get a hold of the secretary of commerce and it will be done. He owes me."

Smiling, the governor replied, "The licenses are for missile technology."

"Missile technology to China? Have you lost your mind?" the president asked aghast.

"No, sir, and this has already been promised."

"I can't do it. Washington is not like here where a couple of good old boys with the right connections can feather their nests with no problems. They would string me out to dry and impeach my ass."

"This is not a request, Mr. President."

"I don't give damn what it is. I can't do it. I have to go to the can. Where is it?"

"The first door to your left at the top of the stairs."

As he came out of the bathroom, Mike was standing there. A cold feeling ran down the president's back.

Mike said, "Listen, you haven't forgot who put you where you are, have you?"

"No, but what he is asking is impossible."

"Nothing is impossible. You get the secretary of commerce to do it personally and I'll arrange for an accident. The blame will all go to him."

"No, I can't do it," replied the president.

Before he could utter another word, Mike grabbed him and threw him down the stairs. Mike walked calmly down to him. The governor ran out and in horror and said, "You killed him!"

The president moaned and said, "No you didn't, but, you son of a bitch, you broke my leg."

"You see how easy accidents happen," Mike replied. "I don't give a damn what you have to do, bubba, but you'll get that thing signed within two weeks or we'll take you out just as easy as we put you in."

Mike walked past him to the front door and opened it and yelled to the secret service, "Hurry, the president's had an accident."

The next day, the president was standing in the window of the White House explaining to the press he had an accident at the home of a friend while on a golf holiday.

CHAPTER 21
Bonn Germany

Helmut stood outside of the Hotel Bonn. It was eight fifteen, and he had already been there for over an hour. He had to make sure no one was following him. He was certain he was alone and made his way into the lobby. The hotel was old and elegant but in need of refurbishing. It reminded him of a beautiful older woman without makeup, still beautiful but could look a lot better. The hotel was famous but no longer in vogue for the locals. It was one of the old grand hotels that were now reduced to being the fifth day of a seven-day tour of Europe. The clientele was no longer international business people but mostly senior citizens from America who seemed to be fond of these escorted tours through Europe.

As he stood there, his mind wandered as he watched the tour guides rounding up groups to take an evening tour around the city. He wondered if at their age he would be able to do such things or would he be broke and living in disgrace for what he was about to do. Just then, an arm went around his shoulders and Ascot Chen was smiling at him with a warm but frightening glare.

"Helmut," he said, "glad to see you're on time. I hate hanging out in lobbies alone. Have you been waiting long? I hope not."

Ascot took his arm and walked him into the restaurant. The maître d' greeted them with a flair rarely seen.

"Gentlemen, it is such an honor that we have two such distinguished persons in our restaurant. Please, this way. I have a nice private dinning room already set up."

As the two of them sat down, Ascot apologized for this restaurant, but it was a good place for a private meeting.

"Not too many celebrities come through here any more, so there is never any press around." Helmut acknowledged it was a good venue for their meeting and tried to get past any pleasantries and right to the point.

"What do you want, Chen?"

Chen, wanting to toy with him a bit, if for nothing more than to put him on edge, said, "Why, Helmut, we haven't seen each other in so long, and you just want to talk about business?"

"I'm not you, friend, and I don't like what you are doing to me, so let's just get to it."

Ascot, seeing he was getting the response he wanted, kept it up.

"Why, Helmut, how can you say that? The few small pieces of business we have done have been profitable for both of us."

"You're blackmailing me," Klieg screamed as he jumped from his seat.

"Now, that's not a good way to view our relationship, Helmut," Chen said with a playful tone to his voice.

"All right, this is what I need of you," Chen continued. "The German Central Bank has just refused a trade with China of three billion dollars worth of US treasuries and some Japanese commercial paper at twenty-five basis points below the euro trading price."

"I can't do anything about that. I'm not in banking anymore."

"Let me finish," Chen said. "In return, the Chinese will give 200 million in technology contracts to German firms, and they will deposit five million euros in an account for you. You will go to the central bank and explain to them this is needed for National Security and instruct them that you will be on the negotiating team to put the deal together. You will demand the 200 million in contracts and come out looking like a hero."

Helmut thought about this for a minute and realized that this was the international visibility he needed to get to the next level of his career while at the same time making him a very rich man.

"And if I refuse?" Helmut asked.

"Then you will soon be working in a café in Berlin utilizing your other talents. Now there is one other thing. How many agents do you have in Hong Kong?"

"Wait. Now you have gone too far." Helmut's face turned red, almost purple.

"No, no, I don't want to know your security apparatus in Asia. I need two good covert agents in Hong Kong. A British solicitor, a young woman, has uncovered some discs containing some very sensitive information, and we need them back. If you can help me with this, I will destroy the tapes and you will never see me again. British and American intelligence are working on it. I only need you to watch those agents and report the information about their investigations back to me. This is a simple surveillance operation, nothing more. If you agree, we are finished. The tapes will be given back to you."

Ascot said this knowing that he no longer needed the tapes. If Helmut took the five million, he would hold that over his head. Helmut thought for a moment and said, "Okay, but I'll never see you again?"

Ascot smiled and simply said, "Deal."

Helmut walked out of the hotel and felt as if the world was off his shoulders, thinking to himself that it was not really a bad deal for his government and it would mean nothing to use two of his covert people for this little job. Sufficiently justifying this to himself, he thought it might be nice to call George, his new young lover, and spend the night refreshing himself.

CHAPTER 22
San Francisco

Peter Fraus was frantic. He had been trying to get John for almost a week, and it seemed as though he'd fallen off the face of the earth. Peter was happy to get so many orders from Asia, but it looked as though they were going to have a hard time delivering on time. The manufacturer of the mast and boom had called, and it looked like they weren't going to deliver on time. He had similar calls from the electronics manufacturer, and Volvo was going to have to ship the last eight motors from their factory in Finland. Sailcraft had cleaned out their entire inventory in Sweden.

With all these delays he was never going to be able to deliver on time. This was the best year they ever had, and with the new designs and the Asian business, the orders were flooding in. The new kid was a whiz, and his ideas were selling. Peter thought to himself the only thing left was to send him a telegram.

When John arrived back in Hong Kong, he navigated *The Lady* smoothly into her slip and surprised himself by thinking he was glad to be home. One short year ago, he would have never believed that he would have thought a yacht club in a foreign country home. After he tied up, showered, and changed his clothes, he went up to the club for a drink. As he walked through the door, the club steward approached him and said, "Excuse me, sir. There is a telegram for you."

He gestured to a clipboard with a receipt form affixed to it and said, "Sir, would you sign here?" and handed over the sealed telegram.

It read:

> John, please call me ASAP. We have a lot of problems, and I need your help. Stop. The problems are all production. Stop. I know if anyone can solve them, it's you. Stop. Your divorce became final yesterday. Stop.

John read it again and felt a sharp pain down in his gut. Peter must have thought this would be good news, but the finality of it gave John a shock deep into his soul. He never felt this alone.

He sat down at the bar, and after four martinis, he knew this would not stop the pain and went back to the boat. John lay on his bed thinking of how beautiful Lucy was and what a good time they had. In the first years of their marriage, he was so happy. After her first affair, Lucy begged his forgiveness and promised it would never happen again, but deep down John knew better. It seemed every time he turned a blind eye to one of her indiscretions she resented him more.

As the years passed, the chasm between them grew wider and he knew the wild streak she had that first attracted him to her was going to split them apart forever. He recalled how sick he felt after overhearing that last phone conversation where she conspired against him with her then-most-recent conquest. He called back every detail of his marriage from their wedding to the day he sailed for Hong Kong, and although he felt a rage that was frightening, he would always love her, but he knew it was in the past and he had to put it behind him and move on.

He was still awake in the morning when Chong arrived.

"Hey, boss, it's good to have you back. What are we going to do today?"

"We're going to Central to visit Tony Wai."

Chong helped lift the box out of the small closet in the galley and said, "What do you have in here? Lead?"

"No," said John. "Gold."

Chong laughed, "You're funny, boss."

When they arrived at Hutchinson House, John told Chong to stay in the car and he would get a hand truck from Tony Wai. John returned a few moments later with the hand truck and put it in the back seat of the car.

"You might as well park at the Furama. I'll meet you upstairs."

Tony's shop was on the second floor right at the entrance to the fly over that connected Hutchinson House with the Admiralty Building, The Bank of America Tower, and the Lippo Building. Tony had already spoken to John about this transaction and had the precious metals expert from Tai Lo, the largest jewelry factory in the world. It was the largest in Asia before Home Shopping Network. Since the American market went to infomercials, their sales had risen to over twelve billion USD per year.

Tony invited John into his office in the back of the shop and introduced him to Cadbury Chen, a well-dressed man in his fifties. They exchanged pleasantries in Cantonese, and Chong arrived with the small box. They put it on the desk, and Cadbury produced an electronic scale from his legal-type briefcase. When they opened the box, Chong gasped.

"You weren't kidding, boss."

They all laughed and proceeded to check out the merchandise. After several tests, Cadbury said, "This is good quality, about 96 percent pure. I'll pay you 90 percent of refined price less refining costs."

John said it was a deal, but Tony said, "No, 93 percent."

Cadbury said 92 percent, and then Tony said, "Deal!"

The price of refined gold was $437 per troy ounce. The total weight was 11.7 kilos. They did the math, and the total came to $1,809,180. They discussed the other metals, and Cadbury agreed to buy them on a regular basis. John asked that the funds be transferred to his account in Wertshaft and Privatbank in Zurich, and the arrangements were made by phone before Cadbury left. John told Tony that he would wire his cut of 10 percent into his account that evening. He couldn't now because of the time difference. Tony said no problem. After thanking him for all his help, John left the shop. Chong was quiet until they got to the car.

"What was that? Where did you get that?"

John said, "Don't ask any questions, but you are getting a raise."

Chong drove back to Aberdeen with a big smile. When John got back to *The Lady*, he called Andre and told him the deal was done and he would follow the instructions Andre had given him before he left Hainan. John sat back in his chair and thought to himself, *I should have come here years ago. This is the wildest place on earth. I've lived a lifetime in the last couple of months. When this is over, I'm going to write a book*, he thought and quietly laughed to himself.

Before leaving Phuket, Imelda and John had made arrangements for a method to contact each other. He would call her on her mobile phone and let it ring once and then hang up. He would repeat this twice. When Imelda wanted to reach him, she would call the Aberdeen Yacht Club and leave a message for him to call John Smith. When either of them was called, they would have Chong meet Imelda's amah in front of the Watson's in the Pedder Building in Central the day after the call at 11:00 a.m. sharp.

After leaving Tony's shop, John noticed the men following them and pointed them out to Chong. Chong told him he recognized them. "They're local British inspectors. They work for Palfrey. Don't worry about them. Do you want me to lose them, boss?"

"No," John replied. "It's probably better to know where they are."

Chong agreed.

After John had finished his business and arrangements had been made to transfer money to Tony and Andre, John called Palfrey.

"What the hell am I being followed for?"

"I am following a request made by Miss Dreed. She wants you safe."

John didn't believe him but said, "All right, as long as those goons don't interfere me."

John decided to have dinner at the club, and as he walked in, the steward called to him and told him he had a message and could he please call Mr. John Smith.

After dinner, John called Chong and asked if he could be at the boat by no later than 8:00 a.m. the next day. As always, Chong agreed without hesitation.

Chong waited outside of Watson's Drug store at the Pedder building. He noticed the man leaning up against the newsstand, and although he didn't recognize him, he knew what he was. Chong went into Watson's and walked through the crowded store to the back and waited. Sure enough, after a few minutes, the man came in and was looking for him.

Chong went down the rear stairs to Watson's grocery store and walked through the store and out through the front entrance. He saw Imelda's amah and walked past her and told her to meet him in the shopping arcade across the street in front of Davidoff's in five minutes. Chong went across the street and went into the arcade and took the escalator up to the lobby level of the Edinborough Tower. From here, he had a view of the entire arcade.

He saw the amah in front of Davidoff's and looked carefully around. When he was certain he had lost the Brit, he took the escalator down and met her. She didn't say anything. She just handed him an envelope and walked away. Chong walked straight out of the arcade and crossed Queens Road and walked a block to Ice House Street where he had the car parked. When he got back to Aberdeen, he didn't tell John about his being followed. He just gave him the letter. It said, "Take me sailing this weekend. Bring Chong. We have to leave Hong Kong." It was unsigned.

John spent the next day mentally charting a trip to the western most islands in the Philippine archipelago. He picked Siamtoa. It was a tiny island with only about 200 residents. The only foreigners they saw there were the occasional scuba divers. John remembered this place. It was where Ian had taken him to go scuba diving before he went back to England. He charted it mentally so there would be no record whatsoever. John thought to himself, *Just because you're paranoid doesn't mean they're really not out to get you*, and he laughed to himself, but in reality, it was better to take these precautions. Imelda showed up at Queen's pier at 7:30 p.m. and quickly jumped aboard. She said hello and went quickly below. Chong climbed up on the rigging to get a better perspective as John sailed south out of Hong Kong Harbor.

After they passed Lantau Island and were approaching Ping Chow Island, Chong was comfortable they weren't being followed. He climbed down and sat next to John in the cockpit. It was a dark night and a good steady breeze. They were making good time. Just as they were relaxing, they had passed Chung Chow about twenty minutes ago, Chong grabbed the binoculars and looked back toward the island.

"Dammit," he said. "We have company."

John sailed toward Macao, although it was in the opposite direction he had planned. John started to call out instructions to Chong.

"Put up the spinnaker. We'll lose them if we can get enough distance between us."

John sailed under the bridge, separating the big and little islands of Macao, and circled around the island. No one was following, so he headed due east. About four hours from Macao, Imelda came on deck with two glasses of gin and a beer for Chong.

"What's up?" John asked.

Imelda said, "Not now, wait until we're off the boat."

John told her Chong had swept for bugs before they left, but she just put her hand to his mouth and said "later."

They arrived at Siamtola Island about 5:00 a.m., and they all went below to get some sleep. John had anchored in a lagoon that looked like a travel brochure. About noon, everyone started to stir and they had a good breakfast and all swam to shore. As they sat on the beach, Imelda said, "Brace yourself for what I'm about to tell you. I got this information from a guy in MI6 that I sleep with occasionally."

The story she proceeded to report frightened them. On

one of her trademark infringement raids with the Flying Squad, they uncovered a dope smuggling operation. That was routine, and arrests were made. What was not routine was the fact that Rebecca found computer disks with an outline of an international drug operation that included government and police officials from Great Britain, the United States, China, Indonesia, Vietnam, Kampuchea, Laos, France, and Germany. It included high-level officials from MI5, MI6, the CIA, and FBI with a trail all the way to Washington, Interpol, and the French DPSD all tied together by the Liddo Group. Evidently, several of the Triads grouped together and were keeping records so they would have some leverage, in case something went wrong. Although not widely known, the Liddo group was a powerful and very dangerous organization, and the Triads were afraid of them. These records were going to be used if Liddo got mad at them. They would have some chips to play in trying to stay alive.

"Rebecca had the forethought to make some copies before turning them in, and that's what is keeping her and you alive as well. This is so far reaching that no one knows whom to trust, but that works in her favor for the moment. Ian Grant transferred over to SAS and is petitioning with the foreign office to take over the responsibility of protecting her. That might work because that would take the light off of everyone in normal channels, although I don't think it would be safe for her. SAS is great for covert operations, but they're not trained to be bodyguards. To outline the entire picture, the Liddo Group, through their hundreds of legitimate businesses launders money for the Triads. They also act as financiers, and through a network of offices around the world, supply Intel to the drug dealers. They have thousands of police and politicians on the payroll. It's not a few pence. We're talking millions of pounds, and it's being paid to every level from street cops to high-level officials.

The Liddo Group originally was a group of Indonesian Chinese who over the years has expanded; using oversees Chinese to build a legal empire funded by illegal means. They started to use the Triad's services of muscle and prostitution to coerce, by friendly or not so friendly means, small business owners to sell out to them. The ones who resisted were killed, and Liddo just took over. The ones that agreed became part of the group. The more they grew, the more powerful they became, monopolizing markets through intimidation and sheer buying power. They became more intertwined with the Triads and drugs just became another commodity. They used their wealth and power over the triads to become the most powerful trading group in the world. They have so many politicians in their pocket, they are now selling their influence and are becoming world power brokers. Their head office is in Jakarta with branch offices in Memphis in the States and London, as their operations center for the European theater."

John was horrified and stared at Imelda in disbelief. "I never even heard of the Liddo Group."

"You never will. They control the world media one-way or the other and enjoy their low profile. They started to get a little press in the States but their problem died quietly in jail, alone."

"Boss, believe it. Remember, I have been a victim of this corruption."

The three of them sat quietly, and finally John said, "What are we going to do? This sounds a little beyond my capability."

Imelda said, "We are probably the only hope Rebecca has of surviving. There is not a government agency or police force we can trust, except for two, PRC and Russia. Liddo has nominal presence in both those countries, and in China, there are still old-line officials who can't be bought. There are a few, anyway. In Russia, the government is not in control, it's anarchy, the Russian mafia can be bought for protection. They are so ruthless that everyone, including Liddo, fears them."

"So what's you're plan?" asked John.

"I don't have the details yet, but in concept, it is to somehow get Rebecca out and hide her in Harbin. Harbin is a Chinese City in Siberia. It's the border-trading city between Russia and China. We'll need some money, but we can buy protection from the Russians and ask for political asylum from the Chinese. They love it when a Westerner asks for asylum. It allows them to wake up the tiger and show the world that people are fighting to live under their leadership. Then we will publish the story with facts and names on the Internet. Liddo controls the media but not the Internet. We'll ask for a worldwide outcry by the public. The politicians will have to buckle, and Liddo will have to back off until the situation dies down. Rebecca can publish the information she has, some crocked cops and politicians will be arrested, there will be an investigation by Parliament and your Congress, and everything will go back to the way it was, and Rebecca will no longer be a threat to them unless something happens to her and the whole mess starts up again. It's her only chance."

It sounded plausible to John.

"How the hell are we going to get her out? I don't even know where she is."

Imelda told him, "Rebecca is in a safe house on Cane Road in mid levels. She is being protected by local police, MI5, and MI6 with the local triads staked out on every corner for a twenty-block radius.

"Great," John said, "and the three of us will just go in and take her."

"Yes," Imelda said.

"You're nuts," replied John. "We'll get ourselves killed, and Rebecca won't have a chance."

Imelda asked Chong if his relatives were clean.

"As clean as any Hong Kong cops," Chong said with a smile.

"Well," replied Imelda, "how many of them can you trust?"

"Most of them," said Chong. "I know the ones I can't."

"Okay then, start to gather information. Find out if they know and have any type of relationship with the triad members hanging around central or mid levels. Get as much information on the British inspectors who are, or might be, in the Triads pockets. Get a list of the French, American, and German security people who are known to be operating with the Triads; there's about 500 last count."

"You're pretty good at this," John said.

"I haven't been with MI5 for fifteen years without picking up something," she replied. "John, you are to go to Zurich as soon as possible. I have been in contact with Ian Grant, and he will meet with you. Check into the Central Hotel and act as normal as possible. You have just made some large deposits and transfers—"

"How do you know?" John asked indigently.

"You're being watched, dear. Don't worry; no one cares about your business or relationship with your IRS. As I was saying, contact your banker and go through the motions of business as usual. When Ian feels it's safe, he will contact you. Do not leave under any circumstances until either Ian or I contact you. Now, Chong, do you have anyone you can trust to act as a conduit?"

"A what?" Chong asked.

"A conduit…a go between."

Chong thought for a minute and said, "Yes, Rose. She is the manager at the New Paradise massage parlor. She is smart, and she has been my mistress for about ten years."

"Good." Imelda went on to say someone would call the New Paradise and leave a message for Rose that would say, "Please call Wai shi Chor."

"When she gets that message, she should go to the Peak Tram station on Garden Road at 11:00 a.m. the following morning and someone will pass her a message for you. If no one approaches her by eleven fifteen, she should leave. They will make another attempt at 3:00 p.m. the same day at the noodle shop next door to the New Paradise."

"How do you know the New Paradise?" Chong asked.

"I go there before hours once in a while. It's one of the perks of working for MI5," Imelda told him. "I will also gather intel and coordinate. It's a little difficult for me right now. It is known in the department that Rebecca and I are best friends, so I'm being watched as much as you are, but at least I have the benefit of their training so I can see them coming. When we go back, I will get off the boat at Silver Mine Bay and take the ferry back. It will look like I was visiting friends there. John, you make arrangements for Zurich immediately. Get out of Hong Kong as soon as you can."

She turned toward Chong and said, "I don't have to tell you to make yourself scarce. Well, that's that, and it's a beautiful day. Let's get some sun."

John looked at her and thought to himself, *She is either the biggest idiot or she has more balls than anyone I've ever met.* He hoped the latter was correct.

CHAPTER 23
Hong Kong

It was about 7:00 p.m. Sunday evening when John navigated the *Hong Kong Lady* into the narrow cove on Lantau Island, about a mile south of the ferry pier at Silver Mine Bay. Silver Mine Bay was a private housing development that looked like a displaced suburb of Cleveland. It was family oriented and mostly inhabited by American and British expats working in Hong Kong. It was only a thirty-minute ferry ride from the outer island ferry pier in Hong Kong, and the ferry sailed every hour on the half hour from 6:30 a.m. to 11:30 p.m. Living in Silver Mine Bay was much less expensive than living in Hong Kong and allowed its inhabitants the familiarity of an expat community. It is like the feeling one gets in a Hilton Hotel in a foreign country; it is a bit different, but you know where the toilet paper is. John felt it was like a holding pen for the more boring and less imaginative people in Hong Kong, but he thought at least they are all bunched together. It was brilliant on the part of Imelda to come here before going back to Hong Kong. If she had been spotted on Queens Pier Friday night, it could be explained away by weekends here at Silver Mine Bay.

John and Chong arrived at Aberdeen about 10:00 p.m., and after *The Lady* was secured, John walked Chong up to the club. Chong got into his car and went home, and John picked up his messages. Among his many messages, John found orders for eighteen yachts of the new design from his new distributors in China. He walked out on the pier and looked out at the blinking lights of the boats in the harbor. He was exited about the orders, but it didn't compare to the feelings of dread and exhilaration from the adventure he found himself in. He picked up his cell phone and called Peter in San Francisco. With the nine-hour time difference, it was still Sunday afternoon in the States.

"Hello, Peter, I received your telegram. Great news about the divorce, and don't worry about the delay in delivery, I got a sixty-day extension on the delivery, and you should receive the amended letter of credit in the bank tomorrow."

"I can always count on you," said Peter. "Where the hell have you been?"

"I have been going nuts trying to get a hold of you," John responded. "I was out of Hong Kong and couldn't get a signal on the cell phone. I just got back, and we got an order for another eighteen boats."

"And here I thought you've been out there having a holiday," said peter.

"Some holiday," John laughed.

"Listen, Peter. I'm going to be away for a while, but I'll contact you when I get to where I'm going, and maybe you can join me."

"Where are you going?" Peter asked.

Trying to be vague, John replied, "I have some banking connections to work on. I'll explain when I see you."

"Oh," said Peter, "I understand. Listen, I want to fill the Superintendent position. There's a kid that has been working here since you left, a friend of our young designer. They went to school together. He's great, and I'll be happy to promote him."

"Good," replied John.

Peter said, "I've been a little nostalgic. These two kids remind me of us twenty-five years ago, and it's scary."

"The next thing you'll be telling me is you just bought a convertible and died your hair." John laughed.

Peter sighed. "I did."

They both laughed. John missed his friend but knew he'd be seeing him soon.

CHAPTER 24
Washington

"Mr. President, the secretary of commerce is here now."

"Good, show him in ... Bob, good of you to come."

"My pleasure, Mr. President."

"I understand Johnny Trong was over to see you concerning some exports to China."

"Yes, sir, but I declined. The commodities they wanted the licenses for were too sensitive, and we would be in conflict with the COCOM treaty."

"Ah, come on, Bob, the COCOM treaty is outdated. The communist threat is over, and we have to make friends with the Chinese."

"Sir, you are asking me to break the law," the secretary said.

"I am not doing anything of the kind. I am simply stating that we need more trade with China, and this is a good start. I've already cleared it with the attorney general."

"Well, sir, you have the power to sign the licenses, but I won't."

"Bob, you'll regret that. It means over a million dollars to the DNC and all the good will of the Chinese people."

"Sorry, sir."

After the secretary left, the president sent for his wife.

"Would you please call our friend in Memphis and inform him I can't help him."

She looked at him incredulously and said, "I'd better go and tell him in person. He is still my client."

As she walked out of the oval office, he realized this wasn't over. The first lady returned that evening and walked into his private office. As the president looked up, she put the papers in front of his face and said, "Sign them."

He thought for a minute and took the papers, and as he signed them, he said, "Are we covered on this?"

"Yes," she replied as she took the signed documents and walked out.

The next day, the secretary of commerce, Bob Bruin, called his attorney and asked if he would come over to his office ASAP. When the lawyer came into his office, the secretary said, "Let's get out of here. This is sensitive."

They took a walk and crossed the street from the Department of Commerce and continued to walk toward Constitution Avenue.

"He's gone completely over the top," said the secretary. The lawyer looked at him and wasn't sure, but he appeared to be either frightened or enraged.

"Slow down, Bob, what happened?"

"The president wanted me to sign export decks for missile technology for the Chinese. Is he crazy?"

"What?' replied the lawyer. "Has he gone insane? Let's think about this for a minute. If you do it, you'll wind up as a fall guy and be doing time in Levenworth for the rest of your life, and if you don't, he'll get you some other way. What did you tell him?"

"I said no, he had the authority, he should do it himself. He said the attorney general had already cleared it, but if he told her to walk naked down Pennsylvania Avenue, she would. What the hell am I going to do?"

"There is only one thing you can do. Get out of town right away. If you are not here, no one can blame you."

"Where can I go? Let me think. I know I was asked to go on that stupid fact-finding tour of Coursivo. They are leaving tomorrow."

"Okay, then, get back and make the arrangements quickly."

Two days later, the attorney picked up the *Washington Post*, and the headline read, "Bob Bruin on fact-finding mission to Corsivo was killed in a plane crash outside of that capital city of Yugoslavia." He dialed the number in Memphis and was asked for the transfer information. Two hours later, he was $250,000 richer.

It was reported that the plane was downed in a horrific storm and all of the passengers were killed in the crash. This was almost true, except there was no storm and two of the passengers had bullet holes in their heads. In the same news day, it was announced that an American company was awarded a large missile contract in the People's Republic of China, which would not only bring jobs to the US but also reduce the costs of sending our satellites into space.

A few days later, a reporter from the *Washington Post* wrote an article about the dangers of having our missile technology sold to the Chinese. This looked like a hot story, but that night it was announced that the president was being sued by a woman for sexual abuse and the media attention was diverted from the missile story to the much more interesting sexual harassment suit. The writer from the *Post* was fired the next day for being drunk on the job. They did it. The Liddo group made wire transfers that day for over 500 million dollars.

CHAPTER 25
Corcevo Yugoslavia

The UN response rescue team was the first to reach the scene. The wreckage of the plane was scattered over an area of at least a mile, and the terrain was mountainous, and the snow made it treacherous. The team was lucky it was such a clear night. They found the main fuselage of the plane and bodies were all over the crash site. It was horrifying, and as the team fanned out through the carnage, a sergeant screamed he had found a survivor, a woman.

She was suffering from shock and what looked like several broken bones, but she was alive. A medic was called, and he immediately started the normal disaster site triage and made her warm and stable. After setting up an IV, he gave her an injection of morphine to relieve the pain and started to attend to her breaks. He determined that there was a compound fracture of her tibia, two compound rib fractures, and what appeared to be a spiral fracture of her fibula. She was saying something about shots fired, but the medic could not completely understand her. Within minutes, a med-evac helicopter was landing.

Before they could move her, an American military helicopter landed and several men in plain clothes flashing US government credentials jumped out and asked the whereabouts of the commanding officer. The officer in charge was a Canadian, and after being shown their papers, he told his men to mount up and they left the area to the Americans. Bob Bruin's body was identified and was immediately put into a body bag and marked for cremation. The bullet hole in the back of his head was never to be seen by anyone outside of this group.

The woman who survived would show up the next day in a morgue in Baden-Baden Germany with a bullet hole in her head, and the police report stated that she was the victim of a jealous lover who was now in the custody of police. The agent in charge reported back to his NSA superior that the mission was accomplished and they were heading home.

The agent in charge in Washington told his subordinates to stand down and close all channels, no memory. This meant that all records or evidence was to be destroyed; even the PCs that were used would be burnt. No record whatsoever. When that was accomplished, the agent in charge left the building and drove to Alexandria and called Manheim from a pay phone, the only message was, "Yugo storm over." Ten million dollars was wired to a numbered account in the Cayman Islands, and the agent smiled. His retirement plan was complete.

The next day, the news media was in a frenzy reporting the downed plane of the secretary of commerce in a storm on a mountainside in Yugoslavia. It was amazing that no one ever looked at the weather report. There had not been a storm or even rain on the entire European continent for days before and after the crash. Manheim's control over the media was absolute.

CHAPTER 26
Sausalito, California

Lucy was pacing back and forth in the bedroom. Frank was watching MTV and had the volume up to deafening proportions.

"Will you shut the thing off?" Lucy screamed. "I can't hear myself think. How can you lay there all day watching that mindless drivel?"

Although she looked more like thirty than fifty, she still wasn't a kid, and he was. She was now coming to the stark reality that they had nothing in common except great sex, and that only lasted for about an hour a day. As she paced back and forth, she kept repeating, "That bastard, that bastard."

Frank asked her what she was saying, and she told him to shut up and get out. Frank said, "Okay, I'll go to a movie, and I'll be back for dinner."

"No," she shouted. "I mean get out. Don't come back. I don't want to see you again."

"But I gave up my apartment. You told me to move in here. What I am going to do?"

"You're a big boy now. You'll figure something out."

She had already pulled his suitcase from under the bed and was packing it as they spoke. She escorted him to the door and said good-bye.

"Don't call me." She slammed the door behind him.

Lucy went into a hysterical rage, and after several hours of screaming and breaking things, she fell asleep on the floor. The phone was ringing, and she woke. It was six o'clock Pacific time. She listened to the answering machine, and it was Tony Cerico, the private detective she hired to find John. She picked up the phone. "I'm here."

"Listen, I think I got a line on your husband, or should I say ex-husband. I went over to the boat yard the other day and a young designer told me they have a slew of orders from Hong Kong. I think he's there."

"No," she said, "he sold his share in Sailcraft to a Hong Kong company. It doesn't make any difference anyway, the divorce is final, and his attorney's made me sign a hold harmless clause that would protect him from further litigation."

"Why the hell did you sign that?" he asked.

"So I could keep what I got," she replied, "and it's really none of your business. How much do I owe you?"

"Are you ending the investigation?"

"Yes. I don't ever want to see him again."

"It will be as we agreed $5,000."

"I'll send you a check tomorrow. Thank you." She hung up.

Lucy went into the bathroom, and when she looked in the mirror, with her eyes bloated from crying, she looked old, every bit of fifty, and she cursed him.

"John, I hate you," she said to the mirror, but in her heart she knew everything that had happened was her fault, and that seemed to make her hate him more.

The next day, she put the house up for sale and purchased a one-way ticket to Sydney. She was going home. Although she hadn't been there in over ten years and knew it was going to be different than she remembered it, she had to get away from here. Everything here reminded her of John. Deep down, she loved him and missed him, but the fact he got the better of her angered her to the point of pure hate. She had abused him and took advantage of his good nature for years and mistakenly took his ambivalence for stupidity. She was wrong, and it was eating at her. The quicker she got away, the better. He left her enough to be comfortable, and with the sale of the house, she should come out with about four million, but she felt she deserved more.

"That bastard," she said to herself, knowing that under the circumstances he was more than fair. She wanted more.

CHAPTER 27
Hong Kong

It was Monday morning in Hong Kong, and Chong came aboard as usual, about 8:00 a.m. On his way to work this morning, Chong thought to himself his life would now surely change and there was nothing he could do about it. It was destiny. He had to be at his best, and if things went right, he could survive and maybe pay back that Quay lo lousy British inspector who ruined his career and his life. He would do everything in his power to help his new friend and boss, and all he wanted was to see that British prick lose everything and leave Hong Kong in disgrace.

As he went below, he saw John was already up and having coffee.

"Good morning, boss."

"Jo San," replied John in Cantonese. "Let's go," John said, and he picked up his small canvas workout bag and started up the ladder to the deck.

As they got into the car, Chong asked where they were going. "Just drive."

When they were underway, John told Chong, "We're going to the airport. There's a flight to London at ten, and I'll buy my ticket there. That won't give them much time to follow me."

"Good thinking, boss."

"As John approached the British Air ticket counter, he saw Palfrey.

"Good morning, inspector."

"Where are you off to?" Palfrey asked.

"None of your business," John replied.

John asked for a first-class ticket to London on the ten o'clock flight.

Palfrey said, "First-class, not bad," and left.

John thought to himself that he would be followed immediately upon his arrival in London, so he had to think of something. The plane had a stop over in Bangkok, and John got off. He went to immigration and got a one-day visa and went to the Shangri-La Hotel. He spent an enjoyable evening, and in the morning went back to the airport, and an hour later was on a Singapore airline flight to Frankfort.

Frankfort Airport was one of the largest airports in the world, and it took John almost an hour to get through it. He took a bus into the city and went to the Eros Center. He knew that here they weren't going to make him register and he could spend the night anonymously.

The hooker he was with was totally bewildered. She never had anyone who actually slept when they *slept with her*, but she didn't care. He was paying the same, and it saved her the wear and tear she would normally get from an overnight trick. John woke up refreshed and took a quick shower and left. He took a taxi to the train station and grabbed the fast train to Zurich.

CHAPTER 28
Zurich, Switzerland

He arrived at the Zurich Bahnhoff an hour and a half after he had boarded the train in Frankfort. He asked directions to the Hotel Central and was pleased he could walk there. He walked two blocks down the Bahnhoff Strasse to the Hotel Central and the porter, with his green apron in the fashion of all Swiss porters, took his bag at the door and asked if there was more luggage.

"No, my luggage was lost, and I'll have to buy some new clothes."

"The hotel will arrange for a driver and guide to help you get what you need."

During his walk to the room, John's mind was racing. *Was he doing the right thing? He was definitely in over his head, but he had committed.* When he arrived back at the Central, he went to his room and lay on the bed thinking about how crazy this all was.

John didn't get to sleep until about 5:00 a.m. but woke at eight o'clock. He was a bit disoriented and had that feeling of not knowing where he was for a minute but then focused and swung his legs over the side of the bed. He drowsily called room service and ordered coffee and croissants. He was just getting out of the shower when his breakfast arrived. While sipping his coffee, he called Peter in San Francisco.

"Hello, Peter, it's John. I'm in Switzerland…Zurich, to be precise. Can you get over here?"

"What?" Peter asked incredulously. "You want me to come to Switzerland?"

"Yes," said John emphatically.

"I guess I can catch a flight tomorrow. What's going on?"

"I'll tell you when you get here. Call me later with the flight number and time of arrival."

John hung up the phone and sat down at the desk and began to write. He listed the events chronologically and named everyone involved as explained to him by Imelda. After several hours, he was finished and went down to the desk and asked if he could make twenty-five copies of his affidavit. The desk clerk told him to leave the papers and the copies would be brought to his room, but John said no, it was of a confidential matter and he would make the copies himself.

"In that case, sir, there is a business center three blocks away on Limmat Strasse number 52."

John took the walk to the business center and rented a fully equipped office for four hours. He sat down in front of the computer and began to type all he had written, and when he finished, he printed twenty-five copies and signed and dated each one. He then printed up twenty-five address labels and affixed them to envelopes and put one copy of the affidavit in each. On the label under each name and address, there was a simple statement, "Do not open this envelope unless I am dead or missing, John."

Inside each envelope was a note that said:

> In the event of my death or disappearance, send a copy of this to as many newspapers and magazines as you can and publish on the Internet everywhere you can.
> Thanks, John.

He then cleared the memory off the computer and printer and paid for the service office and left. He posted twenty-four of the envelopes to friends of his around the world and kept one copy for Peter. He returned to the hotel and left Peter's copy in the safe and told the concierge to alert Frederick, his driver. He would be going out in fifteen minutes. Frederick was in front of the hotel when John walked out of the door.

"Good afternoon, sir," Frederick said as he opened the car door for him.

"Hi! Fred," retorted John.

Frederick smiled to himself and thought how informal these Americans were. He liked it.

"Where would you like to go, sir?"

"Why don't you drive up to Trimmlie. I heard there is a little restaurant on the top of the mountain there."

Trimmlie was just below the village if Eck, about five kilometers from Winterthur. They went as far as you could by car, and then Frederick explained they would have to go the rest of the way by tram.

The scenery was breathtaking. From this vantage point he could see all of Zurich city and past that Zurich See, one of the largest lakes in Switzerland. It was beautiful.

He noticed in the distance a castle in the middle of the lake, and Frederick explained it was a sixteenth century castle, now a museum and restaurant, and you could get to it by either the lake tour boat or by driving along the left shore of the lake. John told him he would like to go there next.

The place was crowded with people—students, tourists, and locals. John was looking around at the crowd when all of a sudden he noticed someone familiar. He looked closer, and sure enough he had seen this guy in Hong Kong. They found him.

He continued his tour and kept a weary eye on the man following him. When they got back into the car, it was almost 10:00 p.m. but it was still light out. John asked Frederick if he could go back on a different road, and the reply was yes but it would take longer. John said that was all right. He wanted to see as much as he could.

On the way back, Frederick drove up to the top of the mountain and drove through the countryside. There were farms, and in a few places, they had to follow a herd of cows walking in the road. This gave John a chance to confirm to himself that they were being followed.

When they got back to the hotel, John asked Frederick to pick him up at 6:30 a.m., as he had to go to the airport in the morning to pick up his partner from America. Once in his room, he called the desk and asked for a five thirty wake-up call and arranged for coffee to be brought to his room by six.

The plane arrived on time, and he was glad to see Peter. He told Peter immediately not to ask any questions, he would explain later. Bewildered, Peter agreed and began to tell John everything that had been going on in Sailcraft. When they got to the hotel, John told Peter they had a busy day.

"Why don't you go up, unpack, and get some rest. I'll wake you in about four hours. God, it's good to see you," John said and gave him a manly hug.

"Man, have you been working out, you look great, and you're solid as a rock. Hong Kong is agreeing with you."

"Yeah," John said, "I kind of joined a gym," and laughed.

It was three fifteen when they walked into Wertshaft und Privat Bank. They approached the receptionist, and John said, "We have an appointment with Peter Tsillman."

"Yes," the young woman replied, "you are expected. Please, come this way."

She escorted them into a round sitting room and left, closing the door behind her. They sat there for several minutes when the room started to turn.

"What the hell?" Peter blurted out unconsciously. When the room stopped, the door was on the opposite side of the room from when they came in. The door opened, and a well-dressed man of about forty entered and said, "Let me introduce myself. I am Peter Tsillman."

He took them into his office, which was decorated with antiques and original paintings from Mattese, Picasso, and a Rembrandt, as well as several of the Dutch masters.

"What can I do for you? Have there been any problems? Are you satisfied with our service?"

John said, "Everything is fine, but I would like to ask you to open another account for my partner here, Peter Fraus."

"Are you any relation to the Fraus family from Bern?"

"No," replied Peter. "I don't have any relatives outside of the US."

"Oh, you're American?" he asked.

"Yes," Peter replied.

"Well, if you would like to open an account here, you will have to fill out this form. It is required by your government, and it gives us permission to show your account information to the US authorities upon their request."

"What?" said John. "I don't do that."

"You're the representative for a Hong Kong interest, I believe. We are not required by the Hong Kong government to do this. I'm sorry, but unless you fill out this form, I cannot open an account for you."

John looked at him and said, "May I please have the full amount in my accounts, and I will be closing them today. Peter, we'll go to another bank."

"Don't be too hasty," said Tsillman. "Let me think. Yes, there is a way I can do it. I'll open a sub account to one of the existing accounts. Would that be satisfactory? Here, Mr. Fraus, just fill in this line that says code authorization. This will be how you access your account. You can do it by fax or give telephonic instruction as to where you want the money transferred. You will be receiving a bearer Amex card that will allow you to access your account. All the credit card bills come directly to the bank and we charge your account. There is no other record."

After the paperwork was done, they were escorted out of the bank. Once outside, John turned to Peter and said, "Not a bad day's work," and they both laughed. As they got back into the car, John noticed the man following him. It was the same man as last night. *This is good*, he thought. *There must not be too many of them following me.*

John and Peter spent the rest of the afternoon at the lobby cafe in the Bauer Au Lac Hotel discussing their business. Peter told John he was able to buy the adjacent land on both sides of the boat yard and he would send the plans for expansion to him before he went ahead with them. John told Peter about his business plan to try by next year to expand the line with larger and more equipped boats. He explained that the social climate in Asia was different and people loved to show their wealth.

"I can't believe we have Lucy to thank for all this. If it weren't for her, I would have never left," John said.

Just then, Peter Tsillman walked in.

"Good afternoon, gentlemen. May I join you?"

"Of course, please sit down."

He ordered a couplet, a glass of champagne, and cucumber sandwiches, which were a standard at the Bauer Au Lac.

"Are you gentlemen staying here?"

"No," replied John, "we are at the Hotel Central."

"Yes, a much more reasonable hotel, but the next time you come to Zurich, may I suggest the Storchen Hotel. It's right up the street on the Limmat, the canal that goes through the center of Zurich to the lake. It is nicer than the Central, and it is more central."

"Thank you. We'll remember that."

"May I invite you for dinner this evening?" Tsillman asked.

He took them to dinner at the Dallder Grand Hotel, the oldest and grandest of all the hotels in Zurich. Both John and Peter noticed that most of the clientele for dinner were old very elegantly dressed women. Tsillman commented on the fact that 90 percent of the wealth in the world was controlled by women who outlasted their husbands. Tsillman seemed to know everyone there, and John guessed that this was Tsillman's target market.

They started off with a bottle of crystal and caviar, then a shrimp cocktail followed by the entire game menu of rabbit, venison, pheasant, and bear roast, each in a different sauce.

"Gentlemen, let me explain. A currency portfolio account has a required minimum balance of 250,000. USD. A portfolio account is divided into major currencies, U.S. dollars, DMarks, Yen and Swiss Franks. We then set up a sub account with Austrian Shillings, French Francs, Italian Lire and Euros. We trade all day, every day. Each night we convert everything back to the strongest currency. We have had an average return of fifty four percent per annum for the past five years."

John was staring off into space and suddenly asked, "Can you substantiate this claim?"

"Of course, why don't you come to the bank in the morning and I can show you the actual figures."

"That would be great; if you can prove this to me I'll move a million dollars to start. Pete, is that all right with you?"

"Fine," Peter answered.

"All right then. What time should we come over?"

Tsillman pulled out his day finder. "Is ten o'clock satisfactory?"

"Ten it is, we will see you then."

The presentation complete, the conversation eroded to small talk, and it was apparent to Peter that John and Zillman were just feeling each other out.

After dinner, Tsillman ordered Brandy and cigars and asked, "If I may be so bold, what business are you in?"

Peter told him they manufactured sailing yachts.

"Do you export at all?"

"Yes, we do," replied John. "As a matter of fact, our export business is substantial."

"Would you consider having an agent here in Switzerland? We have Zurich See; and in Geneva, there is Lake Lamanche and Lake Lugano on the Italian border; and just over the border in Austria is Boden See. We have the highest rate of disposable wealth per capita in the world, not to mention Switzerland has become the play land for the Arabs. I would deliver the clients, and my commission could be added to the price. The clients I would supply would not quibble over the cost, and I would probably negotiate on their behalf anyway. Would it be possible to deliver two boats a month, ranging in price between two and three million dollars each?"

"Yes, that is doable," John said. "Yes, then it's a deal?"

Tsillman responded, "Of course. Wertshaft und Privat bank will offer you trade financing at very reasonable rates to speed your production."

John looked at Peter, and he nodded. They all raised their glasses and toasted to the deal. When they left, Peter was so excited he let out a howl. John laughed. They took the clog railroad from the Dolldar back down to town and walked the length of Bahnhoff Strasse to the lake. Bahnhoff Strasse was lined with expensive shops and banks, and the feeling of wealth surrounded them. Peter turned to John and said, "I can't believe this."

John replied, "Money makes money."

When they got to the lake, they walked out onto the excursion boat pier and watched the people boarding the last boat out for the night. John kept his eye on the man lurking behind the kiosk at the foot of the pier, and just as they were pulling in the gangway, John told Peter to jump.

They were the last two people aboard, and John watched the man who followed him through the newspaper he was holding. The man kicked a trashcan to the ground in frustration. John smiled to himself and thought, *Chong was right. These guys aren't too good.*

He now felt comfortable enough to tell Peter the whole story. They were standing in the bow of the ship alone; the other passengers were on the upper decks. Peter stared at him in disbelief as John related the entire saga.

"How the hell did you get yourself involved in this?" Peter asked.

"Kismet," John replied. "The funny thing about it is that I feel alive for the first time in years, and I think I really love Rebecca and I can't let anything happen to her. I want you to stay far away from this, Peter, but I might have to call on you for help from time to time. I will do it through a third party. You will not know them. They will tell you they are a friend of Lucy's. In the meantime, keep doing what you have been doing. We have a lot of business now, and you have to concentrate on that. If anything happens to me, here are the coded accesses to my accounts. It's all yours."

Peter looked horrified. "Don't say that."

"It could come to that," John said, "but I'm going to do everything I can to prevent it. Don't worry about me. Just focus on the business. I'm depending on you. I'm going to need a steady flow of money if I'm to survive this. Don't let me down."

"I won't," Peter said. The ship pulled into the pier where they had come aboard about 1:00 a.m., and they walked back up the length of Bahnhoff Strasse to the Central. Neither of them could sleep. Peter was trying to digest everything he was told, and John laid in his room thinking about Peter and how long they had been friends.

They were roommates in college, and John was remembering

back to those first days. Peter was originally from L.A. John remembered not liking him at first, but as the semester went on, he began to appreciate his quiet manner. Then John remembered what was probably the strangest day in his life. He was supposed to go home to Sausalito for the weekend and asked if Peter would like to come with him. Peter said no, he had some things to do, and John always had respected his privacy. He left the room and went to catch his ride. About an hour away from school, the car broke down and needed more than a quick repair. He hitched back to school and walked into his dorm room.

Peter was in bed with someone.

"Oh, excuse me."

As he started to back out of the room, he noticed it was a man.

"What the hell?"

Peter jumped out of bed and threw a towel around himself and ran after John.

"Let me explain."

"Explain what? You're a fag. My roommate is a fag. I can't believe it."

John remembered stopping when he saw the anguish on Peter's face.

"Please, let's talk about this," Peter had asked him.

"Tomorrow," John said, remembering the feelings of disgust and bewilderment.

The next morning, John came into the room and Peter proceeded to tell him his life story. He came from east L.A. and was raised by a drunk and a whore. He had what appeared to be a normal time in high school, where he had to fight his way home every day. He was the only white kid in the school, and this made him tough, but when he started to date girls, he knew something was different. He started to feel attraction toward boys and felt very uncomfortable while dating girls. He was terrified. Queers were totally unacceptable in his part of the world. The first real sex he had ever had was in Orange County, where he met a man much older than he who met him in Anaheim and took him home for the weekend.

John didn't want to hear anymore and was assured by Peter

that he would never bother him. The subject was never discussed again, and this unspoken secret seemed to strengthen their trust and friendship toward each other. Peter was John's best man at his wedding and brought a woman he was friendly with as his date out of respect for John's feelings. It was like that for all these years. Both men, so different, knew and respected the other's personality, strengths, and weaknesses. They could not have been closer. With that thought, John fell into a deep sleep.

The next morning, they met and had coffee together. John gave Peter the envelope and explained all the instructions were inside but not to open it unless something happened to him. They discussed the plans for the extension of the yard, and John asked Peter to send him the proposed plans on disc so he could easily make any changes he deemed necessary. They went over the events of yesterday, and Peter told John that Lucy had sold the house and moved back to Australia. John felt very sad but totally relieved. This was the closure he needed.

They had finished breakfast and John asked Peter if he wanted to go for a walk around town and do a little sightseeing.

"Great."

As they were about to leave the Hotel, the concierge called John over to his desk. "Monsieur, you have an urgent message."

John opened the envelope and read the message. "This is to confirm your appointment at the George Clinic off Bellevue Platz 10:00 AM Friday. Please be on time. -I.G."

The George Clinic was a magnificent building. It was shaped like a pyramid and was built directly on the lake. John walked in and announced himself to the receptionist.

"This way," she replied in English and escorted him to one of the private examining rooms. He sat in the empty room for a few minutes, and then Ian arrived.

"Boy am I glad to see you. This cloak and dagger stuff is a little beyond me. You're doing pretty well," Ian said. "That move you pulled on the boat the other night wasn't bad."

"You were there?"

"No, but I have a couple of my men watching the people who are watching you. They are prepared to take them out if they try to harm you."

"Aren't we all on the same side?" John asked.

The answer was a simple no. John looked around and asked, "Is this place tied into the government?"

"No," Ian said. "Dr. George was a military doctor, and I met him years ago on a UN mission. Over the years, we have become good friends. This is actually the largest private clinic in Switzerland, and I can't wait for dinner. Dr. George has all the food here catered by the Eden Au Lac Hotel, and it's brilliant. Let's get to it, John."

"First, I appreciate the fact that you have done what you could have for Rebecca. I still love the girl, even though I had to break it off. The way my career is going, it would have been madness to carry on, so I stopped it before I ruined her life. At any rate, you have performed in an outstanding manner. This is going to be a hard and dangerous operation to save her, and we could all be in the dump if anything goes wrong. Imelda told me she filled you in on the background information. I will fill you in on where we stand now. First of all, do not trust anyone, this is a global conspiracy. It implicates world leaders, autocrats, plutocrats, police forces, the multi nationals, and a loosely connected but extremely powerful worldwide crime organization.

"Drugs and technology transfers have become the power currencies of the world. This far-reaching interconnected group has used these commodities to accumulate more money than anyone can imagine. They have used this hidden economy to buy governments, fund wars, corrupt police, and they are becoming the strongest power brokers the world has ever seen. Both of our governments have been investigating this for years, but they have agents, corrupted officials at every level of government who misdirect or supply false intelligence or simply crush the investigations. Our foreign office has called us in to help ferret these bastards out."

"Wait." John asked, "Who is us?"

"Oh, I'm sorry, old son. The SAS. My government wanted to ask the yanks, I'm sorry, the Americans, to help, but a few of the boys in your CIA told us it looked like this mess might go right to the top of your government, and they begged off. We, the SAS, are operating under a black ops profile known as shadow. Black ops means that if we are caught the government denies our existence. If we are arrested, we are on our own. In other words, we have been thrown to the wolves but with the directive to get the job done. In this case, we are to identify the leaders of a worldwide organization that appears to have no structure other than loosely connected business ties and the government officials of at least five countries who are allowing them to operate, and we are mandated by any means necessary to destroy them."

"Rebecca has discs identifying them and how their operations work," said John.

"Yes she does, at least to the extent of the triad involvement and the Liddo group. That's why it is important to get her out. Not only for her safety, but it should put some of them on the run, especially the government boys."

"You mean you are using her as bait? How are we going to do this?" John asked, feeling very uncomfortable.

"You are going back to Hong Kong and take her out," Ian said.

John laughed.

"Are you crazy? The last I heard, she was being held by MI5, MI6, and the local cops as well as a couple of hundred triad members who are posted all over mid levels."

"Well you're going to have to be careful and good."

"Listen, Ian. I am a yacht builder, not a spy or a soldier. I am not trained for this sort of thing. How do you expect me to do this? I'm fifty-two years old, for Christ's sake."

"You are trained in the martial arts. You speak the language. You're observant, and you have balls, which ought to get you through. You also have Chong; his family is wired into the entire Chinese constabulary of the Hong Kong Police. They will run interference and supply intel. They are competent, and they hate the British inspectors. This will work for you. It seems they hold you in high regard. Here is an outline of the plan. You will go back to Hong Kong and continue to do business as usual. When I have everything in place, I will contact you through Imelda's contact system using her girl and Chong's girlfriend. No one will contact you directly."

He handed John a wallet-sized black device. "Here is a world ban cell phone with a scrambler, that's about the extent of our electronic capability. I can call you, and if you want to reach me, dial one on the speed dial. Do not enter any other numbers. If you are caught, press star three and the scrambler chip will be erased. When Imelda contacts you, you'll have to move fast. Have everything on your boat prepared so you can leave immediately. We have already gotten two of Chong's relatives to move into the flat above the one where Rebecca is being held. Upon a signal from Chong, they will drill a small hole in their floor that goes into a closet ceiling in Rebecca's flat. They will watch for you to arrive, and when you start to enter the building, they will pump in a gas that will put everyone in the flat to sleep.

You will be supplied a gas mask when you get back to Hong Kong. It will be put on your boat while you're out. Put the gas mask on before you enter and locate Rebecca as soon as possible. There will be a Triad round up in that area that night at the same time you go in. Chong is arranging that. We will take out any of the MI5 or MI6 boys that might be around. Chong will start to drive toward Aberdeen. We have located a spot along the way where you and Rebecca will get out and another couple will get in. Chong will drive them to your boat, and they will sail away. We are hoping that if anyone is watching, they will confirm it was you and Rebecca that sailed off. You will be supplied a car at the drop off point." John was trying to take it all in.

"My men will be monitoring your movements to that point. If you get into trouble, they will cover you. From that point on, you will be on your own. Its better that no one, even me, knows your whereabouts at that point. It will take us two to three days to set up a secure safe house in China. When we have that in place, you will have to get her there on your own. If we have to send someone to contact you, they will have a password. They will say, 'Excuse me, my watch has a shadow, is it… o'clock.' They will use the correct hour plus the day of the week, with Sunday being 1. For example, if it was noon Tuesday, they would say, 'Is it 15 hundred hours.' Twelve plus three for Tuesday. Do you understand?"

"Yes," John replied.

"Once you're in a safe place, call me on the cell phone and let it ring twice. Hang up and call again, and let it ring once. I will call you when we're ready in China. I'll be able to give you the address. It will be on scramble."

"It sounds like a good plan," John said, "but there is a lot that can go wrong."

"You will have to improvise if anything doesn't go according to Hoyle. We are all limited in what we can do. I have a good group of men, John, they will back you to the death, and I have confidence you will be up to the job. Do you have any questions, John?"

"No," he said and wished Ian luck and said good-bye. John left the clinic and decided to walk back to the hotel. His mind was racing, and all of a sudden, his chest began to pound and his pulse soared. He started to hyperventilate and became disoriented. He fell to one knee and thought he was having a heart attack.

A man passing by helped him to his feet and walked him back to the clinic. Dr. George examined him and told him he had an anxiety attack.

"Are you under undue stress?" the doctor asked.

John lied and said no.

"I'm going to give you a shot of B12, and it will calm you down a little. I suggest you cut down you consumption of coffee and try to have a glass of wine in the afternoon with your meal. You'll be all right."

John left the clinic for the second time that day and was now thinking of forgetting the whole thing and going home to California. John had just crossed the small bridge across the Limmat and entered the square in front of the church with 1774 on its steeple, across from the Hotel Storchen when he noticed his friend from Hong Kong following him. He ducked around a corner and slid into a small space between two buildings. The man passed him, and John came up behind him.

"Are you looking for something?" John asked.

As the man turned, John hit him. The man jumped back and crouched into a fighting position. John gave him a spin kick and a series of combinations. As he walked away, John looked back and saw the man lying on the ground bleeding. He felt great and was now mentally prepared to return to Hong Kong.

CHAPTER 29
Hong Kong

The entire time John was gone, Chong was meeting with various family members on the police force and forming his game plan. He met with them alone or in groups of no more than three, and everyone was assigned a specific task without knowing the whole picture. The relatives he could not trust he gave misinformation. Knowing they were in the pockets of the triads, he could expect them to pass the wrong information along. He felt good. He was back on the job, and if he could make this thing work, he would get his old job back and probably a promotion. Imelda was keeping him informed of John's progress as she received the information from Ian. Chong was mentally processing the information as he was receiving it from his sources.

It appeared that the triad leaders offered a million HK dollar bounty for Rebecca. They would not do anything while the Brits were holding her, but it was fairly certain the Brits had gotten the same offer. The only thing keeping her alive was the fact that it was known she hid copies of the discs. Everyone she knew was being closely observed, and their homes were being searched. *The Hong Kong Lady* had been searched twice, that Chong knew about.

By the time John got back to Hong Kong, Chong had already put together a small army of Hong Kong cops, all his or his wife's relatives. He was getting information from every level of the police department and was able to monitor the coming and going of all the British inspectors. One of his relatives was the head of ICAC, the internal affairs division of the police force.

He had gotten the list of all the British inspectors who were known or suspected of being on the take. Chong was amazing. He set up surveillance of all the British inspectors and most of the MI5 boys. He set up a head quarters in Rose's flat and received updates on the information almost hourly.

Chong picked John up at Kai Tec airport and told him on the way to the car that he would fill him in later. The trip back to Aberdeen was a quiet one, although John was happy to see Chong, but he noticed something different about him. Chong seemed surer of himself and acted with an air of authority. Chong was really happy; he was finally getting back the dignity, which had been stolen from him.

John had flown back to Hong Kong on Singapore Airlines and was met by Chong at the arrivals terminal. This time, when they got to the car, no one was waiting for them. As they left the airport, John remarked that there didn't seem to be anyone following them. Chong said that there probably was but now they would be MI6 and harder to spot.

"The man you fought in Switzerland was MI5 from Hong Kong. He's in the hospital. You hurt him pretty bad, and so MI6 took over."

"How did you know about that?" John asked.

"I got the report from my cousin who works in MI5. He said they were very upset when they got the news but even more upset when MI6 came in and called them inept and took over your surveillance."

"Before we get back to the club, I want to stop in Repulse Bay for dinner. The food on the plane looked good, but I didn't eat."

"Spices, boss?"

"Yeah, that sounds good."

After dinner, Chong drove John back to the Yacht Club and asked if he could stay for the night.

"I don't want you to be alone, not that you can't handle yourself, but if there are two people, there is less likelihood you will be attacked."

John agreed and actually was happy to have the company.

The next morning, John told Chong to make the boat ready for a day sail. They left Aberdeen Harbor about ten o'clock and sailed for Green Island. Green Island was a small island used as a military base by the British until 1997, when Hong Kong reverted back to China. Although Hong Kong will be self-ruled for the next fifty years, it will be under the sovereignty of the People's Republic of China and will no longer be a British Colony. They set anchor about a half a mile from the island. John turned up the radio so he could talk freely without being monitored. He told Chong what had happened in Switzerland and listened with interest to what Chong had accomplished here. John was very impressed with Chong's work and felt he had grossly underestimated him. Even though John liked Chong very much and considered him a friend more than an employee, he had no idea what an accomplished man he was. They consolidated the information given to them by both Imelda and Ian and formed their own plan based on all the information, including Chong's intel. They had a good idea what had to be done and decided that they would need some money to make sure everything went smoothly with a reserve fund for unforeseen problems. John told Chong they would go back to Hong Kong that night and sail to Hainan Island the next day.

Early the next morning, John called Andre and told him he was coming for a few days. There he was waiting on the Alliance pier as John and Chong pulled *The Lady* smoothly along side.

"Mon Amis," Andre yelled.

Andre was looking as pleasant and laid back as ever, and John was happy to see him. After exchanging pleasantries, Andre drove them to the hotel and waited until they were checked in. He told them he had something he wanted them to see, and they all got back in the car and he drove off. They talked about life in general and the new political climate in China and, of course, women. John asked where they were going, and Andre replied, "Not far." About a half an hour later, Andre pulled off the road and drove through a wide-open field and up a small hill. He stopped at the crest of the hill and turned off the car. He got out and looked around. From this vantage point, he could see about five miles in every direction. Andre walked over and turned the radio up and asked, "Are you in trouble, mon ami?"

John said, "No. Why?"

"Do you remember the two Americans that came into the restaurant that night?"

"Yeah, the guy's name was Wilcox... Charlie Wilcox."

"Yes, that's the one. Well, he and his friend have come to visit me several times and asked all kinds of questions about you. They gave me that feeling that you get when questioned by the police. I would say they were CIA or FBI. What would they want with you?"

John didn't know what to say. He knew he couldn't tell him the truth, but he didn't want to lie to him either. Chong saved him.

"It's the boss's girlfriend," Chong said. "She is a very important cop in Hong Kong. It is probably a routine check they are doing because you are going out with her. When I was on the force, we used to do it all the time."

"Oh," said Andre, "formidable. I thought you might be in trouble. I was going to offer you help."

John said, "Thanks, Andre. It's always good to know you have friends you can count on." Andre replied, "You're my partner. I am with you to the death."

John thought, *He means it.* Chong, wanting to get off the subject, said, "I have some relatives that live not far from here. How would you like to go to their house and have dinner? They are fisherman, and his wife is a good cook. Not bad looking either."

They all laughed, and Andre said, "Just give me directions."

When they arrived at Chong's relatives,' they were all introduced, and a couple of the sons went in the house and dragged out a large round table and enough chairs for them all to sit. Chong was right on all counts. The wife was very attractive, they were all nice, and the food was great.

After dinner, Andre dropped them at the hotel and told them he would be by in the morning to have breakfast with them but he couldn't spend the day because his boss was in from Paris. A few minutes after being back in his room, John had an uneasy feeling that something was wrong. Just then, Chong knocked on his door and came in. He motioned for John to follow him out to the terrace.

Once outside, Chong leaned toward John and whispered, "Someone has gone through our things."

"How do you know?" asked John.

"Before we left the boat, I threaded the locks on my suitcase with a strand of hair, and it's now broken."

"I knew something was wrong," John said under his breath.

"Be careful," said Chong. "Let's leave the door between our rooms open, and I'll stay on watch until 2:00 a.m. then I'll wake you and I'll get some sleep." John agreed and went right to bed. It was almost 3:00 a.m. when Chong woke John.

"There are at least two people watching us. One is across the street, and the other is in a room in the other wing. Sit in the dark, and get your eyes accustomed, and then look out the window from the side here."

John woke Chong at seven o'clock. They met Andre for breakfast at nine. John told Andre he would be back in a week to go over and take a look at their pearl crop and said, rather cryptically, "We can take some of the scrapings back to HK."

Andre winked his acknowledgment, and when they were finished, he pardoned himself, but he had to work once in a while. John and Chong went to the desk and asked if they could borrow or rent fishing poles. They took the poles given to them by the hotel and went to the beach. They spent the rest of the day fishing, and when the sun started to go down, they took their catch to one of the local restaurants and had the fish cooked. After a fine meal, they went back to their rooms.

The next morning, they sailed to Hong Kong. When they arrived at their berth in Aberdeen, Palfrey was waiting for them.

"What do you want?" asked John.

"Can I speak to you alone, sir?"

He took John's arm and walked him out to the end of the berth.

"What's all this about?" John demanded.

"Well, sir, I don't know how to say this, but I think your Ms. Rebecca could be in danger."

"What?" John asked angrily.

"Well, sir, I could get into a lot of trouble telling you this, but as I told you before, I really like Ms. Dreed."

"Tell me, man. What are you trying to say?" Palfrey looked uncomfortable. "Things don't add up."

John asked, "What do you mean?"

"She is supposed to be protected by the MI5 and MI6 boys, but the triads all know where she is, and it's being talked about freely in headquarters. That's not normal. Generally, when someone is being held in a safe house, no one talks. This is out in the open, but when I went up to see her, I was thrown out, and when I demanded to see her, I was put on report and told to take two weeks off. Something is rotten. I don't know what it is, but I know something is wrong."

"What can I do?" asked John.

"I don't know, sir, but I will nose around, and if I come up with anything, I'll let you know."

"What do you think is going on? You can't come in here and give me news like that and just walk away."

"Do you have a private number I can call you on?" he asked.

"No," John lied. "You can call me on my cell phone and tell me to meet you somewhere safe and I'll come immediately," John said.

When Palfrey left, John told Chong what was said. "Either they are trying to ferret you out and find out how much you know or he's on the level." John agreed but said, "I know he has always had a thing for Miss Dreed?"

Chong nodded, "I'll have him followed, and we'll see."

Chong asked, "What do you want to do today, boss?"

"I have to go to Central. I have a meeting with my new distributors from China."

"Where? At the Hong Kong Club?"

"No, at the Pacific Club. They asked to meet there. There is a banker's breakfast they are attending, and I'm supposed to meet them after that."

"Can you make your own way back tonight, boss? I want to get over to Rose's and see what's been going on for the last couple of days."

"Sure, as a matter of fact, it might be fun to go out for a while tonight. I haven't been out in Wanchai for a long time."

"Be careful. Remember the sailors?"

"Don't remind me." John laughed. "I'm still sore in places."

John went to his meeting with the Chinese distributors, and after it was over, he took a walk and was both nervous and happy when he sat at the bar at Mad Dog's. He ordered a pint of San Miguel. Mad Dog's was a British-style pub located in Lan Quay Fan just up from Queens Road. It had become a Hong Kong institution and frequented by the British government employees and newspaper people. The proprietor was a young Scottish girl of about forty named Laura.

She came to Hong Kong when she was twenty with enough money to stay for a month. She took a job as a bar tender and did so well in a year she bought the bar. She took a loan against that bar and built Mad Dog's. She was smart and tough, and over the next couple of years owned several of the most popular nightspots around Hong Kong. The amazing thing was that after twenty years working day and night she still looked like she was twenty. She had the same boyfriend, whom she met her first week in Hong Kong. When anyone asked if they were ever getting married, she would tell them, "No, he won't sign a prenuptial agreement."

Everyone would laugh, but it was the truth. Laura had worked hard, and she invested everything she had into her establishments, and as fond as she was of him, she was not sharing everything with him. Just as John was ordering his second beer, a group of British inspectors came in.

He heard one of them say, "There's that yank that put old Lawson in the hospital in Switzerland."

John figured he better leave before they had too many beers. *There could be trouble.* He walked down to Queens Road, past the Bank of China building, and then around the Lippo Building to Luard Road and across to Locart Road, the Suzy Wong district. He decided to go to another one of Laura's places, Joe Banana's. Joe Banana's was a cocktail bar and dance place. It was crowded as usual, but John liked the anonymity of being in a crowded place. He ordered one of the cocktails Joe Banana was famous for—a fluffy duck. As he stood at the bar with his back to the crowd, someone came up behind him and pinched his ass. He turned quickly, and there was Imelda.

"I told you Hong Kong is a small place, darling," she said.

He looked around, and no one seemed to have any interest in him or her. Imelda looked three sheets to the wind, and John asked if she was all right?

"I haven't been this good in months, and if you play your cards right, you might get lucky tonight."

John laughed.

"It's not that funny," she said, and John noticed she was serious.

He politely said, "Imelda, I'm not the right guy for you. There are plenty of young studs that could do the job better than me. Have you heard from our friend?"

She put her arms around him and gave him a kiss, and while she was close, she said, "Shut up and go along with me."

Imelda backed away a little and said, "Buy me another drink."

John ordered two fluffy ducks. Imelda pulled him to the dance floor and got close to him again and said, "I'm being followed. When I ask you to take me home, come outside with me."

They finished their drinks and went outside. There was an alley next to the bar, and Imelda pulled John into the alley and pushed him up against the wall and whispered to him that she had a message for him in her knickers.

He said, "What?"

She pulled him close again and said, "Reach down in my knickers, there's a message for you. Make sure no one can see it when you pull it out."

John did as he was told and got the message out and into his pocket before anyone could see it. Imelda then whispered, "I'm going to pass out. Just pick me up and put me in a taxi and then get back to Aberdeen."

John followed her instructions. He did not look at the note until he was sitting in his bedroom on *The Lady*.

The note said: "We have to move soon. Get ready, and stay at the boat tomorrow."

He burnt the message and flushed it down the toilet. He waited for Chong to get back.

Chong got in around three o'clock in the morning, and John was glad to see him. Chong looked worried.

"What's wrong? John asked.

"Come outside," Chong said.

John was getting more than a little tired of this cloak-and-dagger shit. Once outside, they walked to the end of the pier and Chong turned on a small portable radio he was carrying.

"Boss, the situation is bad. I've heard that the Brits are ready to turn Rebecca over to the Triads. They will torture her until she tells them where the discs are that she copied. No one is better at torture than these people."

"This is bullshit," John remarked. "Why doesn't she just give them the discs?"

"Well, boss, the situation has become more serious than you could imagine."

"What do you mean? There are no governments cooperating in this, only key officials that have been bought by the Liddo Group. This is mind boggling," John said.

"Those discs must lay out the entire program or so many people would not be involved. Your government has almost 400 CIA guys working out of the consulate here, almost all of them have been deployed to prevent any chance of a leak on this. The Brits have brought over about 200 MI6 guys, and they have taken over completely from MI5 and the other local cops. That means the corruption goes very high. Rebecca is in deep trouble."

They had been standing at the other end of the pier about 500 feet from *The Hong Kong Lady* in a dark spot on the outside of the lights that shone back on the pier. This was probably why the men climbing onto to the boat had not seen them. John went to call out to them when Chong grabbed him and forced him to the ground.

Chong whispered, "Be quiet."

They noticed at least two of the men had guns drawn.

"Wait until they go below. We will get them on their way up."

Three of the four men went below, and the fourth waited outside as a look out. John and Chong silently crept up the pier. When he was close enough to the man, Chong lunged forward and in one smooth motion grabbed him and snapped his neck. He lowered him quietly to the ground and then followed John, who was already on the boat. John and Chong crouched on either side of the boom, waiting for the men to come up. When all three of them came up on deck, they were facing aft. Chong gave John a signal, and they attacked. John knocked two of them to the ground, and Chong hit the third.

Chong made quick work of his target and turned to see John wrestling with both men trying to get the guns away from them. Chong jumped up and landed on the neck of one guy, snapping it immediately. This gave John some freedom to over take the third man. Chong collected the weapons and checked for ID. They had none.

John subdued the last man until Chong came back. John told Chong there was some duct tape in the toolbox. When the last man was taped up and secure, they went out on the pier and carried the body back up on deck.

"Let's bring him below," Chong said and they carried him down. Chong looked at John and said, "Let's get out of here. Where do you want to go?"

"Sail over to Lantau."

John started the twin Volvos and slowly navigated his way out of the yacht club marina. Once in the harbor, they raised the sails and set a course for Lantau Island. John stopped the boat when the depth gauge read 450 feet. He went below and got a long length of spare anchor chain and tied it to the three dead men. Chong helped him get them over the side, and they waited for an hour to make sure they sank. Before going any further, they brought the one man alive up on deck.

"Who sent you?" John asked.

The man said, "Screw off."

John hit him as hard as he could. John turned to Chong and said, "I don't like people to use foul language in front of *The Lady*."

Chong laughed.

"I'm going to ask you one more time. Who sent you?"

The man just stared at him. Chong went below and came back with a blowtorch from the tool locker. John looked at him surprised.

Chong said, "If he doesn't want to cooperate, we have to make him." The blowtorch lit with a popping sound, and Chong moved toward the man, staring at his crouch. His pants actually turned brown and started to smoke before he started talking.

"My name is John Murphy. I'm with the NSA."

John swore under his breath.

Chong said, "What was your mission?"

"To neutralize the two of you."

Chong laughed.

"You mean, kill us?"

"Yes."

John sat down. Murphy went on to say, "Listen, you don't have a chance. Let me bring you in and you might live."

John jumped up and said, "Yeah, my only chance. I'd wind up with a small hole in the back of my neck, and the medical examiner would say it was a heart attack. Or I would be found dead and it would be reported as a suicide, like Vince Foster. No way."

Chong said, "Let's kill him. He came here to kill us."

John asked Murphy, "Can you swim?"

"No," he replied.

"Well, you better learn fast."

Chong was already lifting him up, and John grabbed him. They both carried him up on deck. John cut the tape that was restraining him, and they threw him overboard. Chong figured they were about two miles off shore, and with the tide, he would wash up on shore in China. John looked at Chong and said, "This is nuts. I can't believe my government would do this."

"Boss, you're smart, but I can't believe how naïve you are."

CHAPTER 30
Sydney Australia

Lucy was all settled in to her new home in Sydney. She had been in touch with some of her old friends, but there was too much water under the bridge. She really didn't know them anymore. She had been in America for a long time and had forgotten what Australia was like. She was an American. Lucy had never felt so lost. When she was in America, she was known as the Australian women, and since she'd been back, she was known as a Yank.

When she first arrived in Sydney, she decided to find a flat rather than buy a house, at least until she was comfortable with her surroundings again. She found a nice flat not far from the beach. Her old boss looked her up and asked her to come back to work, good designers were hard to find. She told him she hadn't designed a boat in years. He then made her an offer to let her buy an interest in the company. She said she would think about it but had no real interest. Lucy was smart, and she'd been around. She donated a large sum of money to the Sydney Opera House and immediately stepped into the Sydney social scene. Lucy knew that would be the easiest way to get back in to Sydney society.

Over the next months, she became the chairwoman of several fund-raising committees and was busy every day. She set herself on a course of constant luncheons and formal dinners. Lucy was a social animal, and this was better than work for her. She wanted to forget the past and start a new life here, but every night she went home, her thoughts wandered back to John. It was at one of her fund-raising dinners that she met Niles.

Niles Kent was the owner of two of the largest television stations in Australia, and he had also produced more than a few successful films. He was the most eligible bachelor in Sydney. At forty-five, he was in great shape and a good-looking man. He was known to be a womanizer and an adventurer. He and Lucy were made for each other. They hit it off right away, and for the next several months, they were inseparable. They went ballooning in the outback, scuba diving for great whites, and trekking up in Queensland. They were quickly becoming Australia's first couple. Niles was going on a trip to Kenya to do a documentary and asked if Lucy would join him. They would be gone for three months. Lucy told him she would love to but she couldn't be gone for that long, she had commitments in Sydney. They agreed that she would go for two weeks and come back and then meet him again three weeks before the shoot was over.

Lucy enjoyed her time in Kenya and was looking forward to going back. Back in Sydney, she settled into her philanthropic work. She was a dynamo. She consumed herself with work and was enjoying every minute of it. Her life was turning around. Lucy met Sybil Twang at one of her endless dinners. Sybil was originally from China, but her family immigrated to Australia when she was two years old. She was Australia's most promising women's clothing designer.

Lucy and Sybil hit it off right away. They both had that insatiable zest for life. Lucy invited Sybil to come to her flat for some wine and giggles one night after a formal dinner. When they arrived, Lucy said, "Make yourself comfortable. The wine is over there, and the glasses are in the cabinet there. I have to get out of this gown, it's killing me."

When she returned, dressed more comfortably, she told Sybil to go in the closet and change into anything she wanted to. Sybil came out in an equally comfortable outfit, and they settled into an evening of gossip and jokes. During the course of conversation, Lucy told Sybil she liked her designs and told her she had been working on some herself.

"Would you like to see them?"

"Sure."

Lucy took out her portfolio and opened it across her desk. "What do you think? As you can see from the drawings they are all earth tones so they mix and match. I was thinking of all Egyptian cotton with a few tops in silk."

"These are great," Sybil said. "Where did you learn how to do this?"

"I used to be a yacht designer. Originally I went to school to study art, and I became interested in design and switched to a major in engineering."

"You should have gone into clothing design. These really are great," Sybil said. "How would you like to work with me? I'll teach you fabrics and marketing. Come in as a junior partner, and as time goes on, we'll see what happens."

Lucy gleamed. She said, "I'd love to."

They made a toast to it, and Lucy started the following Monday. Sybil was happy with how hard Lucy worked, and her designs were selling. She was a profitable addition to the firm.

Niles called Lucy to tell her all the arrangements were made for her to come to Kenya, but she told him she couldn't.

"Why?" he asked.

"I have taken a job," she said.

"Where?" Niles asked.

"As a junior partner with Sybil Twang," replied Lucy.

Niles laughed out loud.

"What are you laughing at? It's not at all funny?"

"I am the majority shareholder of that company," Niles said.

"What?"

"Yeah. I backed her when she started out. How do you think she got all that airtime and publicity when she started?"

"Holy cow. What a small world," said Lucy.

"I'll tell you what," Niles said. "You come to Kenya and I'll sell you the entire interest for a million Australian."

"It's worth a lot more than that," Lucy said.

"I know," Niles cajoled. "When are you coming?"

Lucy thought for a moment and said, "When your solicitor brings me the paperwork."

Niles laughed again and said, "Okay."

Lucy said nothing to Sybil the next day. After the papers

were signed, she told Sybil she had a prior commitment and would have to take a leave of absence for a few weeks and prepared for the trip.

Niles was waiting for her at the airstrip in the game preserve. He looked great. He was a little leaner, tanned, and healthy looking. Lucy was not sure if she liked the way she felt when she saw him. Things were going a little too fast for her. She wasn't sure she wanted to be in a serious relationship just yet. Niles looked at her adoringly and said, "What did Sybil say when you told her you were now her boss?"

"I haven't told her yet."

"Why not?" Niles asked.

"The fall line isn't finished, and I don't want to distract her."

Niles laughed and said, "I don't want to go up against you in business."

"It's just that," she said. "Business."

She started to think that if John had brought her into the business, Sailcraft would have been a lot further ahead today and they would have still been together.

The next several weeks were like a fairytale. They went on animal roundups and photo shoots in the most beautiful country she had ever seen. They went swimming under waterfalls and took long walks through the veldt. It was truly magnificent, but the reality of getting back to work came faster then she could have imagined. When she got back, she dove into work immediately. She was tireless and made sure every detail of the preparation for the show was completed. Two weeks before the show, she walked into Sybil's office and said, "I have some good news for you."

"What's that?"

"I have convinced Niles to do a live special on the show."

"Get out of here," Sybil said, smiling.

"No, I really have," Lucy said.

"Oh my God, that's great. You'll get a bonus for this," Sybil told her.

Lucy just smiled.

The show was a great success. Besides the publicity, The Sybil Label Ltd. received 2.5 million Australian dollars for the show. At the end of the show, the MC introduced the owner of the Sybil Label. As Sybil started to walk out, she heard, "Miss Lucy Owens."

Sybil stopped right in her tracks.

"What the hell is going on?"

Lucy took her by the hand and pulled her out onto the stage. After the applause died down and they returned offstage, Sybil screamed, "What the hell is going on?"

Lucy told her she bought the shares from Niles.

"I quit," Sybil said and stormed off.

Lucy knew she would be back, because Sybil still owed over two million Australian dollars to the shareholders, and Lucy was the majority shareholder. Lucy met Niles at the party after the show. Niles was with a group of men, and when she approached him, he turned and introduced her to Mr. Ascot Chen. The three of them went into a private room, and Niles explained to her that Mr. Chen was a financier.

"If you are to have a successful clothing line, you will need financing. Mr. Chen is willing to give you an unlimited line of credit."

"That's very generous, Mr. Chen. What do I have to do for that?"

Niles looked at her quizzically and then realized she was an accomplished businesswoman.

Chen, unflustered, replied, "Please, call me Ascot. We ask nothing from you other than the assignment of your receivables. At time of order, you will be able to borrow up to 80 percent of the purchase order. When you deliver the order, we pay you the balance less 1.5 percent per month on outstanding balance."

"That sounds reasonable," Lucy said.

"Yes, it is. The only stipulation is that your customers remit their payment directly to us."

"Who is *us*?" Lucy asked.

"The Liddo Group," said Ascot.

CHAPTER 31
The South China Sea

John was drained both emotionally and physically. He told Chong he was going down and get some sleep before he even attempted to think of what to do next. He slept for two hours and came back up on deck with two cups of coffee. Until he took a sip of the coffee, Chong didn't realize how cold he was. John saw him start to shiver and told him he'd better finish the coffee and go down and take a hot shower and try to grab a couple of hours of sleep. John told him he was going to call Ian on the untraceable phone and see what he thought they should do.

John told Ian everything, and by the time he was through describing the events of last night, Ian knew John was in a real panic mode.

"Calm down," Ian said. "It sounds like they were rouge operators, not working officially."

John was relieved to hear it, but then he said to Ian, "But he wanted to bring me in."

Ian laughed and said, "Yeah, but to where? John, where are you now?'

"I don't really know," John lied, about six hours out of Hong Kong.

"Go back to Aberdeen," Ian said.

"Are you crazy?" replied John.

"No, I will notify your intelligence boys and find out what's going on. If I don't think I have control, I will ring you back within the hour. In the meantime, you start to head back; everything is almost in place."

"Okay," said John.

He let Chong sleep for three hours. Chong came up on deck and asked, "What's the plan, boss?"

John told him of the conversation with Ian, and Chong looked a little skeptical.

"Give me that phone," Chong said.

He called several of his family contacts and made sure they would be covered when they got back. When he pulled into his berth at the yacht club, several men approached. John started to scramble below deck and then saw it was Palfrey.

"What are you doing here?" asked John.

'I heard you had a close call last night," he replied.

"Not me," John lied.

"Well, I just thought you might like some of my men to hang around."

"That's kind of you, but we're all right."

John actually liked the idea, but he didn't know whom to trust. Just then, Chong came on board again.

"What's going on, boss?"

"Inspector Palfrey has offered his services to protect us," John said.

"That's great," Chong said. "Thank you."

John looked at him quizzically. Chong whispered to him that with all these cops around no one would be foolish enough to try anything. The bonus was that when they were ready, Ian's people could simply tell Palfrey to get lost, and he would listen. John said, "Okay, thank you, inspector." Palfrey replied, "I am still on suspension but I trust these men."

Palfrey positioned men around the club and the berth. They were inconspicuous to the members, but if someone were watching, John thought they would stick out like a sore thumb. After Palfrey had left, Chong told John that two of Palfrey's men were his relatives and that Palfrey was on the level. When he contacted his family from the boat last night, they had gone to Palfrey, and he suggested that they set up a watch. In case anything was to go wrong, Chong's family would be there to help.

John went down and took a nap. He was beat. Chong went home and did the same. The events of last evening took a lot out of both of them. John woke up about noontime and was famished. He walked over to the club and had lunch. It was good, roast duck and orange sauce with a side of hot potato salad. Felling full and refreshed, he decided to go to Central and get some business done.

 The next morning John woke up from a restless sleep. He was exhausted but had to get some work done. He called for a taxi, and within minutes, a red and black taxi pulled up in front of the club. He told the driver in Cantonese to bring him to the Hong Kong Club. The road to Central from Aberdeen is a two-lane road, one lane in each direction. It snakes its way along the coast from Aberdeen to Repulse Bay and then cuts inland and circles around the mountain through a lush forest until it turns into the tunnel that exits in Happy Valley. In Happy Valley, the taxi went halfway around the racetrack and then turned left onto one of the main thoroughfares that go from Central to Causeway Bay.

 The trip took about thirty minutes; traffic wasn't too bad this time of the afternoon. John paid the driver and walked into the Hong Kong Club. He signed in as a guest and went downstairs to the bowling alley. The bowling alley was one of the last places in the club where women were not allowed during the day. John walked into the bar area and saw the regulars sitting there discussing all of the changes in Hong Kong and reminiscing about the good old days when Hong Kong was a colony and the British way of life was ever-present. John said hello, and they all politely nodded and acknowledged his presents. He sat at a table by himself and was soon invited to join the regulars.

 The regulars were a group of businessmen, all British, who had all been in Hong Kong for over thirty years. John Leader was an Insurance Broker; a Dickinsonian character who came to HK in 1950, a young lad of 18 then, and now was the most influential insurance broker in the Far East. He not only insured all of the horses that came to Hong Kong to race, but he was the representative of China's People's Insurance Company. Then there was Mark Tweedy. He had been in Hong Kong since 1948, and he was a shipbroker and made his fortune as broker and agent for Y.K. Pao's fleet of ships during the Korean War. He was now the proprietor of the largest ship brokerage company in all of Asia.

Sitting opposite John was Old Tom Ferris, as he was known. No one really knows when he came to Hong Kong but he is now over a hundred, and he moved to Hong Kong with his family when he was a child. Besides being an old China hand, he was the owner of four English speaking newspapers, two Chinese-speaking newspapers, and about thirty-five magazines in Asia and Europe as well. Directly next to him was J. Gale Peabody, managing director of the Hang Sang Exchange. He had made a fortune in the market, and it was rumored he bought his present position. Nevertheless, he was doing a great job. John thought to himself this was incredible, he was sitting with the whole power structure of Hong Kong, at least they were to the west.

The Chinese had another view. Here at this table sat the heads of insurance, shipping, media, and finance. They ran Hong Kong from the bowling alley at the Hong Kong Club. They were getting old and were now enjoying the fruits of their labor. It must have been exciting to watch so few build an economic empire. John sat and listened to their stories and surmised that these men were so successful because they had the forethought to work with the Chinese and the western business establishment on equal terms.

The more he listened, the more he learned. He loved their stories, and the more he got to know them, the more he realized their stories were true. Leader had just asked John a question when the waiter came over and said there were two Chinese gentlemen asking for him in the lobby. John told the waiter he would meet them in the fourth floor dinning room and excused himself. As he walked away, he overheard one of them say, "Nice young bloke for a Yank," and he smiled.

John walked with a swagger into the dinning room and was seated at the table with the two gentlemen who had asked for him. They were his distributors from China. The tall one was GU Chun Hua, a Mongolian who spoke fluent English without an accent at all, and the other was Xu Yi Jie, a marine architect who graduated from China's famous St. John's University in Shanghai. St. John's was the equivalent of MIT in America.

Mr. GU started.

"We have another proposition for you, John. We have purchased a large dry dock from COSCO in Shanghai. We would like to go Joint Venture in the building of your yachts. Our proposition is as follows, we will supply all labor and material, and you supply the design and expertise. Everything will be done to your specification. We will give Sailcraft 50 percent of the dry dock and put it under your control. We need you to build a complex of buildings to house the molds and fiberglass spray units. We will make money from doing this."

"How so?" John asked.

"Mr. Xu has estimated that we will need approximately four million square feet of buildings. When we purchased the dry dock, it had approximately twenty hectors of vacant land. Although the vacant land is valued at USD $350 per square meter, it has no exchangeable value until something is built on it. We purchased the dry dock through our contacts in the government, and we made a good deal. If a foreigner builds on the property, financing is readily available, especially one that has existing sales in China, such as you. We have estimated the construction cost to be approximately USD $175 per square meter. If you sign the contract in US dollars, we can pay the contractor about 60 percent of that in RMB, the Chinese local currency, so your actual cost is $105 and we will make a construction profit of $70 per square meter. At four million square feet, that is a pre-construction profit of $2.8 million. When the buildings are complete, The Bank of China will extend to you a mortgage of 70 percent of the value, inclusive of the land that would be USD $147 million. This means we can walk away with about fifty million dollars as soon as construction is completed."

"That's a very impressive offer," replied John. "But will the business warrant it?"

"Yes, it will, and the value of the property would not diminish even if we went out of business."

"Give me a few days to think this over," John said. "I would like to discuss it with my partners."

"Of course," Mr. Gu said, "and in the meantime, Mr. Xu will

give you this month's sales report."

They finished their meeting, and John left the two of them sitting at the table. He took the elevator down to the lobby to find it was pouring outside and getting a taxi was going to be tough. He decided to go back down to the bowling alley. The group was still there with the exception of John Leader, who was called away with an emergency. John went over to the table and asked if he could join them, and they all said yes at the same time. John sat next to J. Gale Peabody and leaned toward him and asked if he could make an appointment to meet with him in private to discuss a business matter. Gale told him to come around to the office about 11:00 a.m. tomorrow. From that point, the discussions led to why Jardine left Hong Kong and should the Hong Kong and Shanghai Bank really have spent that much on their headquarters at Queens Road, a monstrosity of a building that looked more like an oil well than a bank? All of these topics intrigued John. As a newcomer, he did not say a word. He just listened and enjoyed the conversation. It was about four o'clock when John said good-bye and thanked everyone for their company. It had stopped raining about an hour ago, and he was certain he would get a taxi.

He walked over to Connaught Street, and within a minute, he was on his way back to Aberdeen. Just as they were coming into Repulse Bay, John heard the shot.

The window exploded and the driver fell over to the side. John looked over the seat and saw a pool of blood where the driver had been seconds ago. He looked up, and the car was headed for an embankment and he could see Clearwater Bay about 200 feet below. John dove over the seat and, with his hands, depressed the brake pedal. He could feel the car swerve and then hit something, and it spun around before hitting a tree and stopping. As he crawled out of the car, he heard the second shot but did not see where it hit. He hid behind the car and looked over the terrain but saw no one. He went to move, and a third shot rang out. He made a dive right over the embankment and slid down the sandy incline until he hit the water.

John started to swim, and there was a small explosion in the water right next to him. They were still shooting at him.

He dove under the water and kept swimming as fast as he could. He came up for a breath and noticed a boat moored about one hundred yards from him. He went back down and swam as fast as he could. He had to surface several more time before he reached the boat, but there were no more shots fired. John finally reached the boat, it had seemed an eternity, and climbed aboard. He studied the shoreline but saw no one. This frightened him the most. There was no one? He sat on the deck of the boat until he was able to wave down a water taxi and asked the woman running it to take him to the marina in Repulse Bay. Once there, he immediately went to see Mike Severson at Spices Restaurant. He explained to him that he had a problem with the boat and could he use the phone.

"Come in," Mike said. "I have an office in the back of the restaurant you can call from there."

While John was on the phone, Mike had gathered up some dry clothes and told him to go in and take a shower right away, the water here was so polluted that one could get real sick real fast. John did just that, and when he came out of the shower, Inspector Palfrey was waiting for him.

"How the hell did you find me here?" John growled.

"Mike called me," he replied. "It's not too often we have a murder in Hong Kong, and we have had quite a few since you showed up. I only presume you were in the taxi when the driver got shot?"

"No, I was touring the bay and I fell overboard from the water taxi."

"Is that right?"

"Well, two of my men witnessed your little swan dive into the bay over the embankment."

"What?" John said. "You had your people watching me and I almost got killed. In fact, someone did get killed."

"They got the shooter. He was a triad member, but I don't think he was working for the triads on this hit."

"What do you mean? asked John.

"He had no identification, and he was carrying foreign cigarettes and using an American rifle. I think the boys that visited you the other night might have something to do with this.

He was probably a gun for hire. Now that the border to China is so open, we have been having this problem more frequently. You can hire a Chinese hit man through local sources, and they come over make a hit and go back to China the same day. Once they are in China, we can never find them. They just disappear. Right now, why don't I get you home? I'm going to see if we can set you up in a safe house?"

"No!" John said. "If you really think it's that bad, I'll just go back to the States."

"That's up to you," Palfrey said.

"I would appreciate a lift home though."

Palfrey drove John back to the yacht club and made a round to see the men he had posted there. He told them all to be very careful and alert. John climbed up on the *Lady*, and after a cursory check, he went below and changed clothes. He took the secure phone and went to dinner. He took a water taxi over to the Jumbo. He walked into the well-decorated reception area and asked for a table for one. The hostess said nothing but motioned for him to follow her. He did, and to his surprise, he was led to a private dinning room. As he entered, he overheard a portion of a conversation in Chinese. He knew no one and turned to the hostess and told her there must be a mistake. She just looked at him and motioned him in.

"John," a voice said in perfect English, "how delightful you could join us?"

"Who the hell are you?" John asked.

"In good time. Please, sit down."

John sat and was served a drink immediately. It was Moutai, a very potent Chinese drink. It was made from sorghum and was 140 proof. The host raised his glass, and everyone at the table did the same. Gombai was the toast, which meant bottoms up, so everyone emptied their glasses. They were immediately refilled. John asked the host again, "Who you are?"

"I am a businessman who wishes to make you a proposition. We know you have found yourself in an interesting set of circumstances through no fault of your own, other than falling in love with a certain lady. We wish you no harm, but we need certain information she has taken from us. To save all of us a lot of trouble and possibly your own life, we would like to offer you a finder's fee of USD $2 million for the return of the computer discs your lady has, shall we say, found. This is, as you Americans say, a no-win situation. My associates, as well as the British and American governments and others, are all trying to get that information. You have proven to be rather resourceful so far, but your situation will only get worse.

"The unfortunate incident this afternoon is only the beginning. We had nothing to do with that. It was your own countrymen who hired him. It was done against our orders, and his family is being punished for that act. We are businessmen. We only want what was taken from us. Your co-operation will keep you alive. The alternative is distasteful. Your lady, Miss Dreed, has been a slight nuisance to us in the past, but she has done her job well, and it made it easier for us to sell our goods at a higher price. When there are tough laws about trademark infringement, it is easier for our buyers to believe the goods are real. In reality, Miss Dreed has done us a favor by being so diligent. I am sorry to say that now she is in a serious situation that she probably will not survive. Sometimes that accompanies the job when you are a crusader."

John flushed with rage.

"Look, you rotten son of a bitch, if any harm comes to Miss Dreed over this, I will personally kill you."

"Please, John, do not get upset. I am not the culprit here. It is the crooks in government you have to be afraid of. We have not tried to kill you; we have made a generous business proposition. It was governments that have made the two attempts on your life. Yes, I know about both. Nothing goes on here in Hong Kong that I don't know about. That's all I have to say, so let's enjoy the meal."

John looked at him in disbelief. How could he be so cold about this? John then realized this guy was right. It was only business to him, but the corrupt officials had a lot on the line here, and in fact, much more dangerous than this guy. After the meal, John told his host he would seriously consider his offer and left. John was pretty upset when he got back to his boat. He went below and tried to sleep. It was impossible.

What the hell have I got myself into? he kept asking himself. All at once, it came to him. *I have never taken any risks. This is my new life, and I'm making up for lost time. Even though I have never been in this much trouble, I have never felt this alive. Maybe you have to be on the edge to really experience and appreciate life? Wow, I'm a philosopher,* he laughed to himself.

Then he shook his head and the reality of it all hit him. He sat alone in the cabin of his boat, in the dark. He felt some comfort in the dark, an anonymous feeling that offered him some physiological protection, a safe haven from the darker side of reality. He felt himself curling up in a fetal position, and he let all his worries and cares dissipate into the nothingness that surrounded him.

John woke with a startle. Someone was on the boat. John leapt from the bed and grabbed the gun that he had taken away from the NSA guy a couple of days ago. He started to go up on deck when the cabin door swung open and he aimed the 9 mm at the man's stomach. His finger was starting to squeeze the trigger when he heard Chong's voice.

"Hey, boss, what are you doing with that gun?"

"Don't ever do that again," John scowled at Chong. "I almost killed you."

He then realized it was he who overreacted to the situation.

"I'm sorry, Chong," John said.

Chong told him not to worry about it but asked if he was all right.

John replied, "All right? Are you kidding?"

John told Chong about the dinner he had had the night before. Chong said, "We're in for it now, boss. The triads were no one to fool with."

Chong did not tell John that just for having that conversation with them he was lucky to be alive.

"I apologize again, Chong," John said.

CHAPTER 32
Washington DC

"Mr. President, your ten o'clock appointment is here. I have arranged for tea in the Lincoln Library. His name is Johnny Trong. He has personally raised over $200,000 for your campaign and $2 million for the DNC. He is a main fundraiser in the Chinese community and a personal friend of the late secretary of commerce. The gentlemen with him are PRC government officials."

"This is a non-official visit when it comes to them. Trong probably wants to show them how important he is to gain some kind of business contacts for himself in China. I hate this, but $200,000 is a lot of money. Oh well, duty calls. Bring them on, but limit it to fifteen minutes."

"Mr. President," Trong began, "this is Mr. Li and Mr. Ma from the People's Republic of China. They have asked me to set up this meeting, as you are the only one who can help them. They have run into a snafu at commerce and need an override from you. A business proposition has been made to your personal attorneys, as we could not get access to the Whitehouse attorneys. The business plan outlines all aspects of the transaction, and I believe you will see the mutual benefit to both parties. We know you will be fair and act in the best interest of the country. Mr. President, I thank you for your most valuable time, and I would only like to impose on you for one more minute. I am having a fundraising rally for you in the Chinese community at one of our larger Buddhist Temples, and I was wondering if you could have the vice president or the first lady, perhaps, attend. We should be raising at least $500,000 in discretionary campaign funds, and a solid presence by someone from the Whitehouse might even double that."

"Why sure, John. I have to check, but I'm sure the vice president could make that. Whatever we can do for the party. Well thank you, John. I can't' tell you how much we appreciate the fine work you have done for the party, and I'll see what I can do for your friends. Here, let's take a picture before you leave." He threw his arm around John and smiled. The flash went off before John knew what happened.

"Gladys, get my lawyer on the line and ask him to look into the business deal that Johnny Trong sent over to him. Tell him I want a report in person tomorrow in the oval office at 2:15 p.m. sharp, and would you ask that intern who was in earlier to come to the office about six fifteen, I have a special project for her to work on."

CHAPTER 33
London, England

Ian Grant arrived in London at 2:00 a.m. London time and was immediately escorted to a military base off of the M6 about fifty miles outside of London. It was in a residential area and hidden so well that most of the people who lived in the area did not know it was there.

"Captain Grant reporting, sir," Ian said crisply to the general.

"Good morning, son. How was your trip?"

"Fine, sir," Ian relied.

"Good, then you will go to the officer's mess and get some sleep. I will meet you at 0800 in Leominster outside the entrance of City Bank's database headquarters. Your driver will know how to get there."

"Very good, sir." Ian turned sharply and left. The next morning, Ian waited outside of the address in Leominster, and at precisely 0800, the general's car pulled up to the curb.

"Get in," the general said through the window. As they drove, the general asked if everything was in order with the American and that troublesome ex-cop in Hong Kong.

Ian replied, "Very good, sir. We will use them to extricate Rebecca, and we will only lend peripheral support." "There is a slight change, Captain Grant," he said formerly.

"You will only do intel, and you will make certain that the girl is killed. We won't kill her. We'll let someone else do it, but we will either kill or arrest the people who do the job. We'll be the heroes and be able to focus attention elsewhere. Use your connections to assist the triads through this man," he said as he handed a file to Ian.

Ian was horrified. He said, "Sir, I can't do this. I have had a long-time relationship with Rebecca."

"Yes, precisely why you were picked for the job. She has faith in you, Captain Grant. This has become a major flap around the world. It just isn't a case of some political Johnny going to jail for corruption. We and several other governments have developed a long-term relationship with this group. We know they are disreputable, but we have used that to our benefit. There are many things in this world that are not black and white, and in many of the gray areas we use these people to get things done that we cannot do as a government. This has gotten out of hand, and your unlucky Rebecca has gotten herself in the thick of it. Ian, she is dead, by the triads, the Americans, French, or Germans. One way or the other, she is dead. It is our job to make sure this incident dies with her. Look, son, I know this is hard for you, but it's your job, and when it is over successfully, you will be the youngest general in the history of the Royal Marines. Set up a com center on Green Island and only communicate through the channels which will be given to you daily by courier."

"Yes, sir."

When Ian got out of the car, he felt like he was hit with a cricket paddle. As he drove to the airport to return to Hong Kong, he remained in that daze.

CHAPTER 34
Paris, France

The DPSD, the French intelligence office, was housed in a rather non-descript building a few blocks off the Champs de Lessee. Inspector Francois Bellignon was about to leave for an important appointment when he got the call.

"Inspector, there is a call from the minister, and he said it is urgent."

"Okay, I'll take it in my office."

"Francois, it is Jean. I must meet with you right now."

"I'm sorry, Mr. Minister, but I have a scheduled appointment, and I'm already late."

"I don't care. Meet me in the north gate of Auburn Park in ten minutes."

Francois hung up the phone and called his secretary.

"Cancel all of my appointments for the rest of the day."

Francois knew this was going to be bad. He could tell from the urgency in the minister's voice.

He arrived at the entrance to the park and saw the minister waiting for him.

"Jean, what is wrong?"

"Come, let's talk while we walk."

The minister looked tormented, and he said "We are in deep trouble, my friend. Ascot Chen paid me a visit."

Francois knew that this was always bad, but he had never seen the minister react this way before.

Francois asked, "How bad is it?"

"This could be the end of our careers and a long prison term for us both," he answered.

"But why? We have always come out on top. The things we have been asked have not been so bad and between us and our group, we have always been able to either cover it up or keep it hidden."

"Not this time, Francois. A list of all of Liddo's payments has been found by a British cop in Hong Kong. She has been somewhat neutralized but has hidden several copies, and they can't get them. You know what this means if this information comes to light? We are screwed. Chen suggested that we contact our friend, the ex-legionnaire, but I told him I didn't think he would be effectual in Hong Kong. Chen told me he did not want to go over my head, and I realized this made things worse. If there is someone higher in our government, that would mean, no matter what, we are the fall guys. Like I said, we are screwed."

Francois looked at him with a look of total desperation, pulled his gun, and shot himself in the head. The minister looked on horrified and then realized he would probably have to do the same.

CHAPTER 35
Back in Hong Kong

"Listen, boss, we should get out of here for a while. Sail over to the Philippines or visit your friend on Hainan Do. I don't want to worry you, but as it stands now, we have the triads, British and American intelligence, and we don't know who else after us."

"Chong, you are right, but the only reason they are after me is that they believe I can get to whatever it was that Miss Dreed is hiding. As long as they haven't found it, both Miss Dreed and I are safe, at least for the time being. I can't leave now, I promised Imelda I would stay here all day and wait for a message from her."

"Okay, boss, but we better be on guard. I spoke to a few of my relatives, and they are keeping an eye on us, and all the information that we can get seems to say Palfrey is on the level, he's the only one we can trust."

"All right, let's get some rest. I have a feeling we are going to need it. Both John and Chong spent the rest of the day lounging around the boat, and it was almost dark when Chong came below and said, "Boss, someone is coming, get ready."

John ran up on deck and saw Imelda coming aboard.

"Hello, Imelda," he said.

And she replied, "I just came by to apologize for last night."

"Don't worry," John said. "Those things happen."

"Not to me," Imelda said.

"Can I offer you a drink?"

"Just tea, please. After last night, I'm off the hard stuff for a while."

As Chong gave Imelda her tea, she passed a written note to

him, and he palmed it so well John didn't even notice. Chong went below, and John and Imelda chatted while she finished her tea. When she was leaving, John asked if he could drive her home, but she declined, saying a friend was meeting her in the yacht club and they would be taking her home. About a half an hour after she left, Chong came up on deck and asked John to go for a walk. When they were at the end of the berth, Chong turned up his portable radio.

"What's up?" asked John.

"Miss Browne passed me a note. Miss Dreed is in serious trouble. Miss Brown said they are taking away all the men guarding her tomorrow except one. That sounds like they are planning to make her redundant, permanently."

"What can we do? We have to start with the plan quickly. Chong, how long will it take to mobilize your relatives?"

"About four or five hours, boss."

"Okay, let's get moving. Round them up personally, and by the time you get back, I'll have the plan set in my head...I hope."

As he went back to the boat, John thought carefully on how to rescue Rebecca, but the real task was going to be what to do when he had her? Thoughts were going through his mind like a wild wind, and he kept trying to focus and not panic. The plan started to come together in his mind's eye.

When Chong arrived back at the boat John went over the plan with him. "It sounds great, boss. Were you ever in the military?"

"No," John replied. "Why?"

"You're quite a tactician."

"And I'm surprised you know a word like *tactician*," John replied.

They both laughed but got real serious real soon.

"Chong, this is really Ian's plan, and don't forget we can't trust anyone, even him."

"Boss, you're learning fast. They went over the plan several times, and Chong said the timing would be tough, but it was the only feasible way to go. They both agreed on the positioning and placement of everyone, and John said, "Let's get some sleep. Tomorrow's going to be a rough day."

They woke at first light, and John made some tea and coffee.

"Chong, why don't you get going and start making sure everyone is in place. I'll meet you at the place we agreed upon. I'll be there at two fifteen sharp."

"Okay, see you then, boss."

The plan was set in his mind. There would only be the one guard left, and Chong's cousin would take him out with the gas. They would go out the front door, and Chong would have a van waiting. Chong's other cousins would run interference in case anyone stayed behind to keep watch until after Rebecca was killed. He had never done anything remotely close to this before, and he was feeling a bit manic, the way you feel when you first run out onto the field in a big game.

CHAPTER 36
Hong Kong, In the Game

It was 11:00 a.m. Chong had already called and said everything was in place. John left the boat and went up to the club and arranged for a taxi. It was there in less than five minutes. He told the driver to take him to the Hong Kong Club. John left the Hong Kong Club at one thirty and made his way to Robinson Road. He paid the driver and started to walk down to Caine Road. He walked passed the Anglican Church and Kings College and crossed the street. He stopped in the pet store just off the corner to make sure he wasn't being followed, but everyone looked suspect. As he turned the corner onto Caine Road, he saw Chong's cousin standing across the street from the safe house where Rebecca was being held. He walked past him and stopped in a noodle shop waiting for the signal. The minutes seemed like hours, and he was getting more and more apprehensive. He was about to jump out of his skin when he got the signal.

Chong's cousin was starting to argue with a shopkeeper and took a wooden packing crate and threw it through the window. That was the diversion, and John started to move. He crossed the street and went into the building. No one was in the lobby, and Chong had already had his team remove the guard. He went up to the flat and listened at the door. There was no sound. He put on the gas mask and looked under the stairwell and found the crow bar that had been placed there the day before by the porter, who was handsomely paid. John used the bar to open the door, and there was Rebecca, passed out on the floor alongside of her bodyguard.

John picked her up and threw her over his shoulder. He ran down the stairs and out the door to the street. Several men started to run toward them, but the van pulled up and John jumped in the open door while the van was still moving.

Going north on Caine Road, just before the Jewish Community center of Hong Kong, a truck pulled out in front of the van and another behind it. Chong jammed on the breaks, and John pulled Rebecca from the van and carried her into the community center. The trucks moved after a few minutes, and Chong proceeded to drive back to Aberdeen. While inside the community center, John told the woman at reception that his wife had a bad reaction from something she ate and could she let them sit for a while. The woman brought them to an office down the hall, and John explained his wife was allergic to MSG and could he have a glass of water to give her an antihistamine. The woman was kind and got the water immediately. As soon as she had cleared the door, John quickly took out a syringe and injected Rebecca with the antidote for the sleep agent that had been blown into the flat from the flat above by Chong's cousin. Rebecca was already coming to when the woman returned with the water.

"Thank you, this is very kind of you."

"Not at all," replied the woman.

She went on to say that the Center had a very reasonably priced dinner prepared western style and it might be safer if they ate there while visiting Hong Kong.

"The food is good, and it's Kosher, as well," she said.

"Thank you again, but we are leaving tomorrow," John replied.

Rebecca was now fully awake and looking at John in bewilderment.

"What's going on?" she asked John.

"Nothing, dear, you had some MSG and you had a bad reaction."

The woman standing over them asked if they wanted a doctor.

John replied, "No, thank you. This has happened before, and she will be all right in a few minutes."

When the woman was gone, Rebecca jumped up and threw her arms around John.

"It's so good to see you. What happened?"

"I'll tell you later. We have to get out of here, and half the world is after us."

John handed Rebecca the flight bag he was carrying and told her it contained a blond wig and some clothes.

"Go in the ladies' room and change. I'll make sure it is safe to leave."

Rebecca was changed in a few minutes, and the different style of clothes and the wig made a remarkable difference.

John went out the door first and stood next to a tree, which was in the center of the front lawn of the community center. From here, he could see the sidewalk in both directions, and it appeared safe, so he gestured to Rebecca to come. He told her to make her way down the side lawn of the Jewish Center, and at the bottom, there were stairs which would leave her at the top of Lan Quai Fun, from there she should walk to Queens Road and through the shopping center at the bottom of Ice House Street.

"Come out on Connaught Road and go into Alexander House. Go up the escalator, and take the bridge to the prince's building and continue on to the Star Ferry. I will meet you on the Kowloon side at the Polo shop in the ocean terminal. Stay in the dressing room and watch for me."

Rebecca said she understood and quickly left. John walked in the opposite direction, down Caine Road, and took his first right turn, which led him to a steep flight of stairs, which went all the way down to Queens Road. This stairway was only used by the people who lived in the buildings on either side. Another block down Cain Road, there was an escalator that was taken by most people who lived in the area. John made another right onto Queens Road and stopped several times to make sure he wasn't being followed. So far the plan was working, but he had a terrible feeling of dread. It was too easy. When he reached Kowloon, he walked to Tsim tsa tui and turned down Nathan Road and went into the Peninsula Hotel. He sat in the opulent lobby for several minutes, just to see if anyone was following. When he felt safe, he went out the door on the opposite side of the hotel and walked to the ocean terminal. Instead of the escalator, he took the elevator to the shopping arcade and went into the Polo store. He looked around for a few minutes and fended off several sales people and then made his way over to the dressing rooms. He walked past them and quietly called to Rebecca, who appeared immediately.

"Let's go," he said, and they walked together to the street level and got into a taxi right outside the door of the terminal.

John told the driver to take them to Shatin and the temple of ten thousand Buddhas. As they were driving, John told the driver to stop in an area of the city that was known for the quick stay motels. This was a pretty undesirable area just north of Temple Street. It was frequented mostly by bar girls and their clients. John told Rebecca to stay outside while he went into a rather dirty-looking hotel and registered as Mr. and Mrs. S. Claus. He returned with a key stamped with the number eight. He told the driver to continue to the temple and explained he had to use the loo at that hotel. They got out of the cab at the entrance to the temple and walked straight through to the other side and went out a small gate and walked a few short blocks back to the hotel.

When they got into the room, Rebecca threw her arms around him and kissed him hard. She started to cry, and John said, "Calm down, don't breakdown on me now. We have just started. He wiped the tears from her eyes and sat her on the bed. Over the next hour and a half, John filled her in on everything that had transpired.

"Hey, look, a hot plate. Would you like a cup of tea?"

"Yes, desperately," she answered.

While the water was boiling, John filled Rebecca in on the events that led to the present. Rebecca looked at him and sighed, "I wish I didn't get you involved in all of this."

John laughed and said, "It's been a ball."

Rebecca threw a pillow at him, and they laughed.

"After you have a cup of tea, we have to figure out what to do next. Do you know St. John's Church down the street from the temple of ten thousand Buddhas?"

"Yes," she answered.

"Well, if we have to separate for any reason, get there and

see Father Chuck. He's an old friend of mine and someone we can trust."

She looked at him in disbelief.

"Where did you meet him?"

"It's a small world, my dear. We actually went to school together in California."

"Okay," she agreed.

The teakettle started to whistle, and just as John poured Rebecca's tea, the window exploded with a gunshot. John hit the floor and screamed at Rebecca to turn out the light. She was diving for the floor and grabbed the lamp and pulled it down with her.

The lamp crashed to the floor, and sparks flew as the room went dark. John crawled to her and whispered, "They found us already. How many do you think are out there?"

"I don't know," John said, "but we have to get out of here soon or there will be an army out there."

John looked around and assessed the situation. He couldn't think for a moment, but then, he noticed the door between his room and the next. He put his back up against the bed and his both feet on the door and pushed. The door buckled and then burst open. He told Rebecca to crawl into the next room, and he grabbed the kettle off of the hot plate.

"What are you doing?" Rebecca asked.

"I didn't get my tea," he answered.

Bewildered, she crawled through the door saying, "I think you've gone mad."

The sad part of it was she wasn't certain he hadn't. Once they were both in the other room, which John assumed was nine, he peeked out of the window and saw one man moving toward the door to room eight. John poured the boiling water into a metal waste paper basket hoping it wouldn't leek. It didn't. Just as the man put his hand on the doorknob, John threw open the door of room nine and threw the bucket of boiling water in the man's face. The surprise and pain made him drop the gun.

John kicked him in the chest, sending him back about five feet, and John then grabbed the gun and fired three times. The bullets hit in a small circle in the center of the man's face, blowing the entire back of his head off. Rebecca screamed, and John told her to shut up and get down. He went through the man's pockets and took all the ammunition he was carrying and all of the money he had on him. The man was Chinese, and John thought this was good. He was probably a local triad thug who wanted the reward for killing Rebecca, and if that was so, there was a good chance he didn't contact anyone before he made his move.

"Rebecca, get to Father Chuck. I'll catch up with you later."

"No," she said. "I'll never make it alone. John I am too afraid."

"Okay, let's get out of here, now."

John took Rebecca by the hand and led her to the back of the motel.

"Let's go through the yards and stay out of sight."

After negotiating several fences and walls, and crawling through about fifty feet of corrugated pipe, they wound up about three blocks from the church. They got onto a crowded street and stayed in the middle of the crowd as much as possible.

They were a hundred yards from the church when the two men came out of nowhere and hit John at the same time. He went down right away but rolled and came up in a crouched stance. He moved quickly toward the one man, and when he was about three feet away, he leapt up and kicked him in the neck. The man folded with a terrible gasp. John kept the other man in view, and as soon as he was back on the ground, he gave him a spin kick to the face and then a forearm to the side of the head. The man went down hard.

John looked at Rebecca and yelled "go," but she froze and stared at him immobile. It was obvious that the whole ordeal was more than she could handle, and John hoped she had not gone into shock.

The first man was now up and running at John. He stepped in toward the man and moved slightly to the side, and with a quick motion, hit him in the bridge of the nose. There was the sound of bone cracking, and then John stepped back in front of the man and hit him under his nose with the heel of his hand. The sound of the man's nose going through his brain was too much for Rebecca. She fainted.

PURCHASED POWER

John looked around, and no one else seemed to be aggressive, so he picked up Rebecca and carried her into the church. It took him a few minutes to find Chuck.

"Hey, buddy. I'm in trouble. I need some serious help."

"I already heard. Quickly, come this way."

John followed Chuck, who was now carrying Rebecca through the church and into his residence, down a flight of stairs and into a storeroom. Chuck put Rebecca down and went over to a wall covered with shelves from floor to ceiling. Chuck pulled a couple of the steel shelves and opened a hidden door that led to a tunnel.

"What the hell is this?" John asked.

"This goes right down to the water. We use it to smuggle political and religious refugees into Hong Kong from China."

John looked at his friend and said, "I don't believe this. You're a smuggler?"

Chuck laughed and said, "At this particular juncture, I think that's the pot calling the kettle black."

They both laughed.

"All right, John, stay here, and I'll be back when I can make the proper arrangements. It will be quite a while, but I'll check in with you every three hours or so. You'll know I'm coming when that red light goes on. If that door opens before the red light goes on, it's not me, and God help you. I'll see you later, and God bless. Take care of her."

"Chuck, thanks."

"Yeah, sure, John," and he left.

The tunnel was dark and damp, lit only by a single bulb that seemed to flicker. John could hear the rats running and smelt the foul smell of rotten food and human waste. Rebecca seemed to be in a daze, and John started to be concerned. He was convinced now that she had gone into shock. He took off his jacket and put it around her and sat her down on a wooden crate that was next to them. After a few minutes, she started to stir and said, "We're in the walled city."

John said, "What?"

"The walled city," she repeated. "It used to be this entire side of Kowloon, kind of an underground city, which was left alone for a long time to keep the hookers and crime off the street. I thought it was completely destroyed back in the 1960s but I guess some of it survived. It was a horrible place and went deep under ground, at least ten stories. It was said you could get anything illegal down here, and it was tolerated because it all stayed down here and didn't effect the city above."

Rebecca went from being totally lucid to a blank stare, but then she started to cry.

"John, you just killed at least two people!"

She now looked horrified, and quickly, John snapped her out of it.

"Hey! It was them or us. They are trying to kill us, you know."

"Oh, John, I am so sorry I got you involved in all of this."

"Lucy, I'm afraid I have fallen in love with you, and I'll do anything to protect you."

"My name is Rebecca." She shook her head. "Oh John, I'm sorry. This is not the time to be like this. We're both upset, but I appreciate everything and I am very happy you love me. I love you too. I have thought of nothing else through this whole ordeal."

John noticed she was starting to shiver, and he sat next to her and put his arm around her. They sat quietly for what seemed to be an eternity when suddenly a red light started to flash and Chuck was coming through the door. He gave them blankets and some food. He handed John a plastic bag and a small tin can with a removable lid.

"Put whatever food you have left in the bag and put the bag in the can or the rats will swarm you." He then said, "Stand against the wall," and he took Polaroid pictures of both of them. "I am arranging for two Canadian passports for you. Your names are John and Mary Mc Kenzie. This tunnel leads to a restaurant barge on the coast."

"You mean the one on the bike path between Shatin and Taipo?" John asked.

"Yeah," Chuck said, "and a boat will pick you up there tomorrow morning. It will take you to a small fishing village about thirty miles north of Saikong. You will be transferred to another boat there and taken to Shanghai. It will take about four days, and you'll be on your own from there."

"Chuck, I don't know what to say but thank you."

"Go to Mass and pray for me. I have been the big loser in cards for the past three weeks."

They all laughed.

"I'm not going to ask what all this is about," said John.

Chuck said, "Sometimes you have to bend the rules to do the right thing, and in this part of the world, it's a way of life. While I was going through the seminary, I had a teacher who had spent thirty years out here, and he liked me, but he saw that wild streak I have always had, and when I was ordained, he said he knew exactly where I could be the most effective as a priest and sent me here. He was right. Now get some sleep. You have a rough couple of days coming up. Rebecca, it was a pleasure to meet you, and please, take care of this guy, will ya?"

She leaned forward and gave him a kiss on the cheek and thanked him. Chuck actually blushed and said good night.

CHAPTER 37

Chong arrived at the yacht club, and a man and woman resembling John and Rebecca got on the *Lady*. Chung jumped aboard, and they immediately prepared to get underway. They had just passed the southern tip of Lantau Island when the first rounds hit the boat. Chung told his companions to get down below, and he ran aft. Chong turned out the running lights and could see the boat that was in pursuit. It was one of those high-speed cigarette boats, and he knew he couldn't outrun them, but he had something up his sleeve. He moved quickly to the built in toolbox on the port side of the boat and pulled out two round objects that appeared to be two garbage can covers. He pulled the tabs on either side of the discs and waited. When the cigarette boat was about fifty feet behind him, he threw the discs into the water. When the boat hit the first disc, the explosion was tremendous, but when the second one went off, the boat went into pieces that went up at least a hundred feet in a huge fireball.

Chong smiled, but his feeling of triumph was short lived. The first blast was only fifty feet behind them, and the second was only ten feet off the bow. The boat actually came out of the water, and Chong fell but was still hanging on to the wheel. He turned the wheel hard to the left, and the boat responded immediately. He rode the wave from the blast and turned around the point of the island. As soon as he was out of sight of the other boat, he spun the wheel to the right and turned almost 180 degrees, but he hit some shallow water and the boat sharply listed. Just as the boat righted itself, the other boat came speeding around the point and was on a collision course with the *Lady*. Chong spun the wheel to the left, and the two boats missed each other by inches.

As the two boats passed each other, Chong pulled the pin on the grenade and tossed it. The grenade landed on the rear deck and bounced into the cabin. As the grenade went off, the flying bridge, with its occupants, flew into the air and seemed to have landed just as the boat exploded. The blast was so strong it threw Chong to the deck, and he couldn't hear and could only see a bright red glare. He lay there for a few minutes and then forced himself up. He could barely see, but he knew they were back in open water, and he turned on the autopilot and fell down. He lay there for several minutes before his companions came on deck and helped him below. The man posing as John was actually Inspector Palfrey, and he took the helm and continued to sail south-southwest. Chong didn't know how long he had been out, but when he came to, Rose was wiping his forehead with a cool cloth. He tried to get up, but she pushed him down and said, "Rest, my darling, the British inspector is steering the boat."

Rose had made some tea and held the cup up to Chong's lips. After half the cup was gone, he sat up and told Rose he was fine, but as he stood, he wavered and fell back into the bed. She said, "Rest, I'll watch the gwuy low."

He touched her face affectionately and fell into a deep sleep. When Chong woke up, he was alone but could see it was light through the porthole. He stood up and surprisingly felt fine. He really needed the rest. He climbed up on deck, and Palfrey was at the helm.

Palfrey asked, "Where did you get those amusing toys you used last night?"

"None of your business," quipped Chong. "Where are we?"

Palfrey said, "I'm not sure, but we should be somewhere near Hainan Island, according to the charts. They sailed the course John had set for them, and by then, should have been there. Chong suggested they sail due north. If they sailed north, and in fact had missed Hainan, they would hit China and would be able to find out where they really were. Palfrey agreed and turned the boat seventy degrees and set the course due north. After sailing about two hours, they saw something out on the horizon. They couldn't identify it, but as they got closer, Chong said, "We're on the right course, that's the Alliance oil field."

It was just four o'clock when they tied up at the Alliance dock on Hainan Island. Two Americans were waiting on the dock. Chong said hello to them, but when they saw Palfrey and Rose, they looked pretty angry and turned and walked off the pier. Chong went into the Alliance office and called Andre, who told him he would meet them at the hotel in two hours. As Andre came into the lobby of the hotel, he smiled, seeing Chong and called, "Mon ami, where is John?"

"I don't know," Chong said out loud. "I thought he was here."

"He told me he was flying over here last night and asked if I would sail over with *The Lady*. Andre, this is Inspector Palfrey of the Hong Kong police. He is an old friend of John's and myself, and this is Rose, an old friend of mine."

"Nice to meet you all. May I invite you all to dinner this evening?"

"Sure," said Chong, "and in the meantime, I'll try to locate my boss." Andre smiled. "I'm sorry, I have to excuse myself until then, but I have to go back to work. I'll pick you up in the lobby at eight."

CHAPTER 38

John and Rebecca stood on the aft deck of the small junk and watched the horizon, as Hong Kong became a small dot than vanished into the sea. The sky was bright red with gold and pink rays of light coming from the setting sun, puffs of clouds lay close to the water, they had no color but seemed to be irregular shaped shadows dancing on the waves. The sound of the sail flapping in the wind while the steady beat of the diesel engine hummed in the background. Rebecca turned to John and told him how sorry she was he got involved in this mess. John did not want to hear this.

He just said, "Be quiet and enjoy this beautiful moment. We will be back in the weeds soon enough."

Rebecca looked up at him adoringly and said nothing, realizing this was the man she was going to spend the rest of her life with. How long that would be was in question. The sky faded into black like the changing of a scene in a movie, and John said, "Why don't we get some rest we will need it." They went below and climbed into the small bunk that was made for them. It was only minutes before they were both asleep, exhausted. John woke up startled from the noise outside. He looked out of the small porthole and realized they were in port.

"Rebecca, we're here, get up."

They both quickly washed and changed clothes. John said, "Stay here, I'm going topside to see what is going on." They were tied up to a small pier in what seemed to be a fishing village. From the villagers' dress and the red flags that seemed to be everywhere, John assumed they were in the PRC, the People's Republic of China, Red China, as it is known in some circles.

There did not appear to be any customs or immigration people, and the crew was not aboard. John got an uneasy feeling he went back below to his cabin. "Rebecca, grab your stuff and be ready to bolt."

"Let's get out of here."

As they went back up on deck, the captain was coming aboard with a military officer. John had a terrible feeling of panic, but the captain waved to him smiling and introduced him to Colonel Ma Jing. The colonel politely offered his hand and smiled with a friendly Chinese greeting, "Ni Hua, Ni Hua."

John took the man's hand, "Ni Hua, Ni Hua." He was still not sure what was happening. The captain invited the two of them to his cabin for a drink, it was 7:00 a.m., but John said, "Sure."

The captain took out a bottle of MoiTai and explained to John that this was special MoiTai from Jansing province. The colonel agreed and seemed particularly anxious to begin sampling it. As the colonel was downing the drink on his own, now the captain explained that Colonel Ma was going to protect him and make certain everything went smooth in the transfer to the next ship to Shanghai. The captain thought it would be a good idea for John to give the colonel a little present about $500 US to show his appreciation.

John excused himself and, on the way out, put five one hundred dollar bills on the table and left the cabin. He found Rebecca in their cabin and told her what was going on. "Rebecca, you get some rest. I'll try to find us some tea and hopefully some food." Just outside the cabin, he saw one of the mates and asked in Chinese, "Yum Cha?"

The mate said yes and he would have it delivered to the cabin. It was best that John and Rebecca stayed out of sight until the other boat was ready for them.

After they ate, they both felt like a nap.

John woke up and got out of bed quietly trying not to wake up Rebecca. As he was getting dressed, he looked out of the porthole and saw soldiers heavily armed, outside on the pier. He pulled the curtain closed and opened the porthole slightly to see if he could hear what was going on. The colonel, who was completely drunk, was arguing with another officer. John tried to concentrate and understand what they were saying, and it appeared that the younger officer was trying to come aboard the ship because there were reports of spies on board. John suddenly realized they were talking about him.

He thought of a plan and went up on deck. Immediately the soldiers aimed their weapons on him. John calmly looked at them and waved hello. He walked down the gangway and went up to the captain and said, "Captain, thank you for letting my wife and I sleep. We needed the rest."

He turned to the two officers and said in perfect Cantonese, "Josan, good morning. My name is John McKenzie. My wife and I are missionaries and have just arrived in your country. Have you come to do the custom formalities? Here is my passport, and I'll go and get my wife's."

The younger officer looked at John incredulously and said, "No, we are not customs officials. We had a report that there were some dangerous people on this boat."

John said, "Except for the crew, I know only of my wife and myself."

The officer looked at the captain and said, "I want to inspect the boat."

The captain said, "Please do," and they all went up on deck. John turned to the officer and asked Excuse me, are my wife and I in any danger?"

The officer said, "I am not sure."

John said, "Please be careful," as the soldiers went below deck. John and the captain followed. For a junk, this boat was large. It was a cargo ship, but in comparison to modern day cargo ships, it was tiny. There was only one main passageway with two cabins on each side and the captain's cabin at the end under the wheelhouse. They searched all of the cabins and, besides the crew, found no one except Rebecca. The officer left without saying good-bye but seemed to be apologizing to the colonel on the way out. When the soldiers left the pier, the captain told John he hoped the other vessel got there soon, as he was sure the young officer was going to do some checking when he got back to his base, about a half a mile south of the village. This could only mean trouble, and he wanted to leave himself before anything happened. The captain looked at John and said, "That was a pretty brave move. Are you two spies?"

John looked at him, and without hesitation, John said, "We are people of God, my son. Don't forget who introduced us," and they both laughed.

Two and a half hours later, they were on a larger steel constructed cargo ship named the Mao Tung. John and Rebecca spent the next ten hours in their cabin. The first mate, a sneaky looking little man, came to get them from the cabin. We have just entered the Huang Po River. We will be in Shanghai in twenty minutes. He brought them to the captain's cabin and they were told to wait. When the ship stopped, there seemed to be a lot of activity from the crew, and then it was quiet. There was no noise except for the low hum of the standby engines. The mate came into the cabin and told them that the authorities were coming on board. The custom's authorities entered, and John rose and greeted them. He presented them with the two passports, and the custom's agent looked at them and put the passports in his pocket. He said, "I will take these to the office and check them. You will wait here until I return."

John said, "Could I save you a trip and put two one hundred dollar bills on the table?" The man sat down and took the passports out of his pocket and stamped the visas in each passport. He got up and took the money off the table with the precision of a magician doing slight of hand. The custom's agent left, and John told Rebecca to get moving.

"I want to get out of here now, right now."

They almost walked off the gangway at the same time as the custom's agent and John never looked back at the ship. They walked several blocks from the pier and realized they were in Podong a suburb of Shanghai on the opposite side of the river from the main part of the city. John had never been here but had read about Shaghai and had seen several specials on cable back in the States. He remembered the tourist area was called the Bund and that was probably the easiest place for them to blend in. He hailed a taxi, and they got in. John asked the driver to bring them to the Bund, but the driver did not understand him. Then John realized they spoke a diffcrent dialect here, and the man did not understand Cantonese. John turned to Rebecca and said, "He doesn't speak Cantonese."

The driver turned to him and in perfect English said, "Where do you want to go, boss?"

"Oh!" John said laughing. "The Bund."

"Anywhere on the Bund?" asked the driver.

"We need a hotel."

"How about the Peace Hotel. It's old, but many tourists like it."

"Fine, that sounds good."

As they drove through the center of Podong, John could not believe what a beautiful modern city this was. He always thought of Shanghai as something out of a Sydney Greenstreet movie, but this was a modern vibrant city with skyscrapers and ultra modern architecture. The people on the streets were fashionably dressed, and everyone seemed to have a cell phone growing out of their head. John was surprised this was not what he expected.

When they walked into the lobby of the Peace Hotel, John turned to Rebecca and said, "This is more of what I thought Shanghai would be like."

The lobby was huge with vaulted ceilings and carved applicaids on the pillars and walls. The main chandelier had to be twenty feet in diameter, and there were smaller crystal chandeliers lining both sides, they were all lit but it still seemed dark. Red velvet was everywhere, and they saw a sign that there was a jazz band in the club off the lobby.

There was no bell boy to take them to their room, but when the reached their floor, there was an attendant who asked for their key and walked them to their room and opened their door and left. The room was huge with a large balcony overlooking the Bund, the waterfront of Shanghai.

John motioned to Rebecca to go out onto the balcony, and he turned on the TV and ran the shower in the bathroom. He walked over and latched the door and joined her. Once out on the balcony, John explained that Chong had taught him to take these precautions in case someone was trying to listen.

"Let's get something to eat, and after dinner, we will go for a walk on the Bund and discuss what to do next. I will only call you Mary from now on, as that's the name on the passport. Don't talk about anything concerning our problems in the room or anywhere that we can be overheard."

Rebecca agreed and said, "Where the hell have you learned about all these procedures? I'm impressed."

John laughed and said, "I'm a quick study. Especially when my life depends on it."

They took the lift up to the eighth floor. They had been told there was a restaurant. It was bright and comfortable with plenty of space between the tables and the decorative columns and carved ceiling appeared to have been recently refurbished. The service was surprisingly good, and the food was fantastic. They started with fried dumplings, which were prepared Shanghai style, then had small dishes of crab, river eel, duck, and Bat Choy. They each had a large bottle of five star beer, a premium beer only sold in Beijing and Shanghai. It was brilliant.

After dinner, they slowly strolled down the Bund and for a good hour. They just walked and talked and forgot their problems. They had walked the entire length of the Bund. They walked over to the next block, Szechwan Road, and followed it until they came to what they first thought was a sports arena, it was actually the old British race track, a remnant of colonial days.

There were many university students who congregated there to practice foreign languages and talk about politics and world affairs. It gave it an almost carnival atmosphere. It is one of the only open forums for these students, and it was crowded. They were approached by a young woman. "Good evening," she said.

"Hello," John replied.

The young woman asked, "Are you an American?

"No," John said. "We are Canadian."

"Oh good! Even better," the girl said.

She asked if they knew the history behind the racetrack, and John said no.

"Let me show you something," she said as she grabbed their arms and started to walk to the other side of the park.

John asked where she was taking them, and the girl simply replied, "You'll see soon."

At the entrance to the park, the girl pointed out a sign that said, "No Chinese or dogs allowed. The Royal Racing Club."

She then pointed to a sign next to it in Chinese that she translated.

"This will never happen again." The girl went on to say that the track was partially destroyed during the Cultural Revolution, but the stands were rebuilt and a commemorative park was built to remind the people of Shanghai and China that they have to depend on themselves and never let foreigners take over the country again. She was delightful, and John asked her for her name.

"Jing Lin," she replied. "And yours?"

"John and Mary McKenzie."

John told her that their luggage was lost in transit and asked where they might buy some clothes and other necessitates.

"Nanjing Road. It has many nice shops. When you go back to Sichuan Road, go straight and walk five blocks to Ulimuchi Nan Lu and make a left turn go two more blocks and you will come to Nanjing road."

"Thank you so much," Rebecca replied.

Jing Lin offered to show them around Shanghai the following day, but John declined. He told her they were leaving Shanghai tomorrow and they would only have time to do a little shopping before they left.

"That's too bad. I was hoping for a chance to practice my English."

"Maybe we can stay an extra day, John. I would love to see this city, and it might give us a little more time to better organize the rest of the trip."

John agreed, and they made arrangements to meet at the same place the following day at 10:00 a.m.

On the walk back to the hotel, they discussed their situation, and John explained that Ian had given him an address in Harbin and they could hire protection from some of his Russian contacts until all of this could be sorted out. John told Rebecca that he would call the bank in Geneva and have some money transferred to Peter in California, and he would have Peter transfer it to John McKenzie here at the Bank of China in Shanghai, funds to be released against presentation of passport.

"Tomorrow we'll buy a car and drive to Harbin."

"How far is it?" Rebecca asked.

"I have no idea. We better get some maps and try to figure out our route. Driving will be a lot safer than any public transportation. The plan was set with the understanding there were still many details to work out, but in principle, there was a plan."

The next morning, they were both up early and had breakfast in the room. John called down to the desk and asked about a car for the day. They came out of the side entrance of the lobby, and their car and driver were waiting for them. John asked the driver where they could buy a car, and he told them it was difficult and could take a week to get all the paperwork done. John handed him a twenty-dollar bill and asked if he could help? The driver looked at the twenty and said, "For this, I could help a little."

So John gave him two hundred dollar bills. The driver smiled and said, "Do you want to buy it for cash?"

"Yes," John replied, "US dollars."

"What kind of car do you want? Mercedes?"

"No. What is the most common car?"

"Toyota, Corolla, answered the man."

"Okay, a Toyota…black."

"That will cost $28,000 US."

John laughed.

"Are you crazy?"

"No, here in China there is 100 percent tax on imported cars. If you don't pay the tax, you can't get the registration plates. I can deliver the car in one day from the time you pay for it, and I will only ask for five hundred dollars."

"Whatever happened to communism?" John laughed.

The driver said proudly, "This is Shanghai, the capitalist center of China."

John agreed. He had called Peter last night and was told the funds should arrive in Shanghai today at about 1:00 p.m. John asked the driver his name, and he said Pete. John went into a fit of laughter.

PURCHASED POWER

They met Jing Lin at ten and began their tour of the city. Jing Lin asked where they were staying, and John said the Peace Hotel. She told them that the Peace Hotel was the Cathay Hotel before the war. During WWII, it was the command center and officers' quarters for the American fleet during the war. They circled back to the Bund, and when they passed the hotel, Jing gave them the history of every building on the Bund. They passed the old British Shanghai Club that was now the ministry of Animal Byproducts and on to the park hotel, which was the first British Hotel in Shanghai, then the Bank of China's head office in Shanghai, where John asked to stop to transact some business but was out quickly when he was told the transfer would not be ready until later in the day.

As they drove around the city, Rebecca was getting more and more fascinated by the stories, realizing how much British history was in Shanghai. They followed the road and then made a series of left turns pass modern skyscrapers and entire sections of the city that were under construction. Traffic was heavy, and the going was slow, but it was a great way to see the city. When they pulled onto Nanjing road, the driver explained that he could not stop here so he would let them off around the corner so they could shop. Both John and Rebecca were surprised at the international flavor and quality of the shops. They were able to get everything they needed and enjoyed shopping in these high-end boutiques. While they walked down the street, John noticed a Sassoon Beauty Salon and told Rebecca that he wanted to see her as a blonde with a new short cut.

At first she said no, but John said, "Mary, do it for me," and she reluctantly acquiesced. While Rebecca was being transformed, John and Jing went into the old section of Nanjing Road and John saw the tea house where the boxer rebellion started. John and Jing walked back to the shop, and Rebecca came out just as they walked up.

"Mary, I can't believe it. What a difference," Jing said. "Cool, you look great."

"Yeah," said John, but actually he felt kind of bad. This new do showed how young Rebecca really was, and he felt a little self-conscious being with her. At first she made him feel a little old, but he got over it fast. On their way back to the car, John spotted a shop that sold maps.

"I'll be right back."

He came out of the shop with bags full of maps. Jing and Rebecca continued to tour while John went to the bank and then to the old French Concession with Pete. The French Concession was a beautiful section of the city, which was at one time actually controlled by the French. In the nineteenth and early twentieth centuries, England, France, Russia, and Japan divided Shanghai into fourths, with each country taking care of its own concession.

This was a colonial city paid for by foreign business concerns that were protected by their respective governments. John found this interesting and told himself if he lived through this he would like to come back and really learn about the place. Pete pulled into a drive and up to a gate. An attendant came out and asked what they wanted, and Pete told the man he had an appointment. The gate was opened, and Pete drove in. The driveway ran along the border of a beautiful manicured lawn and up to a house, which would probably cost twenty to thirty million dollars in California.

They were met at the door by an old woman who just kind of whisked them through the door. She pointed to a parlor door, and they went in. The room was probably 100 feet square with thirty-foot high ceilings. There were sofas and overstuffed chairs, all red velvet with white doilies over the backs. Pete explained that the man who lived there was a high-level official.

Mr. Gu came into the room and motioned for them to sit down. Mr. GU was at least ninety-five years old and was wearing a tee shirt and plain blue pants that he hiked up over his knees when he sat down. He and Pete verbally battled for over an hour, and John was not sure if they were truly negotiating or was this show for his benefit.

The shouting stopped, and Mr. GU walked the to the door and, almost as if it were an afterthought, pulled out some papers from his pocket. After he unraveled them, he asked John to sign them in several places, and when they were signed, he simply walked back into the parlor. Pete motioned for John to leave. When they were back in the car, Pete simply said, "Your car will be delivered at seven fifteen this evening where I picked you up this morning. Have the cash."

John thought to himself how wild it was and that he loved Asia. They picked Rebecca up at the racetrack, and John said good-bye to Ling and slipped her some money. Ling looked down at her hand and back at John and said, "No, take this back. I appreciate the fact you let me practice my English, and that's enough."

"No, please take it. You have been so kind to us, and we have taken up your whole day."

"Thank you very much, but I can't. It is too much, but I would like to keep enough to take my friend to the American movie theater, and that's all."

Rebecca said, "No, please keep it. You have made us truly enjoy our experience here."

They both got into the car, waving good-bye to Jing.

Pete suggested a good restaurant close to the hotel for dinner. After they dropped off their packages at the hotel, they walked over to the restaurant. After their meal, John said, "Pete has to be thanked. This was a great restaurant."

After dinner, they went for a short walk on the Bund and then back to the hotel and picked up their new car. Rebecca went straight to bed, but John stayed up half the night studying the maps he had bought and decided on the best route for them to get safely to Harbin.

They would drive to Sochow and Wuxi and on to Nanjing; the roads all appeared on the maps as two lane back roads. The going would be slow, but they had no time constraints. From Nanjing he would drive to Hofie and take the coast road to Tianjin. They would pass through Guilen and Xian, where the Terracotta soldiers were discovered.

From Tianjin, John decided to stay along the coast and go all the way to Dalien. It was much longer, but the other way would take him through Beijing, and John thought there might be too many intelligence people there. From Dalien, he could travel almost due west to Harbin. He went over the maps once more, and when satisfied his route was good, he went to sleep.

CHAPTER 39
Hainan Island

Chong met Andre at the door of the hotel and asked him to take a walk outside before joining the others. Chong explained that John was in some trouble, not of his own making. He was actually helping a friend, but it was a very serious situation. The two American intelligence agents on the pier that day were part of it. They were looking for John.

"Mon Dieu, how can I help?" Andre asked.

"I'm not sure, but if he makes it through alive somewhere along the line, he's going to need all the friends he's got. When I first met John, he helped me out of an embarrassing situation, and since we have been partners, he has been always honest and strait forward. I truly like him, and I will do what it is I am asked."

"Thanks, I knew we could count on you, Andre."

They walked back to the hotel, and Palfrey and Rose were waiting on the veranda. After a fine dinner, Andre gave Chong all of his contact numbers and address. They exchanged pleasantries and retired for the night. In the morning, they sailed off for Hong Kong. Chong discussed the situation with Palfrey, and both agreed that since the opposition knew John and Rebecca were not on the boat, there was no danger. Chong thanked Palfrey for his help, and both agreed that the plan had worked. It gave John at least a two-day head start and redirected some of the oppositions' resources away from John completely. They arrived in Hong Kong with no surprises or resistance.

Chong and Rose left the Yacht Club without anyone following, and Palfrey went home and remained there undisturbed. The next morning, when he showed up in the

Wanchai police station, he was told to take the rest of the week as vacation days, and he did so without hesitation, other than that there were no repercussions. Chong had stayed at Rose's that night, and in the morning, he was feeling pretty good.

He left Rose's house about 10:00 a.m. and was driving home, but as he reached Causeway Bay, he realized maybe he should at least check on the boat and make sure no one was tampering with it.

He drove through Causeway Bay and past Wanchai onto Cottonwood Drive, and just as he was passing the American consulate, he spotted that bastard that he and John threw overboard that night, the NSA agent. He slowed to take a better look, and just as he was passing the guy, Chong recognized his companion. It was Ian Grant.

Chong went around the sharp curve just past the consulate, so he was certain he was out of sight, and stopped the car. He got out and walked into the grounds of the Helena May and hid in the garden between the old and new residences. From there, he could see the consulate and both Grant and the other man. They seemed very friendly. After about five minutes, another man joined them, and they all went into the consulate.

"What are you looking at?" The voice came from behind him.

Chong spun around and said, "Missy Imelda, you frightened the hell out of me."

She laughed that kind soft laugh that just made one know she was a good person.

"Missy Imelda, I just saw Ian Grant with one of the men that tried to kill the boss and me on the boat that night."

"What do you mean?" she asked.

"Just what I said. It was him."

"That doesn't sound good. You stay here, and I'll go over to the consulate and see what's going on."

She came back and said, "Chong, you were right, it was Ian, and he almost shat his pants when he saw me. This is bad, this means that Ian is with them. Can you get in touch with John?"

"No," he said lying. At this point, he could trust no one, and it was better she did not know anyway. Imelda looked at him, and she knew he was lying but decided not to pursue it.

"Chong, why don't we go home and get a good night's sleep. I'll meet you at the boat tomorrow. I'll bring a friend, a Yank. I've known him for years. He's not in the trade. He imports Christmas ornaments into the States, or some such thing. I don't really know exactly, but he will be a good cover, and he can't see anything past my tits, so he'll be occupied and won't bother us at all."

Chong laughed and agreed. Imelda showed up with her friend about ten thirty, Chong had arrived at eight and had everything prepared for the sail. Imelda told Chong they would like to go to the beach at Lantau, and he set sail. Imelda was a good sailor, and she was a great help to Chong on the way out of the harbor. They arrived at Lantau about twelve thirty and Chong dropped anchor about 200 yards off the beach.

Imelda said, "Les, darling, I am going below and put on my swimming costume. Would you be a dear and swim to the beach and arrange for some towels and chairs? You can get them at the restaurant on the beach. I'll be along in a while," and she kissed him on the cheek. Lester dove off the boat, and it looked like he was a good swimmer. Imelda turned to Chong. "Have you swept for bugs?"

"First thing, as soon as I came on board."

"Chong, don't lie to me. I know you can get in touch with John. I will not ask how, but you have to do it, and soon. The address they were given in Harbin is a set up. They'll be killed as soon as they arrive. Ian has been in on this from the very beginning."

Chong looked really upset. "I knew it, that son of a bastard monkey. If you are using the phone Ian gave John, tell him to put the scrambler on as soon as you make contact. He will have to destroy the phone after that because they will use a descrambler as soon as they locate the phone. That only gives you the one call."

"Okay, I'll do that, Missy."

"After I leave the boat, think about what to say and let John know you only have less than three minutes before they can track the signal. Tell him to destroy that phone by crushing, melting, or submerging it after your conversation, and give him a safe phone number to contact you. Don't forget, by now they know everyone you do, so you have to use a number they don't know, like a restaurant or tailor shop or something like that, and change the number each time you make contact. Okay?"

Imelda went below and came up in a two-piece swimsuit that hid nothing. Chong smiled, and she just said, "Don't say it. I know … nice tits." They both laughed, and she dove off the boat and swam to shore to meet Les.

Chong sat and thought out exactly what he was going to say and repeated it over and over again until he had it down cold. He went below and dialed the satellite phone that piece-of-shit Ian had given John and called the number of its companion that John was carrying with him. After giving John the instructions he just heard from Imelda, he said, "Boss, where are you?"

"About 200 miles south of Tianjin," John replied.

"How the hell did you get there?" Chong asked rhetorically.

John simply answered, "I drove."

Chong was a little confused and thought maybe he was giving him misinformation in case they were somehow listening. He told John that Ian was part of the other side and not to go anywhere near Harbin, it was a trap. He gave John a telephone number to call if he needed him and said good-bye and good luck.

John went over a small bridge over a river and stopped the car. He got out and stepped hard on the phone, and it crushed under the force. He then kicked it in the river, and when he got back in the car, Rebecca asked, "What that was all about?"

"I hate cell phones," John said and drove on.

They drove along the coast, and it was difficult because most of the road signs were in Chinese, and although he spoke a bit, he could not read at all. In the distance, he saw a large city, and the next sign was in English. It said Tianjin ten kilometers. John saw a hotel and stopped.

"Let's stay here tonight."

"Alright."

They were in luck. This was a joint venture hotel, which meant it had a foreign partner and it appeared to be duplicated of a Holiday Inn Express.

John got a room on the ground floor in the back of the hotel away from the road and was able to pull the car right up to the door... room 19. They got settled, and John suggested a walk before dinner. While walking, John told Rebecca what Chong had told him, and Rebecca cried out, "No, it couldn't be true."

"I'm afraid it is."

Rebecca felt faint. She couldn't trust anyone, even old friends and lovers, and she felt cold and afraid and shivered, as if a cold wind had just hit her. She was never this alone in her life, and she thanked God for sending her John, her white knight, her protector. John noticed her reaction, "It's alright, we will go to plan B."

"What is plan B?"

"I don't know yet but I'm working on it."

CHAPTER 40
Hong Kong

The two triad thugs were getting tired. They had been beating him and reviving him for hours. Father Chuck's face looked like a slab of Kobe beef, and he was already missing four fingers. They looked at their boss, and he said, "Stop for a while. If we kill him, he'll be of no use to us."

He thought to himself, *If the priest dies before I get the information, I'll be next.* They stopped the bleeding and put the priest on his bed.

"Rest for a while, father. We can start again tomorrow. You'll tell us what we want to know."

Father Chuck glared at the man, and the thug saw it in Chuck's eyes. *This priest is tough. Most men would have been broken by now. He still has a lot of fight in him. This is going to be harder than I thought.*

They let him sleep for about four hours and woke him by throwing a bucket of cold water on him.

"Will you tell us?"

"Drop dead," Chuck snapped at him.

"Okay, we'll do it the hard way. Tie him down."

Chuck tried to fight, but he was weak and racked in pain. When they had him tied, spread eagle on the bed, one of the men produced a large bolt cutter.

"We are going to cut your fingers and toes off digit-by-digit. Why don't you tell us what we want to know, and you'll be spared."

"Go screw yourself," Chuck replied.

The man put the bolt cutter around the first digit on the last remaining finger of his right hand.

"Will you talk?"

"No," he replied, and the triad boss nodded. The man squeezed the bolt cutter, and a piece of Chuck's finger flew across the room, and blood squirted everywhere.

"Will you tell me?"

"No," was the answer, and the second digit was gone.

Chuck let out a horrifying scream, and just before he passed out, he saw the man smiling. They revived him and started on the other hand. After fourteen cuts, all his fingers were gone, and he was asked again, incapable of speech he spit at them. After he was revived, he was asked again, and again, he spat at them.

"Start on his toes."

All of the toes on his right foot were gone, and they began on the left when Chuck couldn't take it anymore. His last word was "China." The man dialed his cell phone immediately, and Ian answered on the other end of the phone. Ian hung up and told the group of men he was with, "We got them, and they are in China."

Calls were made to triad members, police, and intelligence operatives from several countries. Descriptions were given, and the largest international dragnet in history was underway, with instructions that simply said, "Locate and dispose of these two packages."

CHAPTER 41
The People's Republic of China

Rebecca woke up and John was at the desk working on something. He heard her get out of bed. "Good morning. I think I have a plan."

They would backtrack and go south toward Shanghai. There seemed to be a series of small roads that were single lane roads off the beaten path.

"I'm not sure they all connect, the maps are unclear, but the farther we stay away from civilization, the better."

They drove in shifts six hours on and six off, stopping to eat and use the facilities when they found them.

After two days, they were both exhausted. Rebecca was driving and John was asleep when he woke to a crashing thud and realized Rebecca had fallen asleep at the wheel. It was dark, there were no outside lights, and it was difficult to assess the damage. Everything appeared all right, other then some dents and scratches, but John suggested they stop at the next village or town. They were driving in the dark for several hours when a city just seemed to pop up from nowhere. John looked at the maps and said, "This is strange. Unless we are really lost, the maps don't show a city in this area or anywhere within a hundred of miles around. We must be really lost."

They drove into the city. It was bigger than a town. It looked as if it housed about a million people. They drove well into the center of the city, but they hadn't seen even one hotel. They stopped at a rather large building with an obvious lack of signage, and John went in to see if it was a hotel or at least find someone to help him locate one. John came out of the building and said, "This is some kind of hospital for terminal patients. It was awful."

They drove a little further and stopped at another building, John reappeared and said, "I don't know what's going on, but these people looked worst than the others."

Several blocks down, John saw a church, and the light was on.

"Let me go in and see if there is a priest or someone who can help us."

John went into the church and was happy to see a priest up on the altar. It appeared he was setting up for tomorrow's mass.

John yelled from halfway down the middle isle of the church, "Hey, Father, do you speak English?"

John was happy to hear a reply in English, "Yes, I do," and as John came closer, it appeared the man was American. John stopped dead in his tracks. The priest had turned toward him and John couldn't believe it, his face was half gone, and the remaining skin was bubbled and distorted. The priest saw the shock on John's face and said, "Don't be alarmed, my son. Didn't you know you are in a leper colony?"

"A what?" John asked in horror.

"You don't have to be alarmed, most of the leprosy here is not communicable. You are safe. There are 450,000 people living here, about 200,000 have the disease, and the rest are their families. They are sent here from all over China."

John could still not believe it.

"Father, how far would I have to go to find a hotel out of this area?"

"About five hundred miles."

"Oh my God," John said under his breath.

The priest went on to say that the roads were dangerous at night in that part of China and it would be safer for him to stay there.

John thanked him but said, "I think I'll try to move on."

"I can give you the room only used by the bishop when he comes up here from Shanghai. I assure you, he is not a leper."

"Well, okay. I guess," said John, "but I have my wife with me."

"She is also welcome."

Rebecca was horrified and refused to stay, but John reminded her she had just gone off the road and he was in no better shape.

She reluctantly agreed. Rebecca thought she would vomit when she saw the priest, and he unconsciously covered his face. The priest told them he had contracted the disease while working as a missionary in some of the most remote areas of China.

"As you must have noticed by now, the sanitation is poor outside of the major cities and disease is rampant. We do our best to treat the sick and train the people in safety and sanitation. I was treating several severe cases, and I stayed too many hours with them in the same unclean surroundings, so it was inevitable I would contract it."

"You are a very devoted man, Padre," John said.

The priest replied, "Just doing my job."

"Father, where are we on the map. It doesn't show this city at all."

"You are here," and he pointed to the map, careful not to touch it directly. "The leper colony is about thirty square miles. This is the main city with a population of almost 300,000 people, and the rest are scattered in smaller villages, depending how serious and communicable their disease is. No one with transmittable leprosy is allowed in this city."

John said, "Father, I don't want to be troublesome, but I have to admit I am not very comfortable here."

The priest said that was understandable but he was in no real danger.

"Come, I will show you to your room."

John and Rebecca looked at each other, and they both knew how uncomfortable the other was, but now they were committed. They followed the priest through the church and to the rectory. Once inside, the priest handed them a set of sheets and blankets sealed in a plastic bag. They had been boiled and were sterile. He also gave them cups and silverware wrapped in the same plastic.

"Be well, my children," he said as he retired to his own room.

John turned to Rebecca and said, "I don't care if this stuff is sterile, I am not getting in that bed."

They took the blanket and sheets out of the bag and wrapped them around each other, and they sat on the wooden chairs that were stacked in the corner. Sleep came surprisingly easy. John woke at first light and shook Rebecca. She jumped up startled. They quietly made their way toward the front door, and just as John was about to open it, the priest came in. John thanked the priest for his kindness and said good-bye. They almost ran to the car, but neither of them said anything until they were about fifty kilometers away from that terrible place. John spoke first and simply said, "That was horrible. I can't wait till we get to a hotel and I can take a nice hot shower and throw these clothes away."

Rebecca agreed and looked as though she was going to be ill.

They drove for about two more hours, during which, neither said a word, both feeling rather emotionally drained after spending the night in that terrible place. They were coming into an industrialized area, but John could not identify it on his map.

It appeared to be a mining area, and John thought to himself if it was, there must be a hotel of some sort there. He was relieved to see the sign "Occidental Petroleum, Coal Mine Number Two." He stopped the car and told Rebecca to wait, he was going to go in and see if there was someone who spoke English or Cantonese and maybe they could direct him to a hotel. As he walked into the office, he saw a young man who was obviously American.

"Hello, I'm a little lost, and I thought you might help me."

"Sure," answered the young man, "I'll say you're lost. There aren't too many tourist attractions around here."

"Where are we?" John asked, and the young man started to laugh.

"I ask myself the same question about ten times a day. You are 125 kilometers due west of Tianjin. The closest city is Shandong, which is about five minutes down the road. You are right smack in the center of Shandong province, which is the coal-mining province of the PRC."

"Can I get a hotel room in Shandong City?"

"Yes," the young man said. "Holiday Inn just finished a hotel there, and it's pretty good. We all go over there to the bar."

"Are there many Americans here?"

"Oh yeah, about 125 engineers, equipment specialists, and geologists."

"Great! Thank you very much."

"Don't mention it."

Ten minutes after they left the mine, they were checking into a brand new hotel. It looked like any other Holiday Inn, but in its drab surroundings, it looked like a five-star hotel. The check-in formalities were quick, and within minutes of their arrival, they were in their room. Rebecca ran for the bathroom, and seconds later she threw her clothes to John and said, "Burn them."

He laughed, but it actually wasn't a bad idea. He flipped on the TV and was surprised it was in English. "Holy cow!" he yelled to Rebecca. "We have HBO."

As he channel surfed, he saw Rebecca's picture and immediately turned up the volume.

"This person, Rebecca Dreed, is traveling with a male companion by the name of John Moore, and they are suspected to be hiding in China and are being sought by various governments for the murder of several government officials. They are to be considered armed and dangerous. Ms. Dreed was a solicitor who had worked for the Hong Kong police, and it is believed she was under investigation for corruption and drugs."

"What the hell is this?"

He went into the bathroom, and while Rebecca was showering, he related the news story. He was surprised at her reaction. She said, "Yes, that would be normal procedure. They will try to discredit us before we can discredit them."

"Chong was right, I am naïve. I can't believe all this bull."

"It might be bull, John, but it is reality, and we have to think about what we're going to do next."

"Well," John said, "our pictures are all over the screen."

Rebecca interrupted, "Both our pictures?"

"No, just yours."

"Good, do I look that much different with my new hair color and cut?"

"Yes, and the picture they showed of you was in one of your frocks. In jeans, you look thirty pounds lighter."

"Good," she said. "Did they show your picture at all?"

"I don't know," John said. "They had your picture as a background in the studio, but I believe they only gave a verbal description of me, but I came in at the middle."

"I will get dressed and go shopping. I'll see if I can find some black hair die for you and some sunglasses."

While she was out, John was developing a plan.

John looked in the mirror and could not believe the difference. With the gray gone and all of the exercise this past year, he looked twenty years younger. He was pleased.

"Rebecca, even though we look a little different than the descriptions on TV, we still stick out here in China. There are not throngs of Caucasian couples running around this part of China, and I would assume that any good intelligence person would be able to pick us out of a crowd. As soon as that happened, with even a cursory inspection, we would be caught."

"What do you propose?" she asked.

"Well, I think we have two alternatives. One is that we split up."

"And the other?" Rebecca quickly asked.

"We go back to the leper colony."

"No," she said. "There must be something else we can do."

"Wherever we go from here, they'll be watching, especially now that we made CNN. If we go up there and hang out for two of three weeks, we have a better chance."

"Oh God!" cried Rebecca.

"We have some alternatives, get shot or worse if we get caught trying to get out of here or catch leprosy. That's about it," John said. "Remember what the priest said, no one with communicable leprosy was allowed in that city."

"John the man telling us that had half a face."

"Good point! Is there a business center in this hotel?"

"Yes there is why?"

"I want to find out something on the web. I'll be right back."

John was gone for more than an hour. When he returned, he had good news.

I did some research on leprosy, and I found out it is a virus that can attack you only when you have a severe bacterial or fungal problem. It is caused by poor sanitation and untreated bacterial and fungal infections. Bottom line, you have to be dirty for a long time. There are doctors and missionaries treating people in Malacai for forty and fifty years without themselves ever contracting the disease. The prophylactic is simple. Antimicrobial soap, like the soap here in our room, and at least 500 milligrams of vitamins C, D, and E every day, and we can pick up some antibiotics just in case."

"John, please think of another way."

"I have tried to, but this seems the best. No one would look for us there."

They checked out, and John thought he would have to literally drag her into the car, but she got in under her own steam. Four hours later, they were knocking on the door of the priest.

"Hello, please come in. Have a seat. Would you like some tea?"

"No thank you, Padre," said John. We have a problem, and we were wondering if you could put us up for a while. We could pay you?"

"No need. I'll be happy to have you. I don't get many visitors here."

John thought to himself it was odd that the priest never asked what their problem was but dismissed it. *I never really understood priests anyway.*

He showed them back to the same room and gave the several cardboard boxes of sterile sheets and blankets. He told John to follow him and brought him to the kitchen.

"Use only this refrigerator. It is used for non-infected persons. I will have it stocked for you with imported prepackaged food, the same way I do when the bishop comes."

"Please don't go to any trouble for us," John said.

"It is no trouble. It is actually good for me to get out of routine once in a while, otherwise I could get stale."

John wasn't sure if that was a joke or not, so he just smiled.

"Padre, let me pay you something for all your trouble. Here."

John tried to hand him $500.

"No, thank you, but if you could buy some medical supplies, I would be very thankful."

"Father, do you have a list?"

"Yes, but it is too large. Just some quinine and penicillin would do. There is a shop in the city, and I can have someone bring you there."

"Father I really am a little frightened to go tramping around here. Could I just give them the money?"

The priest looked a bit disappointed but said "okay."

"John, if you are staying here any length of time, I suggest you get as much sunlight as possible. We have a rooftop deck, and you and your wife should spend at least four hours a day up there. Also, I have vitamins you should be taking."

"Thank you, Father, but we have plenty of C, E, and D vitamins, as well as antimicrobial soap."

Before they left the hotel in Shandong, John raided the maid's closet and took two full cases of the soap.

"Oh good, wash several times a day."

"We—" John paused, "thank you, Father."

"If that's all, I have some things I have to do in the church."

"Can I help you, Father?"

"No, thank you. That was kind of you, though."

"No," John said, "I don't know how I'll ever repay your kindness, Father."

"No need," and he walked away. John went and got Rebecca and brought her up to the roof. They looked out over the countryside, and Rebecca remarked, "If you were just dropped here without knowing what this place was, one would think it's quite beautiful."

"Yeah, but this is a perfect place to watch who comes and goes. Look, there is only one road north and south and one road east and west, and we can see both of them. We will be able to see every car or truck coming into or leaving the city from here."

They started to get into a daily regime: breakfast at seven thirty, and a walk around the grounds of the church until eight thirty, and up to the roof until lunch around 1:00 p.m. and then back to the room for exercise until three, shower, and back to the roof until seventy thirty and then dinner. At eight o'clock, John would go down the hall and visit with the priest, Father Paul. They would talk about various subjects, and John was surprised at how well versed Father Paul was on so many topics. It was almost the same every evening. At about nine thirty, Father Paul would say, "John, I think you have left Mary alone long enough. I'll see you tomorrow."

It got to the point that John looked forward to his conversations with Father Paul.

They had been there for almost two months, and Rebecca seemed to be getting more depressed by the day, and John was getting concerned.

"John, we have to leave here soon. I can't take it any more, and I can't get comfortable here."

"Please try to understand, we don't have too much of a choice."

"John, it's been months. I am sure we are no longer a daily topic on the Telee."

"You are probably right. I have never asked you this, but where did you put the discs."

She looked at him and said, "I destroyed them."

"What?" John said as he jumped from his chair. "Are you kidding? We have gone through all of this and you never even had them?"

This was the first time John had actually been angry with her.

"Please, calm down. I destroyed the discs, but not the information."

"What?"

"I downloaded the discs to a Web site that I was working on. The information is sitting on a server somewhere, but I can retrieve it or pass it on to someone else from any computer anywhere."

"That's brilliant," John said. "You never cease to amaze me. Okay, we will leave tomorrow."

Rebecca did not say a word. She walked toward him and reach up and pulled his face toward hers and gave him the most sensuous kiss he ever remembered.

That evening, he went in to see Father Paul.

"Good evening, Father, how was your day?"

"Fine, and yours?"

"Father, we are leaving tomorrow."

Father Paul looked sad and said, "God be with both you and Rebecca."

John looked at him quizzically.

"You should be safe now. There has been nothing on TV about you two for almost a month."

"What, Father? You knew all along?"

"Yes, but after meeting the both of you, I didn't believe it, any of it."

"How did you know?"

"I have very few pleasures in life, but TV is one of them. Didn't you ever notice the satellite dish outside my window?"

John was almost in shock.

"Father, Rebecca is a good person, and she did everything right. Corruption has caused her problems, and I'm just trying to keep her safe."

"I understand. Even the church, several times in history, has suffered from corruption. I will pray for the both of you, and let's hope that the outcome is positive and the right people are punished."

"Thank you, Father. I would tell you all about it, but the less you know, the safer you will be."

"It's nice you're concerned for my safety, but there is nothing anyone could do to me to make me suffer more than I have already. John wanted to reach out and hug this saint of a man but restrained himself and just said, "Father, I have few friends, but I am proud to think of you as one of them. When this is over, I will contact you, but until then, I think it best not to."

"I understand, John. Thank you for the compliment."

John returned to his room and told Rebecca to get ready to go.

CHAPTER 42
The American Consulate, Hong Kong

"They could not have fallen off the face of the earth, goddamn it. We have 450 agents, Ian, you Brits have almost as many. The entire goddamn Chinese police force, and no one can find them. They are obviously somewhere else. That priest in Kowloon pulled one over on you."

"I don't think so," said Ian.

"I don't care what you think; if they were in China, we would have had them by now. I really don't care what you think, Ian, you're the one who told everyone you had it under control. Well, maybe I can lean on Chong, I'm sure he knows where they are."

"Bullshit, Ian, we've been on him like white on rice. He hasn't had any contact in months, and he's working for Imelda Brown now, isn't he? That would be just great, rough up a driver of one of our own Intel specialists, Ian, you got your head up your ass."

"Well, what do you propose?"

"Well, we know he has a partner in California, an ex-wife in Australia, a bank account in Geneva…let's start there. Miss Dreed has family in the UK, several friends in Ireland, France and Portugal lets go there, but goddamnit, if you don't have anything by Friday, your ass is out of here. I have the president himself on my ass, and I don't need any more cuts in the department. We're working with a skeleton crew now. My agents are losing their assets and connections because they don't have the resources to keep them, and I'm not going to let a boat builder and a woman lawyer bring me down."

Ian didn't say anything. *Why does the President of the United States have a direct interest in this? Maybe it wouldn't be a bad idea to get out of this now before it hits the fan and I'm standing in front of Parliament answering questions I'd rather not. When the big guys are involved, it's always the guys in the field who take the heat. Ask Oliver North*, he laughed to himself.

"Ian, what are you going to do?"

"Well, sir, how many men can you deploy in the countries you mentioned? I will establish strike teams in each area and have them liaison with your personnel. I will have MI6 set up airport and train watches. Can we use your people to man credit card, wire transfers, and cell phone monitoring?"

"Yes, you have all the resources of the agency at your disposal. Get these two."

Ian called his superior in London and gave him a report on a secure phone.

"The Americans are playing hardball. Be careful. They could be setting us up."

Ian wished he never took this assignment. He was a soldier not a spook, and he was starting to have a bad feeling about the whole thing. Ian left the consulate and went to Taimar, the British naval Station in Hong Kong and called in Lieutenant James.

"Lieutenant, get over to Green Island and set up a base camp for us, complete autonomy, set up sat com, a complete field Intel pack, and round up our crew. We have work to do."

"Yes, sir."

The lieutenant jumped to attention saluted and spun around as if he were on a lazy Susan. As he walked out, Ian thought to himself all spit and polish that young man, and still one of his best men in the field.

Ian began to put together a multi-national Intel force, which he would run from Green Island. Green Island was only a couple of hundred yards from Hong Kong Island, right in the middle of the harbor. It had been restricted to all civilians since World War II. The British used it as an auxiliary naval and intelligence station. Several ships were sunk around the island during the war, making it unsafe for civilian water traffic, and it was easy to keep people out because there was only one narrow channel threw the wrecks to access it. When Ian's team was in place the lieutenant contacted him and he joined them. He called a briefing and when they were all assembled he began.

"We have two targets. This woman is primary, and the man in this picture is secondary. These people are a real danger to both the American government and ours, and we have a green light to eliminate them. Their whereabouts is not known; they slipped through our net in Hong Kong and China. The local Triads have been unreliable to date. The Americans are angry, and we cannot trust them at this juncture. Do not share any intel with the Americans unless it is cleared by me personally. You each have a coded list of your American counterparts with their contact numbers. Contact them immediately and inform them you have joined the operation, meet with them, and get to know their contacts. Give them nothing. I will give each of you daily script sheets to feed your American counters through Lieutenant James. Give them this info and only this info, everything else comes to this office only. Have I made myself clear?"

A collective "yes, sir" rang out in the small room, and Ian simply said, "Dismissed."

CHAPTER 43
Washington DC

The president called for his assistant and said, "Cancel my appointments this morning and get the first lady on the phone."

When the intercom rang, he picked up the phone and said, "Get our friend from Memphis. I need to see him now. I don't give a damn; get him here today. We'll meet in your office."

He slammed the phone down. Two hours later, Mike Manheim walked through the door of the first lady's office.

"Mike, it's good to see you. Sit down."

He glared up at her and said, "Is he nuts?"

"Ah, Jim," the first lady quipped. "Let's make sure the scramblers are on."

After checking her electronics, she said calmly, "He's upset. They are investigating him, and that special prosecutor is a pain in the ass."

"I know," he retorted, "but we have been able to defuse him every step of the way. The American public loves a sexual harassment case, it trumps anything that can happen, and thank God your boy is as horny as all get out."

"That be as it may, if any of the investigator's pick up on this Liddo thing, we are screwed."

"Tell him not to worry; if anyone gets close, we can ruin them before they can get the information out. I am leaving; I don't think it's a good idea for me to be seen here in Washington with him. Send him my regards and tell him to be cool."

With that, she turned off the scramblers and started to walk him to the door, saying, "Mike, don't worry. My assistant in the Memphis office has completely filled me in, and she is competent and able to finish those negotiations for you."

CHAPTER 44
Tianjin, The People's Republic of China

John turned to Rebecca. "I got the tickets. We leave for Osaka in three hours. It appears the Canadian passports are good, no red flags went up when they typed our names in the computer. This is great! They don't know about our identities. God bless Father Chuck."

Rebecca laughed and said, "Do you see a trend here where priests are protecting us?"

"God is our co-pilot," John said. "We should stay in Osaka for two days; we can do that on a temporary visa and figure out where to go from there. The safest places would be South America, they would never expect us there, or New York."

"New York?"

"Yeah, neither of us has any connection there at all, and it's big enough to hide. With Canadian passports, we don't need visas. Let's work it out in Osaka."

"All right," she said, "we have just enough time for a good screw and a bath. Are you up for it?"

"Always." John laughed.

When they arrived at Osaka International Airport, John spotted several Caucasians milling around, seeming to be studying everyone coming into the airport.

"Rebecca, strike up a conversation with that woman over there and stay with her until you're outside. I will meet you at the Nikko Airport Hotel; you catch the bus right outside the door. I read about it in the in-flight magazine."

John waited until almost all the passengers were in the terminal and asked one of the stewardesses to help him. "I'm sorry to be a bother, but I have a bad leg. Is it possible for me to get wheel chair assistance?" She took him to baggage claim in a wheel chair.

John was being wheeled through the airport, unnoticed by the watchers.

He met Rebecca at the hotel, and they registered as Mr. and Mrs. John Mc Kenzie, Canadians. Pleased with himself, he said, "Why don't we just order up and eat in the room? I'm feeling a little romantic this evening."

Rebecca smiled; she did want to talk about what had been gnawing at her for these past months. John was in the shower when dinner arrived. She signed for the dinner and let the bellhop out. John came out of the bathroom and asked, "Did you give him a tip? I know how cheap you Brits are?"

"Oh my God, John, I signed my name on the bill."

"What? Oh hell," John ran for the phone, "Moshie, Moshie, the voice on the other end called."

"Yeah, hello, a bellman just brought dinner to our room, and I'm afraid there was a problem with the bill, could you send him back please with the bill?"

"I'll connect you with room service."

After John had repeated himself three times, the person on the other end said, "I'll send him right up."

A few minutes later, there was a knock on the door. The man said in Japanese, "Ohio go say hemasta."

John clearly agitated said, "Yeah, hello, do you have the receipt?"

"Yes," the man replied and gave John the bill.

He looked at it and said, "Where is the one my wife signed?"

"It was already put into the system," he replied.

"Here is a hundred dollars to get it back. When you bring it to me, I'll give you another hundred."

The man smiled and said he would be right back. As soon as the door closed, John said, "Get packed, we have to leave."

"Where are we going to go?"

"I don't know, but we can't stay here."

A few minutes later, there was a knock on the door. After looking through the peephole, John let him in.

"Here it is, sir, I caught it before it was recorded."

"Thank you," and John handed him the hundred. "Good, it should be no problem, but let's get out of here anyway. Okay, Mary?"

"Yes, I'm sorry. It won't happen again."

"Hold on, I have an idea. Rebecca, get me the phone book."

Luckily it was in English.

"What are you looking for?" she asked.

"Here it is, Hatch brokers. Osaka is a port; we can buy a boat and sail to Vancouver."

"John, you don't have much money left."

"No problem, I'll get Peter to wire it."

"Do you think that's wise? They would be able to track the money right to us."

"I'll figure that out later, let's go."

They went to the address shown in the phone book; it was a marina just outside the city in what appeared to be a local resort area. The taxi dropped them at the marina and left. John looked around and there was a sign in Japanese and English, "John Motioshi, Yacht Sales."

"Mr. Motioshi, I am looking for a sailing vessel at least forty-five feet with deep-water certification."

"We have several. Please come this way."

John picked a forty-eight-foot Ocean Runner, an Australian boat that he was familiar with and he knew was seaworthy. He inspected every inch of her and asked if he could take her out on a trial. Mr. Motioshi agreed. "I only have to get the owner's approval. It will not be a problem. We can sail her tomorrow morning say 9 a.m., is that satisfactory?"

"Yes very."

"Mr. Motioshi is there a hotel nearby?" asked Rebecca.

"Yes, there is a nice one near here. I'll bring you over myself."

It was a nice hotel right on the water. When they were comfortable, they went out onto the veranda and Rebecca asked, "Have you figured out how to pay for this yet?"

"Yes I have. I'll tell Motioshi that we buy all of our boats from Sailcraft and the transaction will have to go through them. The fax will read, 'Your Chinese agents have a client who desires to purchase one of our yachts. They instructed us to have the funds wired by you from Peter Tsillman. They are interested in blue water sailing and need this done immediately before the weather changes. John Motioshi.' *Blue water* is the code word for our Swiss account."

"Brilliant, John, you should have been a spy."

"Don't even say that in jest."

"I'm sorry. John, I am sorry about everything. This is costing you an enormous amount of money and probably your business and possibly your life. Why are you doing this?"

"Because I love you, Rebecca, and partly because this whole thing is wrong and we have to figure out a way to make it right."

After a good night's sleep and a great cup of coffee, John called Motioshi. He would there to pick them up in minutes.

"Did you like the hotel?"

"It was very nice," Rebecca answered.

John did another inspection of the boat and said, "Well, let's see what she can do." After about two hours, John headed back toward the marina, satisfied this was the right boat. John Motioshi was excited, especially since there was no counteroffer to his price, which was way over market price for the boat. The papers were signed, and John explained that because of the time difference, the funds would not arrive until the next day.

"No problem. Please allow me to take care of your hotel bill tonight, stay as my guest."

"That is kind of you," said John, thinking to himself that this guy was making enough money off of the deal to rent them a house. The funds arrived as expected the next day, and after securing a full set of charts and provisions, they were off. The *Flying Gull* was his.

Once underway, John put the boat on autopilot and set a course due north. He plotted a course around Hokkaido, Japan's northern most island and then due east to a point at the Alaskan-Canadian border.

This route was relatively untraveled, and although a little dangerous this time of year, it would be the safest route for them to take. They would stop at Hokkaido and pick up some warm clothing and foul weather gear. It was a three-day sail from Osaka.

They had to provision in Hokkaido, because once they started on their eastern tact, there would be nowhere to pull in until they hit North America. If they did have to stop for repairs, they would have to sail north to either big or little domino, which were islands that were part of the archipelago that stretched from Russia to Alaska. John hoped that didn't happen, if it did, they could be stuck there all winter.

While John had been checking the rigging and equipment on deck, Rebecca was below stowing the provisions and getting ready for a long hard trip. She was an accomplished sailor and knew what had to be done.

When John was satisfied they were in Open Ocean, he went below. Rebecca was already cooking lunch, and it smelt good. We are in open water. Our course is due north along the islands of Japan. We should be in Hokkaido in a few days. We'll provision there before we take the eastern tact to North America. Make a provisions list for at least sixty days, just in case."

While they ate lunch, John explained that Hokkaido was an interesting place, and although he had never been there, he had read a lot about it. It was the northern most inhabited island in the Japanese archipelago, and the people there had a totally different culture than the Japanese. Even their appearance was different and some anthropologists believed they were a fourth race, being neither Asian nor Caucasian. Their historical culture and religion were interesting. They worshiped the bear.

"I would like to stay there for a couple of days and look around, but we are very close to safety zone weather wise." John walked over to an instrument panel and told Rebecca, "It is already fifteen degrees colder than it was when we left Osaka five hours ago. Keep a careful eye on the temperature and the barometer readings. If I'm on deck, check them every hour or so, although on the eastern tack you are going to have to be up top and looking for ice. After tomorrow, do not go on deck without being in a safety harness, rouge waves and small cyclones, water spouts, are common in these waters.

We will be covering some of the unfriendliness water in the world. When we get to Hokkaido, we'll get some foul weather gear and diving dry suits. The water will get so cold that if we get to wet we could die of exposure in about three to four minutes. The dry suits will give us protection more so than the foul weather gear."

"How do you know so much about these waters?"

"When we graduated from college, Peter and I fished these waters. We never came this far west, but pretty close sometimes. We followed the fish. It's brutal out there. When we get to Hokkaido, we'll get some blankets, warm clothes, socks, gloves, and hand and foot warmers. Stow everything in heavy plastic bags. It will get rough, and we can count on taking on some water. I'll get some additional batteries and we'll set them up in series. It will be your job to keep them fully charged. If we lose power, they will be the only thing we can run the pumps on. I'll also get some tools and lumber and raise the bunks sailing in this kind of weather you have to be certain you have some place to get warm and dry or you're dead. When you buy the provisions, make sure you get plenty of vitamins, especially vitamin C, in the highest dosage you can find. As far north as we are going, we won't get all that much sun."

John turned to Rebecca and said, "Let's get some sleep. We are going to need all the rest we can get right now."

John woke up about eight o'clock and went up on deck. They were traveling at about nine knots, and the seas were high rolling waves. They were right on course, and if the weather held they would reach Hokkaido about three o'clock the day after tomorrow. The boat handled pretty well, *it was yare*, John thought. It reminded him of his father. He remembered the first time he sailed north to Seattle with his father. The boat was similar to this one, and they were sailing in seas very much like these. He was about eight or nine years old, and he remembered his father saying, "This boat is yare," and he asked him what that meant, and when his father explained it, he thought his father was the smartest man on earth. John smiled to himself at the memory. He missed his father.

Rebecca came on deck and looked around without saying

anything. John looked at her and thought she looked beautiful with the wind in her hair, and that fearless look and attitude made her appear that much more attractive. John knew he loved her, but up until this moment, he did not realize how much.

She turned to him and asked, "John why have you done all this?"

He thought about a response, but he simply said, "I wanted to."

They were both quiet for a while. It was about 2:00 a.m., and John called, "Rebecca, get up here now he said."

She hurried onto the deck and said, "What's up?"

"Look, we are in a heard of whales."

"Wow, they're huge."

"Yeah and dangerous, if one of those things come up to close, they can flip us. Climb up top and tell me what you see."

Rebecca climbed the mast up to the look out like a veteran. Once she was set, she yelled back, "We are right in the middle of them. I can see their shadows below the water, and it looks like there are a lot of them."

"Which way should I sail to get out of them?"

"Hard to port," she yelled.

As John turn the wheel hard to port, the boat hit one of the whales and almost stopped dead. Rebecca fell, but she had already secured her safety line, and she hung by her waist for a moment before she could get a foothold. She was a little sore, but she climbed back into the lookout unharmed.

John had fallen hard. His arm went through the wheel and was jammed between it and the console. John heard a snap and felt the pain; he was sure he broke it. The mast flew over his head and was coming back hard. He ducked just in time. He kept his head and was able to regain control. He looked up and saw Rebecca was safe, and he yelled to her, "Are you all right?"

"Yes, and we are almost away from them."

As soon as they were in the clear, Rebecca climbed down and came to John's side.

"That was close," she said, and then she saw the pain in his face. "Are you all right?"

He took his jacket off and she gasped, his arm was already blue and swollen almost twice its normal size.

"Damn, it's broken," she said.

"Set it."

"What? Are you crazy?"

"We won't be near land for at least another day, and by then, it could go septic."

She ran below and took all the ice from the freezer and put it into a plastic bag. She put the ice pack on his arm and said, "Let's get the swelling down before we do anything else."

They waited about an hour and the pain was subsiding and the swelling went down considerably. When the swelling went down, you could clearly see the humorous was broken about four inches from his elbow. The bone did not come through the skin and was still partially connected.

"Okay," John said, "I'm going to hook my arm around the rail. You have to pull on it until the bone snaps back into place."

Rebecca was reluctant but knew it had to be done. She pulled in a swift but strong pull and the bone found its way back into position. John passed out during the process, and when he woke, she had already put on the air cast she found in the first aid kit. She had five aspirins and a glass of water ready. John took the aspirin, and Rebecca told him she was taking him below. He started to argue and then realized she was right. She put him in the bunk and pulled the blankets tight around him.

"I don't want you moving around too much. Is this too tight?"

"No," he answered.

"All right then," she said. "I'm going up on deck and get back on course, you get some rest." He did not argue at all, he was asleep before she got to the ladder. Rebecca was getting tired but felt pretty good. It was almost light, and the seas were relatively calm. *Thank God*, she thought to herself. She had been thinking on how much has happened since all this started. *I owe my life to him. Am I ever going to be able to repay him?* She remembered the first time she met him at the Aberdeen yacht club and thought that was a lifetime ago. She heard him stirring below and went down to check on him.

"What are you doing up?"

"I'm making a cup of coffee."

"Sit, I'll make breakfast. John, you have to rest, I need you back in full form before we take the hard part of this trip."

"You're right. My arm is sore, but it feels pretty good."

"We'll have to change the cast when we get to Hokkaido."

"Yeah, while you go through the formalities I'll find a doctor as soon as we get into port. Rebecca, by the way, where are we?"

"I put us back on course last night, but I think we lost four or five hours. We should get to Hokkaido about eight o'clock tonight if we can maintain this speed. We're doing ten knots. I let out the mainsail a tad, and she seems to respond better."

"Great," John said, "she'll be more stable that way as well. I feel better than I thought I would. You're a pretty good bonesetter. You might have another profession when we get back to Hong Kong."

"Oh John, do you think we ever will?"

"Sure, we'll be back before you know it."

He didn't believe that himself, but it was good to hear. Rebecca, even though she knew it was a total lie, was happy to hear it to.

John brought his coffee up on deck and sat in the cockpit and watched Rebecca expertly maneuver the boat.

They came into Hokkaido exactly on course. John got on the radio and informed the harbormaster they were arriving and in need of provisions and medical attention. The harbor master came back and told him not to come into port but continue on three and a half nautical miles due north from the channel buoy. There was a marina there with a clinic and would be better suited to meet their needs.

The marina was actually in a fishing village, and there was a medical aid station right on the main pier. After they tied up and fastened her down, they went to the aid station. The doctor was impressed; he told them the x-ray showed the bone was perfectly set and already healing nicely. He put on a plaster cast and told them to make certain it was removed in three weeks.

Once the cast was hard, they went shopping. They were able to get almost everything on the list they had compiled and had it all delivered to the boat. After they took inventory and stowed everything properly, they went to look for some place to eat. They found a nice little Inn and the food was fantastic. They decided to stay ashore that night, and the inn accommodated them nicely. Rebecca opened the sliding door in the room and called John to come out on the small wooden deck outside of their room. The view was out of a dream.

The village was in a protected lagoon lined with pine trees. The village itself had a Japanese flair but different from anything they had seen in Osaka, it was beautiful. John turned to Rebecca, "I only have less than $1,000 left after we fuel up tomorrow. We are going to be real low on cash. I'm afraid to contact Peter, I have to assume they are watching him and monitoring all his transfers."

John went quiet, and Rebecca left him alone. She knew he was trying to think this out.

Rebecca said, "I'm going to take a shower and get some sleep." She leaned over and kissed him on the top of his head. John sat there for hours and finally fatigue got the better of him and he feel asleep in the chair.

Rebecca woke him up in the morning and gave him a massage to get the stiffness out of his tired muscles. When she finished, John took a shower and they went to the dining room in the Inn for breakfast. "I have a solution, I know how to get some cash."

I'm going to call Father Paul. There is no connection to him that we are aware of; I don't believe anyone knew we were there."

After breakfast they went back to the room and John called Father Paul. "Father Paul, I need your help."

"Anything, my friend."

"Please call this number in California and ask for Peter. Tell him I just left, but before I left I asked you to call him and to send you a donation for your kindness to me of USD $50,000. Father, take half of it and send the rest to me John McKenzie, Canadian passport number L43762 at Sumitomo Bank, Hokkaido, Japan. Please don't send it the same day. They will be tracking that money."

"I will not send it."

John's heart sank. "You won't send it?"

"I will not send it directly. I have a friend at the bishop's office in Beijing. He is familiar with blind transfers and those kinds of financial matters; it will look normal for me to send half of the donation to the bishop."

"Father Paul, I can never repay you for all your help."

"You're repaying me most generously, as I see it," and they both laughed. "John, I really miss you," said Father Paul.

"I'll stay in touch, Father."

"I'm praying for the both of you." John hung up the phone.

"It's done," he told Rebecca. "We have to wait until the money arrives. Why don't we do a little exploring?"

"Great idea," voiced Rebecca. They went to the manager of the inn and asked if he could arrange for transportation.

"My son has a jeep, if that would be acceptable."

"Yes, that would be perfect."

"He is young, only twenty-four, but he knows the island quite well. He will meet you in front in about an hour."

"Fine," John said.

The boy introduced himself as Hiroshi; he was a pleasant looking young man with a warm smile and inquisitive eyes. He asked where they wanted to go or was there anything in particular they would like to see. John was impressed with his knowledge of English and asked him where he learned it.

"I went to school in England."

"Oh? Where?" Rebecca asked.

John nudged her when the boy asked if she was British.

"No, dear, I'm Canadian. My family was originally from Scotland."

"Oh, I went to Cambridge. I studied literature. I want to be a writer."

"How fascinating."

Hiroshi asked, "Where would you like to go? Is there anything special you would like to see?"

"This is our first trip to Hokkaido, We'll leave it up to you. I do have to stop at the bank though." The bank was only down the street from the inn. John had seen it the night before. He went in and was greeted by the manager. John explained that he was expecting a wire transfer the next day, and even though it was a dollar transfer, as long as a portion of it was dollars, he would take the rest in yen. The banker said he would be happy to accommodate him, and John thanked him and left.

Hiroshi took them on a great tour of the island. John and

Rebecca were both impressed with his knowledge and demeanor.

"The people here are noticeably more hairy than typical Asian people and their features are more European."

Hiroshi explained that the origin of the Hokkaido people is unknown but their culture and stories are decidedly different than the Japanese.

"The Japanese people can trace their origins to China, but the people here are different. Our ancient religion is based on worshiping nature with the bear the most revered animal; it is different than anything ever recorded in Asia. As you can see, our architecture is more European than Asian, which is strange, as we are an island and our history shows that we had no contact with Europeans before the nineteenth century."

John was fascinated, and Rebecca was totally impressed with the young man's slant on things. They drove past large horse farms that looked more like a Marlboro ad than actual working farms in Japan.

"Would you like me to ask my parents to fix you an authentic Hokkaido dinner?"

"That would be great," John said. The day was the best either John or Rebecca had had in a long time, and the best was yet to come. Hiroshi dropped them off at the inn. "I'll call you when dinner is ready." They went back to the room and recapped the events of the day, took a shower, and made love. They were lying in each other's arms when the phone rang.

"Dinner will be ready in an hour."

"We'll be there," John said.

Hiroshi met them in the small lobby and started out the door.

"Where are we going?" John asked.

"To our ranch."

When they drove up to the house, John could not believe how beautiful the place was. They were about a twenty-minute drive from the coast. The house was quite small, but it had nice clean lines. It overlooked large pastures with wooden fences dividing them into about two acres each and in the background was a snow-covered mountain. The sun was just setting and the sky was pink and yellow going into shades of orange. John and Rebecca stood there and took in the scenery; it was nothing like either of them ever imagined.

Hiroshi said, "Please," and motioned for them to come into the house. Hiroshi's mother greeted them and apologized that her husband would not be joining them, as he had to be at the inn. They sat at a hand carved table and the food started to come. It was a game dinner with pheasant, venison, bear, and rabbit. Each prepared in a different sauce. The meat was served with local vegetables and potatoes, not noodles. It was a truly magnificent meal.

They had a pleasant conversation, and Hiroshi and his mother enjoyed John's questions and was surprised he knew as much as he did about their culture.

"Hokkaido has intrigued me ever since I first learned of it," said John. Hiroshi's mother excused herself and came back with a book, which she presented to John, *The Complete Written History of Hokkaido*. She explained that her brother was the foremost expert on Hokkaido and he authored the book. "Yes, it was my brother who influenced Hiroshi to go to school in England."

They sat for a long time after dinner drinking tea and a local plumb wine. Rebecca helped with the dishes and seemed to enjoy the domestic chores of clearing the table and cleaning up. It was the first time in many months that she looked relaxed. She was truly enjoying herself. John asked Hiroshi how much he owed him for dinner, and he looked insulted, "Nothing, you're a guest in my home."

"I'm sorry," said John, "thank you very much, I can't remember when I enjoyed myself as much as I did this evening."

Hiroshi smiled and said, "You're welcome, any time."

They slept in the next morning, and John didn't get to the bank until almost noon. As he entered the small bank, the manager got up to greet him.

"Your wire has arrived, $40,000 USD."

John smiled. *Father Paul, you are a truly remarkable human being.* The bank manager told him he could only give him $5,000 in US currency and the balance in yen, but if that was not acceptable, he could arrange to have it all in US dollars in three days. John said this would be fine and took the money, less the bank's commission of 1.75 percent. John thanked the banker and left.

When he told Rebecca what Father Paul had done, she said, "I think I'm going to convert to Catholicism."

They checked out of the inn, and John left an envelope with a sincere thank you note and the equivalent of $200 for Hiroshi. John knew he had to leave, but he really wished he could have stayed for a while. *This is another place I have to come back to some day.*

They inspected the boat and made sure everything was in perfect order. They went below and John had Rebecca read the checklist as he took inventory. He went over everything in his head a second time, and when he was certain they had everything they might need, they were ready to set sail.

While they were fueling up and taking on potable water, John spotted something and told Rebecca he would be right back. He returned a few minutes later with a man on a fork lift carrying a spare mast following him.

"Can't be too careful."

John spent the next two hours lashing the spare mast onto the gunnels and headed out of the lagoon. Within six hours, they were leaving the Sea of Japan and entering the northern Pacific. It was getting cold. The temperature had already dropped twenty-two degrees. John told Rebecca to go below and put on the dry suit and foul weather gear. When she returned, he did the same. The difference in temperature was already making his arm ache. This was going to be a tough trip. They were already into twenty-foot seas but the waves were rolling and the boat was handling them beautifully. "Get some rest. By tonight, we are going to have to take alternate watches, four hours each. How does the barometer look?" asked John.

"It's good, we're in a high-pressure system, and it looks steady we're good for at least the next four of five hours."

"Check it every hour. Things can change real fast out here." John set a course due west and plotted his course just south of the Domino Islands. He figured they would reach that far in about four days. There was nothing but water between him and those islands, and the frigid weather made it that much harder to navigate. He thought it was smarter to plot the course closer to the islands than he originally wanted to.

The wind was up to about twenty miles per hour and at full sail they were moving at about eighteen knots. John called down to Rebecca and asked her to check the oil levels in both engines and check the batteries and make sure they were on charge. If either engine went down, they could be in serious trouble. John thought, *at least those extra batteries will keep the pumps going.*

When going on a trip like this, one always had to be making mental checklists and follow up on every detail. Rebecca came up on deck and climbed up the rigging and perched herself in the lookout. After an hour or so John called her down. Her face was already chapped and swollen from the cold wind.

"Go down and cover your face and any exposed skin with grease or petroleum jelly, it will save you problems later."

She did and came back with a jar of Vaseline and started to coat his face, neck, and wrists. It was starting to get dark, and they were both preparing for the night. The seas were getting rougher, and the deck was awash with frigid water. They both secured their safety lines and checked each other's. Rebecca climbed out to the bow walk and stared out at the horizon.

She started to get a little sick and realized she had to set her sight on the night sky just above the horizon, following the line of waves would make her sick. There was nothing out there but black. She would not have known she was in the ocean except for the salty, freezing spray that hit her about every thirty seconds. She felt bad for John; he was taking the brunt of the waves that were breaking over the side of the boat. At one point, a large wave split and hit the boat from both sides. The boat straitened up and literally came out of the water. It hit tail first and John almost lost control. The boat surfed down the other side of the wave and when it hit the bottom almost rolled. John turned her hard into the wave and she righted herself. His arm was throbbing from the strain and his hands and feet were so cold they were going numb. *We better get some rest and warm up or we won't be any good tomorrow.*

He signaled to Rebecca to come aft. Rebecca started back to him, but it was not easy going and took about five minutes. He told her they better go below and get some rest. John set the autopilot and turned on the alarm system, which would ring in the cabin if they were going off course or the boat was listing too heavily. He joined Rebecca below.

"Rebecca, take off all your clothes and get up in the bunk. I'll join you in a minute."

"Are you kidding?"

"No," he said, "we will get warmer with our own body heat and we will stay warmer when we get dressed to go back out."

"Not very romantic, are you?"

She smiled and did as ordered.

"Take your clothes up there with you, they'll stay dry and warm. Give me your slicker; I'll hang them down in the engine room to dry."

They lay together and neither could sleep. They were happy to be warm and dry. They listened to the boat bang and creak and slip through the waves. The boat was taken a brutal beating from the waves. John looked into Rebecca's eyes. "I hope this wasn't a mistake." Rebecca kissed him. *I just had the same thought.*

After several hours, the seas started to calm and the boat maneuvered itself into a steady pattern, rolling softly through the waves. The steady slapping and easy roll finally put them to sleep. John woke and didn't know how long they had been sleeping. He was warm and rested and got up and dressed. Rebecca looked so comfortable and content he decided to leave her there.

He went up on deck and could not believe his eyes. They were becalmed in a misty black pool in the ocean. The fog was thin enough to see through, but it gave an eerie sense to the picture in front of him. There was a deafening quiet that actually frightened him. The boat was barely moving, the sail hung limp, and there was no wind whatsoever. There were icicles hanging from the lines and the mast. There was a thin layer of ice over the entire boat, making it slippery and cold. John had a strange thought, am *I sailing into hell?* He felt very alone and for the first time in his life, very insecure. He heard a noise. It was a welcome distraction. Rebecca came up on deck. He curiously watched the look on her face as she took in the scene.

"Why don't you use the engines and get us out of here? This is spooky. It looks like something out of an old movie."

"No, I want to save the fuel. The engines are on, and we're probably going at about two knots. I have to check our position, why don't you go below and make us some breakfast. We might as well take advantage of the calm."

John unbolted the cabinet below the console in the cockpit and took out his sextant. He looked through it and made notations on the plastic coated charts with a wax pencil. After checking his calculations, he made the adjustments to the autopilot. They were only five degrees off course, not bad. Rebecca brought up a thermos of coffee and some bread she heated in the toaster oven, along with some bacon and roasted tomatoes.

They felt much better after eating, and they topped off breakfast with a handful of vitamins. It was almost noon when John felt the first breeze, and within minutes, they were flying through relatively calm water. Rebecca came into the cockpit and snuggled close to him, it was as if they were pleasure sailing in San Francisco Bay. "This is a relief after yesterday. We should be about fifty nautical miles south of Big Domino by tomorrow evening. I think I will change our course to land at Big Domino. We can go ashore and rest for a day or two," John said. "This is a lot worse than I thought it would be, and we better take every chance we can to rest."

Just before dark, they saw it, an ice field that seemed to go on forever.

"Get the sails down, hurry."

They worked together as a well-trained team, and John was surprised at the efficiency and speed at which they worked. Rebecca put on her headset and they checked the receiver that John had before she climbed up top. They hit the ice about 8:30 p.m., and John revved the engines to get as much torque out of them as possible. Rebecca directed him around the larger pieces over the intercom.

"I don't know how long I can stay up here," she called to him, "my hands are numb and my feet are killing me."

John shut the engines down to an idle. He went below

and got two pairs of electric socks and what appeared to be a beanbag but was actually a hand warmer. He climbed up to the lookout and gave them to Rebecca. He said, "Hold on, we can't get through this without you up here."

She was already squeezing the hand warmer and getting some relief. She sat down and put the socks on, and by the time John was at the helm, she called down to thank him and said she was doing great now.

They sailed deeper and deeper into the flow, and John realized that it was getting more and more solid and the pieces of ice were getting bigger. He looked over the charts again and decided that he better start sailing north and try to get out of this. Taking a northern tack here would mean the next closest land was Little Domino and as far as he knew that was uninhabited. It wasn't good, but it was their only chance now.

They started to come out of it just at first light. There was still a lot of ice but now you could see water and the pieces of ice were no bigger than a basketball. John called over the intercom to Rebecca, but there was no response. He looked up and could not believe what he saw. It looked like there was a big snowball at the top of the mast; Rebecca was completely encased in ice. He climbed up to her as fast as he could but could not break through. He climbed back down and went to the tool chest and got a hammer and started to break the ice away with it. He finally broke through and threw Rebecca, unconscious, over his shoulder and brought her down to the deck. She was a strange, bluish-gray, and it scared the crap out of him.

He leaned his face close to hers and he could feel she was still breathing but quick shallow breaths. He put the boat on autopilot and carried her below. He took her clothes off and put her in the shower and ran the water as hot as he could. He rubbed her as hard and fast as he could, and with the hot water running on her, he could see her skin slowly turning back to normal color. He sat her carefully on the floor and let the hot water run on her while he went into the galley and started to brew a big pot of tea.

He ran back and kept rubbing her extremities, alternating between her hands and her feet. Her ears were pure white, and he knew they were frost bitten.

He heard the water boiling. John ran to the galley and made a big mug of tea. He returned and began to pour it down her throat.

She gagged and coughed and then started to sip it on her own. She was coming to, and John breathed a sigh of relief. After two cups of tea, she started to become coherent and John took her out of the shower and began to dry her off. He had just wrapped a blanket around her when the alarm went off; he whirled and ran out of the cabin leaving Rebecca on the floor. He jumped into the cockpit but saw nothing wrong. He was still on the same course. Then he realized it was the potable water alarm, the hot water in the shower was potable water and the alarm meant that is was getting dangerously low. He ran back down below and turned the shower off.

He picked up Rebecca and put her in the bunk. He covered her with several blankets and coated her hands, feet, and face with petroleum jelly. He went over to the first aid kit and took out some painkillers. He gave them to her and said, "Take these, it might not hurt now but when you start to thaw the pain will be bad."

He also knew he gave her enough to sleep for a while. He covered her with another blanket and covered her head, her own breath will warm her face and ears, he thought. He went back up on deck and got back into the cockpit. He was exhausted, but he knew he could not rest until he was long out of this ice. It was starting to get dark and he was nodding. *I'd better get some rest now, because by morning, we might be back in the ice.* He checked the autopilot and as he went below he checked the barometer and temperature. He turned on the stove to make himself a cup of coffee and realized that he hadn't checked on Rebecca in hours.

She was still sleeping, but her color and breathing were fine. He checked her fingers, toes, and ears, and they all had normal color. He checked her pulse, and it was a little slow at fifty-five beats per minute, but that might be average for her. He made a mental note to check again later. He continued working off his checklist. He made sure all battery levels were good, checked oil levels, and that everything was still properly stowed. When he was satisfied, he climbed into the bunk and fell asleep immediately. He was awakened by the smell of bacon cooking and coffee brewing. He opened his eyes and saw Rebecca cooking in the galley. He swung his legs over the edge of the bunk and he felt dull aches in every joint. *It sucks to get old*, he thought. He got dressed and went into the galley.

"Morning, how are you?"

"Fine," Rebecca replied. "I have a little pain in my ears and fingertips, but otherwise, quite well. What time is it?"

"About 2:00 p.m., have a cup of coffee?"

"Yeah, and then I have to make sure we're on course. We can't afford any screw-ups now. We have no water left. I have switched the sink and shower to seawater, and if you feel up to it, you can collect ice and snow from the deck and bring it down here and boil it. After it cools, pour it into the desalinization tank over there, it will only produce one gallon of drinking water every three hours, so we have to watch what we use, and by using the ice and snow, it will taste better than just using sea water. We're going to need it; we shouldn't hit land for at least four days according to weather."

"I thought we were going to reach Big Domino today?"

"No, because of the ice, I had to tact north. We'll hit Little Domino in a few days." John didn't have the heart to tell her it was uninhabited. After his coffee, he went back up on deck. It was beautiful and clear and the temperature was brisk but pleasant. The boat was doing a steady twenty knots. The seas were only about eight feet and rolling smoothly. The boat was cutting through the waves like a hot knife through butter, and John was able to relax and enjoy the sail. He took out his sextant and studied the charts and he was dead on course.

If the weather held he would hit Little Domino at about four o'clock in the afternoon three days from now.

Rebecca came up on deck, and after her chores were complete, she joined John and they spent a pleasant afternoon. It started to get dark but the temperature had risen about fifteen degrees and it was getting rather comfortable. Rebecca asked John if he would like some dinner, and he replied quickly, "Yeah, I'm famished."

"One gourmet meal coming up."

John laughed and asked sarcastically, "A British gourmet meal, does that mean we're having bangers again?"

"You got it, sir, and if I had more water, I'd have made mash too."

John thought to himself he'd better check the barometer, if the temperature was rising so fast, he could be heading into a storm. The barometric pressure was on the high side. The air was dry, and no bad weather was indicated, but John turned on the radio and listened to the weather reports.

The weather reports were good, and the seas were unseasonably low. John felt good and put the boat on autopilot and went below and decided to relax. After dinner, John asked Rebecca to give him a message. He was tight and sore. Rebecca rubbed him down with a mixture she came up with that seemed to have real therapeutic value. It was baby oil with a little witch hazel and avocado oil. She heated the oil slightly before she applied it, and the warmth of the oil under the soft pressure of her hands was all the elixir John needed. The pain left his body, and the stiffness turned to a pleasurable feeling of well-being. It wasn't long before he was asleep.

They woke together, and as they lay there, they began exploring each other's bodies. It was almost noon before they went up on deck. The temperature was up to about sixty degrees Fahrenheit, and the wind was at a comfortable fifteen knots out of the east. They could not have better sailing conditions. The next couple of days were pretty much the same, and they arrived at Little Domino four hours ahead of schedule.

CHAPTER 45
Little Domino Island, the Alaskan archipelago

Little Domino was a desolate landscape with a few birds and many sea lions. They had reached the northern tip of the island and sailed close to shore to the southern tip. At one beach, they witnessed a group of killer whales actually beaching themselves hunting the seals. It was about 5:00 p.m. when they hit the southern tip of the island, and except for the whales and a seal, there was no sign of life. As they turned the southern tip, the wind picked up and the temperature dropped sharply. John said, "Let's sail a little north and see if we can find some shelter. Let's sit this one out."

Rebecca quickly agreed. About fifteen miles up the coast, they saw a sheltered cove with a pier, their spirits soared. They secured the boat and walked up to the house at the end of the pier. There was a sign, which read "In case of emergency, take fuel and water, leave a contact number and name of vessel on the log at the fuel station. You will be billed by the US National Geological Society."

The house was well equipped, and John had the fire going in the potbelly stove in minutes. Let's go down and get all of our clothes and bring them up here to dry thoroughly before leaving again. When they had carried up all the clothes, John found some rope and made a clothesline near the stove. He surveyed the room and told Rebecca to start up the coal stove. Rebecca investigated the ancient stove.

"It will take some time to get it hot enough to cook on."

John looked at the stove. "You get it started, I'll be right back. I'm just going to take a look around."

John found some crab traps on the side of the house and took them down to the pier. He got some bacon out of his galley and tied it in the traps and lowered them into the water. While he was waiting, he fueled the boat and filled the fresh water tanks. He went on board and checked all the battery and oil levels then checked all the lines. The boat was secure and ready.

He walked back to the house and told Rebecca they were going to have a feast. He had brought wine, butter, and canned vegetables up from the boat. They busily prepared the house, cleaning and washing utensils, checking lights, and making sure they had enough coal. After about two hours, John went down to the pier. He went to pick up the first trap and it seemed to be stuck on the bottom but as he pulled he realized it was just heavy. When he got it to the top of the water, he saw it was full of king crab. He pulled up the other two traps, and they were just as bountiful. He started to laugh to himself. *I'm not leaving until every one of them is gone.* He found a wheelbarrow and put the traps into it and brought his catch up to the house. He opened the door and smiled at the look on Rebecca's face.

"The mighty hunter is home."

They both had a good laugh and started to boil the crabs. They truly had a feast. They ate for what seemed hours and then feel into bed and slept. They woke up the next day feeling both refreshed and full from the night before.

John went into the bathroom and yelled, "There's no hot water," It was heated by the pot belly stove that went out early that morning. He lit the stove and the heater and waited for them to get hot. Rebecca walked out the door and stood looking out at the bleak surroundings. John came along side of her and put his arm around her.

"Would you like to do a little exploring today?"

"Sure," she replied, thinking it would be better than getting right back on the boat.

"Okay, let's take a shower and have a cup of coffee and go."

While they were having coffee, John remarked that the clothes were dry and it would be nice to be in dry clothes again.

They got dressed, and John took only one of the traps down to the pier, last night's catch was too much. After he set the trap, they started on their trek.

They followed the coast and came to a cove. The beach was cover with sea lions, and they didn't seem friendly, so they walked up a hill and from the rise they could see the entire colony. They sat and watched the interaction between these huge animals. Rebecca remarked, "This is interesting."

There seemed to be a defined hierarchy, and as big as they were, they moved rather fast to defend their territory and harem. Rebecca wanted to go inland and see what was there so they walked away from the shore. The landscape was almost a moonscape, barren, and colorless. It was the most inhospitable landscape they had ever seen. The terrain, mostly rock, was interspersed with patches of tall brown grass. There seemed to be no life away from the shoreline. They traversed some streams, which broke up the monotony of this dull landscape. They walked for hours and the terrain was the same. On the walk back, the colorless shades of gray and brown depressed them to the point they both went quiet.

Finally they came to the shoreline at a different spot, and this bit of shore was covered with penguins. Watching them brought their spirits up again. Rebecca said it looked like a colony of nuns and butlers, and John laughed. He actually needed that laugh, because as he looked back at the landscape, the only thing more foreboding than the land was the blue, black sea they were going to challenge tomorrow. After another dinner of king crab and a couple of glasses of wine, they went to bed and made love. They were both insatiable; it was like they were trying to prove they were alive in this dead place. It was hours before they finally stopped, both spent and ready to sleep. John had just lost consciousness when he heard the noise; it was rain. The rain was hitting on the roof so hard that it sound like drum rolls. He unhooked the door to take a look, and the wind blew it open with a horrific force. It took all his strength to close it again.

Dammit, he thought to himself, *I hope we can get out of here tomorrow*. Knowing there was nothing he could do, he went back to bed. He slept well even though the storm had gotten worse during the night. Once he fell asleep, nothing was going to wake him. In the morning, he looked out the door and it was sunny. When he stepped out, he realized it was warm. He went back in and woke Rebecca.

"Come on, let's get out of here before there's another squall."

The boat looked a little beat up, but after close inspection, there was no real damage. Rebecca went down below to check and found everything in order and ready.

The barometer reading was falling, and John was concerned. He listened to the radio and there was a storm coming out of the east but much father south.

"We must have gotten the tail end of it last night," he told Rebecca. "Let's get out of here if there is weather coming from the east. We will be better off sailing north again to here," he pointed to his chart, "and then take an eastern tact to here and then south southeast to Vancouver. We have an alternative route if the weather is bad. When we reach the first point, instead of going south, we can go due east and we'll hit Valdez, Alaska, the end of the oil pipeline. If we have to go into Valdez, we will be there in two days. The downside to that is we will have to check in with the US Coast Guard, and we may be met by unfriendly people. It will take us five days to get to Vancouver, it will be much safer, at any rate, let's get going now."

They cast off the lines and headed off into the choppy black Pacific. The temperature was dropping again, and it was cold. The seas were rough, but the boat handled them. Rebecca thought to herself, *Thank God John is such a good sailor; if it weren't for him, we would have been dead days ago.*

When you are navigating a small boat through these kinds of seas, there is literally no rest. It is grueling, hard work and it takes a toll on even the strongest. John's arm was killing him, his feet were numb, and his hands were throbbing. He thought to himself, *I hope we get into better conditions soon, I don't think I can last too much longer. Rebecca is a good sailor but not good enough for this.* Just then, Rebecca brought him a cup of coffee and she took the wheel while he drank it. The hot cup felt good in his hands, and he moved around and stomped his feet to try to get some of the circulation back into them. Stay at the wheel. I'm gong below to get some socks and take some vitamins."

He went back up on deck and realized he just needed a break. He was feeling fine. "Rebecca, go down and get some rest. I'll get you in two hours to relieve me."

John let her sleep for almost three hours before he went below and woke her. "I have some bad news. The barometer is falling fast. I think we are headed into a big storm." They stayed below for a short time and had a cup of coffee. When they went back up on deck John said, "Oh hell!"

The sky was black as night and flashes of lightning were visible even at that distance. "I figure it is about twenty miles away, and we should hit it in about thirty minutes."

The seas had already gotten worse, and John checked his charts.

"I'm going to go further north, if I'm right we can go around it."

The further north they went, the calmer the seas were. Rebecca came up on deck and said, "The barometer is rising, we are back into a high pressure system. It should be clear sailing now."

John didn't tell her but he had lost all the feeling in his hands up to his wrists.

"Could you get me one of those hand warmers?" he asked.

While she went below, he removed his gloves and his hands were purple. *Good*, he thought, if they were white, he would have been frost bitten and probably lost his hands. He had to be careful now, it was really cold and he would probably be running into ice again. John checked his chart and thought the safest route was to now go due east and when they reached a point about a day's sail to Alaska he would change to a heading of due south. He stayed at the helm through the night with Rebecca bringing him hot coffee and messaging his hands and feet to keep the circulation going, the foot and hand warmers were a life saver.

At first light, the temperature had already risen thirty degrees from the night before and the seas were much smoother. John now knew they were going to make it. He put the boat on autopilot on a course due south and ask Rebecca to stay on watch while he went down for some sleep. It was about two in the afternoon when Rebecca woke him.

"John, it's the US Coast Guard. They are calling us. There is a cutter following us now."

John got up and got on the radio.

"This is the *Flying Gull*. Over. Can I help you? Over."

"This is the US Coast Guard asking permission to board your vessel."

"Please do come aboard."

"Oh my God! John, do you think it's them? Have they found us?"

"I don't think so," John replied. "If they were going to do anything, they would have blown us out of the water by now. The boarding party came aboard, and a young officer asked for their papers. He studied them and said, "Canadians?"

"Yes," John answered.

"What the hell are you doing out here?"

"What do you mean?" John asked.

"I mean, this is some of the most dangerous water in the world, and you're sailing around in this little boat."

"Yes, my wife and I are writers, and we are writing a book on sailing rough water, rough weather."

"Well, that's great, but do you know how dangerous this is?"

"Son, I have been sailing since I was a child, and I have sailed around the world twice."

"Sir, I meant nothing by it, but we get a lot of weekend warriors out of Alaska who get out here and the next thing you know we have to bail them out. Where are you sailing from, sir?"

"Japan," John answered.

"Japan? Did you come through that storm?"

"Partially, and we partially sailed around it."

"Well, it's obvious you know how to sail. I'm sorry to have bothered you."

"No bother, it was good to see another human being. Would you like some coffee?"

"No thank you, sir, we have to get back and make a report."

John walked him up on deck and said, "Listen, you know

these waters better than I do. Could you tell me the best course to Vancouver?"

John pulled out his charts, and the young officer pointed out a route.

"Stay out and you won't encounter too much ice. This time of year you will only see the big bergs, but if you stay west of this line, you'll only run across the real big ones."

He pointed at the chart.

"I would go back west to here and then southeast from here, which should be the safest route. There is no bad weather expected for the next four or five days so you should be all right."

"Thank you."

"Not at all, sir."

The two men shook hands and the boarding party went back to their ship.

Rebecca came up on deck and said, "John, do you think it's okay?"

"I don't know, but I don't think I'll take the route he suggested. If someone puts two and two together, they would know exactly where we are."

Over the next three days they had to dodge a few ice flows, but nothing eventful happened. They both had to stay on watch and were cold and tired. John decided to go into shore and get some real rest for a couple of days.

They hugged the coast and stopped at the first place they could. It was a fishing village, mostly enuks, Canadian Eskimo's but it was a sportsman resort, where people from the states and Canada came to fish for big halibut and salmon. The hotel was rustic but warm and clean. They took a hot shower, went down to the dinning room, and had a great dinner and went up to bed. They were in heaven. They decided to stay for a few days and rest to get their strength back.

The hotel was much better than either of them expected. It was clean, with two bedrooms two baths, a living room, kitchen, and a wraparound porch. It was right on the beach, and you could actually sit on the porch and watch the people kayaking after the dolphins. John paid for a month's stay and explained to the owner that this was their honeymoon, and they sailed up from Vancouver and would be doing some day sailing. Thinking this would offer them some privacy as newly weds.

During the next few days, John and Rebecca tried to relax as much as possible and get their strength back. John made a visit to the local doctor and had the cast removed from his arm, and Rebecca went to a beauty parlor and had her hair colored and trimmed. They also cleaned up the boat and did some painting.

With their chores behind them, they settled in and relaxed. No one would think they were not on their honeymoon. They took long walks then they would disappear for hours to their room and then surface again for a meal then disappear again. John realized that he had to try to enjoy the time they had together because it could end at any time.

CHAPTER 46
Bonn, Germany

Helmut took the first day off since he was installed as director. He went through all of his accounts and thought to himself, *they have ruined my life. Everything I have worked for all these years, and now I have to resign and leave before I'm found out.*

He kept glancing over to the letter of resignation he had just signed, and his hands shook. Trying to compose himself, he went back to the task at hand and in almost disbelief he totaled his accounts to see an amount of $ 14,745, 812 USD. He could not believe he had received that much from the Liddo Group over these last ten years. He really was a traitor and a crook. No, he told himself, he was just weak, but was that worse? He woke with his head on the table and quickly realized he had to rush to get everything done and still catch the four o'clock flight to India. He supposed he had plenty of money and now was as good as time as any to retire. Just as he was leaving the house, the phone rang, it was Ascot Chen.

"Helmut, my friend, I just called to tell you I don't think it's a good time to leave."

"How do you know I'm leaving," Helmut demanded.

"My friend, you should know that I am always trying to protect my friends."

"Screw you. I had enough, I'm getting out."

"That would not be advisable at this time. There are many sensitive issues that must be finalized."

"Damn you, I'm out."

Helmut slammed the phone down and ran out of the house. The next day, the headlines of all the German papers read,

"Helmut Kleig, Dead!" Heir Klieg had died of a heart attack in the airport yesterday afternoon. He will be remembered as one of Germany's best intelligence directors. The coroner who did the autopsy was paid a handsome sum to leave out the fact there was a small syringe hole in the back of his neck.

CHAPTER 47
Vancouver, Canada

The two-day sail down to Vancouver was easy and uneventful. They tied up in a nice marina right in the city. John spent a few days cleaning and doing repairs, while Rebecca hunted for a flat.

Vancouver was a beautiful city. It is fashionable and quietly dynamic. It has the largest Chinese population in North America and with John's knowledge of Cantonese, it was easy for them to assimilate into the Chinese section of the city. Rebecca remarked it reminded her of a quite Hong Kong.

Rebecca found a flat to rent and within days of their arrival they were set up in the community. The flat was quite nice and it was only a few blocks from where John had moored the boat. It was on East Pender Street and Carrall Street and had a view of Dr. Sun Yat Sen Garden.

The garden was the largest Chinese garden outside of China. It was just what they needed. They spent a few days shopping and decorating the flat and by the weeks end they only wanted to relax. John went out early Saturday morning for a jog through Stanley Park down to the tip of Brockton Point, which was famous for its totem poles. He continued through the park and looped around past the aquarium to Alexander Street at the foot of Columbia Street, where the boat was moored. John had made it a point to check the boat daily. After checking the lines on the boat and making sure it was secure, he started to jog back.

On the way back, he would stop to buy a paper. He jogged about five miles, and although it felt good, he realized how out of shape he was. He went into a local coffee shop where he could get a cup of coffee, which he drank while reading the news. The shop was pleasant and John decided to sit at a table near the window to read. He was almost finished his coffee when he noticed a sign that said Kung Fu and kickboxing. John took down the address and decided to investigate. After he had showered and changed his clothes, he told Rebecca he was going to see if he could join the martial arts class he had read about in the shop. He walked a few blocks and found the place was closed but there was a young, strong looking young man inside. John knocked on the door, and the young man waived him away.

"We're closed," he yelled with no noticeable accent.

John knocked again, and the young man shook his head and came to the door.

"We're closed, old man. Come back after twelve."

John stuck his foot in the door and pushed it open farther.

"I'd like to talk to the manager or owner."

"That's me, and we're closed," the young man repeated, getting noticeably annoyed.

John began, "I want some private sessions. I'll give you $100 per hour."

The young man smiled, "Come in, sir. My name is David Song, and I am an eighth degree black belt."

"Hi," John replied, "my name is John, and I use my belt to hold up my pants."

The young man looked at him incredulously and said, "Yeah, I saw that movie too."

He went on to ask John, "Do you know what a black belt is?"

"Yes, it has to do with the levels of ability in the martial arts. I don't really care to be rated or compete, I just want to work out. I have some knowledge of the martial arts, I used to work out with a friend in Hong Kong, but I haven't worked out in months and I feel a little rusty."

"When would you like to start?" the young man asked.

"How about now. I'm dressed for it, and I just jogged, so I am warmed up."

"Okay, but you have to sign a release form and answer some

health questions."

After the formalities were over, John and David stood on the mats.

"This is the proper stance," said the young man. "When I say go, I want you to attack me. Go!"

John took one step forward and pushed David. David tried to pull him forward, but John countered and David lay on the floor. The young man looked surprised and thought to himself, *Beginners luck*. They faced each other and again. David said, "Go." Before he could respond, John had hit him and flipped him onto his back. David got up a little embarrassed and angry, "Okay, old man, let's see what you got."

David attacked him, and John countered every move but was impressed by the speed and strength of the young guy.

David pulled back and said, "Who are you, Superman?"

John laughed, and David attacked, trying to catch John off guard, but again, John countered every move. John laughed and said, "Son, where did you get your black belt, in the girls' school?"

David attacked him viscously, and John again countered every move, but being a little rusty, was getting tired. After an hour, David was sore and frustrated. John was exhausted but happy to be back training. David said, "Your hour is up."

John thanked him and asked, "Are you up for another session tomorrow?"

David looked at him and said, "Sure, what time?"

"The same time as today?"

"Okay, but tomorrow I'm not going to be easy on you."

John laughed, and David thought to himself that he better keep these sessions private, if anyone saw how this old man was beating him, he could lose his business. John jogged the rest of the way back to the flat, and Rebecca was waiting for him at the door.

"Where were you? I was worried."

John told her he had found the gym and went on to tell her of his training session. He would be doing this every day. He went in and took another shower and came out leaning to one side and limping.

"What's wrong?" Rebecca asked.

"I didn't realize how much I have gotten out of shape. That kid hurt me. I'll never let him know that, but he hurt me."

John's competitive side showed through. Rebecca laughed and said, "Come here, you baby, Mommy will fix you all up."

After Rebecca rubbed him down with her magic oils, they made love, and John felt strong and young again. They lay in the bed, and John said, "I really love you." Rebecca smiled and let out a soft moan and rolled over, thinking to herself that she really loved him too and felt guilty that she had gotten him involved with all this. A tear came to her eye, and she put her face in the pillow to hide it from him.

It was almost 9:00 a.m. when John called from the shower, "It's a beautiful day, don't waste it in bed. I'm going to train, and I'll be back in an hour."

Upon his return, they had a quick cup of tea and decided to go out and explore Vancouver. It was a good practice to know your surroundings very well in case of an emergency. It was their knowledge of Hong Kong that saved them there, and it was John's knowledge of the sea that saved them. They walked the streets surrounding their flat and stopped in the shops and enjoyed sampling the restaurants and cafes. They were in no rush and lingered and talked to the shop owners and began to become part of the neighborhood. Each day they would go a little further and learn the area a little more. John was becoming very friendly with David Soong, and he and Rebecca would double with David and his girlfriend Mai Lin. They went to dinner, the movies, the theater, and sometimes they would picnic in one of the many parks in Vancouver; their favorite was Lynn Canyon, it was full of hiking trails and a suspension bridge over the Canyon. John and Rebecca were enjoying their time there but never forgetting the danger they were in.

One morning, after their workout John and David were having a cup of coffee and David asked if John was retired. John laughed and told him no but was taking an extended holiday. David looked at him and asked, "Are you in some kind of trouble in the states?"

"No," John replied. "Why do you ask that?"

"Well, it seems kind of strange that you would come to

Vancouver and move into Chinatown, and you don't seem to have any friends except for me and Mei Lin."

"Oh, is it that obvious?" John asked. "The truth is that I got a divorce last year and it was nasty, so I kind of dropped out for a while and went to Hong Kong. That's where I met Mary. I own a yacht building company, and my partner and I are lifelong friends. He has continued to run the business while I set up a Hong Kong operation. My wife is still trying to get control of my share of the business, so I disappeared for a while. It was easy for Mary and I to pose as a Canadian married couple. My wife hired several private detectives, and they found me in Hong Kong, so we split. I would really appreciate it if you didn't tell anyone about this."

"Not a word," replied David. "I'm sorry I asked. It's your business and I apologize for prying."

"Not at all," John replied, "as a matter of fact you might be able to do me a big favor. I have a man working for me in Hong Kong and I knew my wife had his phone tapped so I haven't called him since I left. His name is Chung, could you call him and give him your number as a contact in case he really needs me for something. You might say you're his cousin and that you have received his gifts and thank him, tell him they both arrived by boat and that nothing was broken. If he wants to talk tell him to call here tomorrow morning, he'll know enough not to call from his place or the office."

David agreed and called Chong. Chong was a quick study and picked up on the code immediately. They arranged for him to call back some time tomorrow morning. John thanked David and left. He jogged back to the flat and after a shower, he and Rebecca went out for their morning exploration. They took the bus to MT. Seymour Park and took the chair lift to the top. They were alone on the lift and John said, "We have to come up with a plan soon on what to do with the discs."

"I know, but what?"

"Come on, Rebecca, you are a solicitor and a cop, you must have some ideas."

"Well, I was thinking we might post it on the Web. Once it's out in the open, we should be safe."

"But where would you put it on the Web?"

"That's what I've been trying to come up with in my head. I don't know."

"It's a good idea in principle, but how do you do it," John replied. "Let's buy a computer this afternoon and get to work on it."

That evening the computer was installed and they were on the Web. John asked David to use his credit card for the set up so there would be no trail back to him then he set up a personal Web page entitled Blue Waters, thinking it might be a way to communicate with Peter and Chong without being noticed. They could use computer cafes and probably couldn't be traced. When the Web page was completed, he reimbursed David and began to research lists of government agencies, newspapers, and magazines. He started to get tired and asked Rebecca to find out how to send mass e-mails. She worked on it through the night.

The next morning, John woke at about 7:30 a.m., and Rebecca was still at it. She had come up with at least ten different ways to send mass e-mails and had found existing mailing lists that you could plug into that reached about two million households in the US and there were others for the UK and Europe. John told her she did a great job, but they still had to finalize a plan that would get the information out without getting them killed. John went out for his exercise and when he arrived at David's he was told Chong had already called and would call back in twenty-five minutes.

"Great," John said, "and while we're waiting, let's get in a work out."

David laughed and said, "I thought I was going to get away without one this morning. I'm getting tired of getting beat up every day."

They both laughed but went into battle, John trying to keep his edge, and David trying to beat this old man. John was happy to hear the phone ring. He was running out of steam. David was either getting better or he was getting slower, knowing the latter was more reasonable. David answered the phone and then handed it over to John.

"It is good to talk to you, how are things there?" Chong said, "I'm being covered like white on rice."

John laughed, but he knew what Chong meant.

"I have developed a personal Web page. You and I can stay in contact through it," John told Chong. The address is www.bluewaters.ca. "Don't call me again, we are working on something now that might end this whole thing but it is still in the planning stages. How is everyone there?"

"Fine," Chong said, "but they are intent on getting you. They have set up an entire control center and your old friend Ian is in charge. That's all I know the security on their side has become very tight. I think it all has to do with the current sale of missile technology to China by the US. There are rumors that the American secretary of commerce would not sign the export papers and he was killed. There must be something on those discs that implicates a lot of people in that deal. They are watching me, but I am also watching them. Their command center is out on Green Island, so it is easy to see if people are coming and going. I have their routine down pat so I will report to you on any variances in their patterns. I'll use the Web page."

"Good," John said, "lose this number or memorize it and only use it in extreme emergencies and only contact the Web page from someone else's computer."

"Okay, boss. Bye."

John put the phone down and realized how much he missed Chong. They had become great friends.

CHAPTER 48
Green Island, Hong Kong

"Sir, we got them. Our man that was following Chong got the number he was dialing on a pay phone, well not the whole number, but enough to know he called Vancouver, Canada."

"Lieutenant, how do you know he wasn't calling a relative or a friend?"

"We don't, Sir; but if he were, wouldn't he call from home or his mobile?"

"Good point and good work. Get our people in Vancouver on this immediately and to make matters easier for them notify the Vancouver police and the RCMP that John is wanted here in Hong Kong for the murder of a Catholic priest. Send his picture by fax and e-mail."

"Yes, sir, right away."

Ian thought to himself, *This ought to be the end of this, and I'll get that promotion to general and then maybe I'll get listed on one of those discs.* Ian was from a British working class family and had worked his way up to this position. It was almost impossible to make the rank of general in her majesty's services coming from his background, but he was going to show them, show everybody and make a fortune of his own.

CHAPTER 49
Vancouver Canada

After their workout, John and David went for a cup of coffee, which had become their ritual.

David asked, "You are pretty tight with Chong, aren't you?"

"Why, yes I am. Why do you ask?"

"I don't know, but you two seem like unlikely candidates as friends."

"How so?" John asked.

"Just from his accent I heard on the phone, he sounds like a working class guy from Hong Kong, and you seem a little older and more sophisticated."

John laughed.

"You're wrong on both counts, and I'll leave it at that."

David laughed but thought to himself there always seems to be another layer to this onion; every time he thought he had John figured out, some little thing would come out to show he didn't have a handle on him at all. David thought this guy has to be the most interesting guy I have ever met. He seemed open but at the same time secretive. *I can't figure him out at all.*

John, seeing that David was thinking a little too much said, "Don't try to figure me out. I'm so simple I'm complicated," and he laughed.

David thought this was funny but true. "Listen, I come from a middle-class family and have made some money, but I worked hard for it and I have friends form every level of society and because of that, I have developed into what Mary calls a social chameleon. I call it a varied background. I'm a renaissance man," he said with a big smile.

David laughed and took it as a sincere explanation and the subject was dropped; John asked David if he would like to go sailing.

"Sure. When? Right now? I have a one-hour class then the rest of my day is free."

"Great, meet me at the boat in two hours."

"Okay, John, see you then."

David came down to the boat about noon and they cast off and sailed around the Peninsula to Stevenson, an old fishing village that is in the southwestern corner of the suburb of Richmond. This is where the property of the Canadian Japanese was auctioned off when they were sent to internment camps during WWII.

They tied up and got off the boat and visited the Gulf of Georgia Cannery, a National Historic site. There was a museum showing the nautical history of the region. John enjoyed this immensely and thanked David for pointing it out to him. It was a great day, they got back to the berth about 5:00 p.m., and John was surprised to see Rebecca on the pier waiting for him. When the boat was secure, John and David got off the boat. David said hello to Mary, but she just stared at him blankly. John gave her a kiss and said, "What do I owe this honor?"

As he spoke, he saw the look on her face and then noticed she had brought their bags and their computer.

"What's all this?" he asked.

"Oh, I just wanted to store some of this stuff. The flat is getting crowded."

"Oh," John replied, knowing that something was wrong. David thanked John and said good-bye.

As soon as David was out of earshot, John turned to Rebecca and asked, "What's wrong?"

There were tears in her eyes as she answered him.

"Mrs. Wu—their landlady—said the RCMP was circulating a picture of you with you real name and told her that you were wanted for the murder of a priest in Hong Kong."

"Oh my God, they killed Chuck," John said.

Mrs. Wu, being Chinese, had an aversion to telling anything to the police and just told them that she had no American tenants.

"Oh my God, John, they know we are here."

"Maybe," he replied, but if they are using my real name, they don't know about the Canadian passports."

John walked to the end of the pier and after a few minutes he came back to Rebecca.

"Okay, get on board, we're out of here."

She followed those instructions without a word. Once they were under sail and out of sight of Vancouver, she asked, "What are we going to do?"

"We are going to sail to Seattle and grab a flight for Australia."

"What?" she said surprised.

My ex-wife is there, and she has been dating a guy who is a media mogul. She hates me, but I think if she knew I was in real danger she would help me out. Her boyfriend controls almost the entire media of Australia, and he might want to release the news we have, and if we get enough celebrity, it will be difficult for anyone to kill us."

Rebecca thought for a while and said, "That's great plan, but what if your ex doesn't wan to cooperate. A woman scorned and all that."

John said, "That's a chance we'll have to take. The world keeps getting smaller for us, and we don't have too many options left."

About two hours out of Seattle, John threw the computers overboard, his depth finder read 800 feet, and he figured no one would find them there, and if they did, they would not be able to retrieve anything from them anyway.

"Did you save everything to the Web page before you disconnected it?" John asked.

"No, I was in such a panic I just ran."

"Well, that's understandable, but we lost three weeks' work. We'll have to try to work as fast as we can when we get to Sydney."

They reached the marina in Seattle and quickly processed all the necessary paper work with the harbormaster. John took the title to the boat and put it in a FedEx envelope with a note to Peter to please sell this boat and transfer the funds in the name Blue Water enterprises, blue water was the password on their Swiss account, and Peter would know immediately what to do. When they got to the airport John told Rebecca to buy the tickets for the next flight to Sydney via Seoul Korea as most flights go through Hong Kong John thought it would be safer to take that route. While Rebecca was on the ticket line, John handed her two new passports they were German and the pictures did not look to unsimalar to them, John simply said, "I'll tell you later."

John went to the computer shop where they had Web hook ups and e-mailed Peter Tsillman at the Wetrshift and Privat Bank to transfer $200,000 to Franz Wederiel, German passport number 1396347prg at Barclay's Bank Sydney, Australia to be released with presentation of passport only. The funds should be drawn from account T237458hp password, Blue Water 32. The code 32 was gotten from adding the numeral equivalent of the day of the week plus the month plus the time, this always had to be added or the transfer would not go.

With that taken care of, he went to the pre-arranged spot to meet Rebecca. They boarded the New Caledonian flight and sat in first class. The flight was pleasant, but John was apprehensive. *How did they find us in Canada?* he kept asking himself, and then it dawned on him, they somehow bugged Chong.

"It won't be long before they get to David and now they'll know our Canadian identity." It was lucky that John had noticed the couple in the airport, when he saw them he thought they had an uncanny resemblance to him and Rebecca. Looking at them closer, he noticed their passports sticking out of the bag the man was carrying and on pure impulse took them. John kept that to himself figuring Rebecca was upset enough and he needed her to be as calm as possible. She was tough but when you're under this much pressure for this long you loose your tolerance little by little and it grinds you down until you can't take the pressure anymore, she was almost at that point, not quite but not far either.

They had a two-hour layover in Seoul, and they got out to stretch their legs. John went immediately to the newsstands but there was nothing in any of the papers about them, he was more than a little relieved. When they got back on the plane Rebecca fell right to sleep but John could not stop thinking about Father Chuck. He was a great guy and a priest, don't these people have any morals at all.

He started to think about the people named on the discs, president's of the most powerful countries on earth, the heads of almost every police and intelligence force and throngs media people. The light bulb went off in his head. *Before we make contact with Lucy, I better make sure her boyfriend is not on the list.*

He thought about that for a while and then he thought are all the people who are after us in on this conspiracy, do they know they are protecting these really corrupt politicians, probably not, their being duped and made to believe we are the criminals? They have people in the media so information is not thoroughly checked; it came from high-level government sources. This was pure unquestioned power, and it appeared to be worldwide, which meant criminals were running the world and we are at the mercy of their puppets, our national leaders. The thought of it all made John nauseous. He called for the stewardess and ordered a double martini. After two of them he went to sleep and woke up on the descent into Sydney.

Before they left the airport John made a reservation at The Salty Anchorage in Port Stevens, about an hour and a half drive from Sydney. They took a taxi to the main office of Barclay's bank and John picked up the cash, all of it $200,000USD which was almost $400,000 Australian. The banker arranged for them to be taken to a car dealer who was a client of the banks and within three hours of landing in Sydney they bought a car for cash and were on the way to Port Stevens.

"Why are we staying out here at the beach?" Rebecca asked.

"Because I can pay cash, and there will be no records, just in case."

"Brilliant, John, I don't know how to thank you for all you've done for me, without you I would have been dead a long time ago."

"No worries, as they say down here, I have had the time of my life. I was getting too complacent; I needed something to jump-start my life again. I should be thanking you."

Rebecca looked at him adoringly and thought to herself, *that was rubbish, but I love him for saying it.*

CHAPTER 50
Green Island, Hong Kong

"Sir, MI6 has sent a notice to Canada and the RCMP has already been canvassing all the cities in British Columbia as well as Toronto, Montreal and Halifax. They have been supplied with warrants for their arrest for the murder of the priest. Pictures and descriptions have been supplied."

Ian nodded. "Good, who's our man on the ground there?"

"That would be one Colin Briggs. He is posing as a Hell's Angel and runs a string of topless establishments all over Canada. His cover allows him access to both the Russian Mafia and the Chinese Triads."

"Is he good?" Ian asked.

"The best, sir. He did a tour in Vietnam with SAS and he ran a recon group in Ireland for three tours, he's seasoned tough and smart."

"He's got to be for this one, that yank is brilliant and tough. That SOB has no known military training, no intelligence or police training and has out smarted and beat MI5, MI6 the Intelligence forces of three nations, the triads and the police. He is one wild piece of work as the yanks say."

"Yes, sir."

"Send Bradshaw to Vancouver and have him work as the outside man for Briggs. We got them now; Vancouver is a small place, with their background, especially Rebecca, they're going to gravitate towards Chinatown, put a net around that part of the city that a fly can't get through. I want to end this now."

"Yes, sir, I'm on it."

The lieutenant turned swiftly and went to his office.

"Send in Bradshaw."

It was about five minutes before Bradshaw arrived; the lieutenant had the complete file ready for him.

"This is a non-recourse op," he told Bradshaw. "We will not take responsibility for you or your actions. You are completely on your own. Contact Briggs as soon as you get there. Here is a phone number where you can reach him. When you call him, just say you want a private party at Bad Girls and you would like to meet him at 8:00 p.m. the night following the call. The address of Bad Girls is in the file. Study the file, commit everything to memory, and put it in a burn bag and leave it on your desk, your flight is at 2200 hours."

"Okay, sir, but one question—do I capture for interrogation or do I delete the targets?"

The lieutenant stared at him with dead eyes and simply said, end it.

Bradshaw was only off the plane about three minutes when he called Briggs. "Hello, my name is James Bradshaw, and I would like to arrange a party at Bad Girls could we meet there tomorrow at 8 p.m.?"

"Yeah, I'll be there just ask the hostess on the way in to call me."

"Fine good-bye," said Bradshaw, and he put the phone down and left. From the airport, he rented a car and drove to the Holiday Inn Crown Royal in Chinatown. After checking into his room, he went out and walked around the area familiarizing himself with any and all possible locations to make the hit. He returned to the hotel about three o'clock in the morning and went over his notes and thumbed through the pictures he had taken, there was nothing more to do until his meeting with Briggs so he decided to get some rest.

CHAPTER 51
Washington DC

They met in the White House residence; the scrambler had been set along with another electronic device, which sent a swooshing sound out for a radius of fifty feet. When they were certain no one could overhear them Manheim began, "The situation is serious, and we have to act quickly. That women and her friend have eluded us and we are quite sure they are going to be letting the information out. I think I have come up with a plausible deniability that should work but we need a high level fall guy."

The first lady spoke up, "What about the VP? He can't think on his feet, and if questioned, he looks guilty. Remember when he told the media he didn't know it was a fundraiser, he was in the bathroom when they collected the half million."

Manheim chuckled but said, "No, he's too close. What about the speaker of the house. He'd be perfect, and he's a Republican."

"Well," said the president, "he has been having a long time affair with one of his aides, if it was presented properly in the press where it looks like he is being investigated for corruption and this came to light…"

His voice trailed off, and Manheim said, "Great idea, it's done. I know just how to do it, now how about some law enforcement people?"

"They are easy," said the first lady. "They're always into something they shouldn't be. By the time they had finished they had comprised a list of over 300 people who could take the fall, and as the icing on the cake Manheim told them he had three women who were going to bring suit against the president for sexual harassment and it would hit the news the day after the headlines of widespread corruption hit the streets, this would completely deflect any fallout that might come his way."

By the next day, investigations had begun by hand picked men from the Justice Department, who were told they only answered directly to the attorney general. Manheim had prepared hundreds of press releases and all he had to do was pull the trigger and over a hundred major newspapers and three of the network TV stations would be reporting it all as they gathered their information from high level government sources.

CHAPTER 52
Port Stevens, Australia

John and Rebecca had worked most of the day compiling lists and adding them to their e-mail address books. It was now 5:00 p.m., and they had identified and catalogued almost seven hundred e-mail addresses of news paper editors, government agencies, TV station managers, radio talk show hosts, and twenty or thirty open chat rooms which were devoted to open political forums. John turned to Rebecca and said, "I am bleary eyed. I need a break. How about you?"

"Brilliant," she replied, "Let's go out for a walk and dinner."

"Great," John replied, "let's take a walk down and watch the people shooting the rapids on the river. I'll get a bottle of wine and some cheese and we'll have a picnic."

"John, I love you. You always know how to brighten my mood."

He actually blushed and they both looked at each other adoringly. John thought to himself, *She is twenty years younger than me and she's caused me more problems than anyone in my life, but I truly love her. If we make it out of this, I'm going to ask her to marry me. I wonder if she'll say yes.*

They packed up some wine and food, two glasses and utensils and were off. They walked down the path from their hotel and found a beautiful spot overlooking the bay. They sat on a blanket between two huge trees and from their vantage point, about ten feet higher than the water; they could see all the people in tubes and canoes as they passed. When the food was gone and they had drank about three glasses of wine, Australian of course, John said, "It won't be over when we send out this e-mail. We will have to get some newspaper or TV station to guarantee to run the story and feature us. If we get enough publicity and recognition, we should be safe. The trick is making enough people aware of the situation and put the information out in a way it can't be disputed. We won't be able to surface until a few indictments have been made, that should give us some authenticity. We're going to piss off half the governments and police forces in the world never mind the Liddo group and they play for keeps."

"Oh! John I am so sorry I have gotten you involved in all of this, but without you, I'm afraid I would be dead by now."

"We're far from out of the woods on that one," he replied. "When I met Peter in Zurich a few months ago, he told me that my ex-wife is dating some kind of media mogul down here, the one I told you about. She hates me, but I don't think she would want me dead. Tomorrow I am going to look her up and she if she can get her boyfriend to help us, I could not find him on the disc."

"Whatever you think is best, darling."

"I think the best thing we can do right now is go back and screw our brains out for the rest of the night."

Rebecca laughed and said, "God I am glad I didn't know you when you were younger, you must have been insatiable."

"Are you calling me an old man?"

"Well, you are old enough to be my father," laughed Rebecca getting up to run. John laughed and ran after her catching her before she made it back to the path.

He pulled her into his arms and said, "I was just thinking about our age difference myself, but I have never felt closer to anyone in my whole life."

"I feel the same way, darling. I was only kidding, and I have never met a more vibrant and virile man in my life." He pulled her closer and they kissed, a long lingering gentle kiss, the kind that makes you feel as if you're the only two people alive. After that kiss, they said nothing to each other, they just went back and made love for hours. When they were both totally spent, Rebecca fell asleep in John's arms and he looked down at her studying every detail of her face until he to fell into a deep sleep.

John was up early and dressed quietly as not to wake up

Rebecca, he put on his running shoes and went for his morning run. He ran about five miles and when he came back into the room Rebecca was up and making breakfast.

"This is very domestic," he said and she just turned toward him with that angelic smile and at that point he only wanted to repeat last night but he knew he couldn't he had a lot to do.

After breakfast, he drove alone into Sydney and looked for an out of the way pay phone; he found it just inside a small park. The phone booth was enclosed and at least a hundred feet from a bench and had glass walls so he had a complete 360 degree view of everyone around him. He dialed the number and a receptionist with a Chinese accent answered the phone, "Good day, Fashion," she said.

"Lucy Moore, I mean Lucy Owen, please."

"Who is calling please?"

"John Moore," he answered.

Lucy was standing at her desk and talked into her headphone when the intercom buzzed.

"Hold on. I'm sorry, I have another call."

"What! I mean...who? Just put the call through," she said into the intercom.

"John Moore is on the phone," the receptionist replied.

"Ask him to hold," she went back to her original call and said, "I'll call you back, I have to take this. Put him through."

She heard his voice through the phone, "Hello, Lucy."

"John, is it really you?"

Lucy felt faint, all the blood in her body seemed to be draining out slowly, and she fell backward into her chair.

"John, is that really you? Where are you?"

"I'm here in Sydney; I would like to see you."

"Come up to my office, do you have my address?"

"No," John replied, "but I don't want to meet you in the office. Do you know the lower entrance to the symphony?"

"Of course," she replied.

"Okay, can you meet me there in an hour?"

"Sure, but—" John cut her off in mid sentence.

"I'll see you in an hour," and John hung up.

Lucy sat there dazed, she could not believe the impact he

had on her after all this time. She started to go into a rage, but then she just started to cry. She would always love him, and she was excited about the thought of seeing him. Lucy picked up the phone and told her secretary to cancel all her appointments for the rest of the day, this was a first for the hard-driven woman executive that she was.

CHAPTER 53
Vancouver, British Columbia

The phone rang at 8:30 a.m., and Bradshaw woke a little startled. He was disoriented, and he didn't pick it up for about four rings. In a sleepy husky voice, he simply answered, "Bradshaw. This is Briggs, I have to postpone our meeting tonight until 11:00 p.m., is that all right with you?"

"I might have a line on the package you inquired about and I will research it today but something came up and I won't be back to the club until about ten thirty or eleven."

"Okay, I'll see you then," Bradshaw replied, and he hung up the phone and went back to sleep.

Colin Briggs was a seasoned and cold operative; the cover of a Hells Angel suited his personally perfectly. He had gotten some information about the possible targets from some of his street guys and he wanted to check it out before he told Bradshaw. He understood that guys like Bradshaw didn't want to investigate, they wanted to see their target, hit it and leave, the less contact he had with anyone the better for him. Two of his street guys, as he called them, told him they were down near the ferry terminal smoking some dope and saw a couple that looked a bit strange. The man had a distinct American accent and the woman had a British accent, although they heard them telling someone on the pier that they were Canadian. Briggs wanted to check this out, he could be lucky, and it sounded like the two everyone was looking for.

When he got down to the pier, he saw an empty berth and asked the harbor master if the boat that belonged there belonged to an American.

"Why do you ask?" the harbor master inquired.

"There was a couple at my club last night and they left a package there. The guy sounded American and his lady sounded British, I don't know their names, but I was talking to them, and they mentioned they had a boat here. If there is a reward, I'll split it with you."

"Oh," said the Harbor Master, "that could not be the boat, this one belongs to a Canadian couple, although the woman's accent did sound British or Scotch but it couldn't be them they sailed out of here four days ago and haven't been back."

"Thanks," and Briggs walked away. He knew he had to verify the information and to make certain it was the targets; he turned and asked, "Did they ever come her with anyone else? Maybe I could find them."

"Yeah, there was a Chinese guy that sailed with them often, he ran a gym or something he told me, wait, he gave me a card maybe I still have it." The harbor master went into his office and came out with a card.

Briggs reached into his pocket and pulled out a twenty-dollar bill and handed it to the man in exchange for the card. "Thanks," he said as he took it. "Buy yourself a drink."

"Thank you," the man said and returned to his office.

Briggs walked into the studio and David said we're closed. Briggs said, "I'm a friend of John's and I was just wondering if you have seen him or his lady. No I haven't seen them for days. Who are you? I'm a friend of John Moore's; we knew each other in the States."

"Oh, I don't know any John Moore; my friend's name is McKenzie."

"Was his wife's name Rebecca?"

"No, Mary, John and Mary McKenzie, not Moore."

Briggs looked at him and knew he was telling the truth; at least what he thought was the truth.

"Okay, I'm sorry, someone told me that they saw my buddy, but I guess it wasn't him. My buddy is a sailor and lives on a sailboat down at the ferry pier."

"Wow, that's a coincidence, my friend sails too."

As soon as he said that, he knew he shouldn't have. There

was something strange about this guy, but he just couldn't put a finger on it. If you'll excuse me, I have some work to do. Sure sorry to inconvenience you. When Briggs got into his car, he got on his cell phone.

"Hello, inspector, Briggs here. I have something for you, but I need something back."

"What is it, Briggs?"

He explained that he probably had some good Intel on the guy who murdered the priest in Hong Kong but he needed the RCMP to go to see this guy David, he runs a kung fu studio in Chinatown, he told me there was a Canadian named John McKenzie working out there but I believe it is Moore, I couldn't push him to far without blowing my cover. Within the hour David was being interrogated in police headquarters. When Briggs received the information back from the RCMP, he called Bradshaw immediately. Bradshaw was not in his room so he left a message for Jim to call him ASAP at 902-992-7876, which was a secure cell phone.

He waited for Bradshaw to call all day but he didn't, Bradshaw walked into the club at 10:45 p.m. Bad Girls was a typical topless joint, a lot of chrome and velvet and a lot of Tits and Ass hustling drinks. The hostess approached him and said welcome that will be $20, which allows you to have 1 beer included in the cover charge. I'm here to see Colin Briggs, oh, yes sir this way please and she led him to a private room in the rear of the club. Briggs was sitting on a couch with a girl on his lap.

When he saw Bradshaw, he yelled, "Oh Jesus, let me get some pants on. He told the girl to leave and pulled his dirty jeans up. "Jim, it's been a long time."

"Yeah, Colin but you haven't changed a bit." The two men laughed. "Jim, I got some bad news, your package has flown the coop."

"What!"

"Yeah, they sailed out of here four days ago on a sailboat named the *Flying Gull*. No one knows where they went; they are posing as Canadians named Mary and John McKenzie."

"Thanks, Colin, I'll put in a report to HQ."

Bradshaw left and went back to his hotel room, he put

a scrambler on the phone and when the operator in Hong Kong answered he said, "Give me Grant, and make sure the line is virgin."

CHAPTER 54
Sydney Australia

Lucy saw John as she walked up to the Symphony entrance. Her legs went weak and she almost lost her breath. She hated him for the way she felt right now. No man had ever made her feel like this, and it annoyed her. She ran up to him and latched on to him with a death grip. John stiffened. Realizing that she drew back and composed herself.

"John, it's so good to see you. I miss you and after I got over the fact that you disappeared on me and screwed me out of my rightful alimony, I realized that it was my fault and I wanted to apologize, after all you were and still are the only real love of my life. I was a fool and it was my fault all my fault. I am so happy you are here and I have the chance to tell you this, it has been haunting me since the day you left."

John looked at her and he remembered why he was attracted to her. She was now pushing fifty but was still as beautiful and sexy as she was when she was thirty. He snapped back to the present and said, "Right you're forgiven."

"God, haven't you got cold in your old age," she retorted sarcastically.

John laughed and said, "No, I mean it; I have forgiven you a long time ago. You always had a wild streak and that's what drew me to you in the first place. It was stupid of me or maybe egotistical of me to think I could keep you all for myself."

"Well that's big of you."

"Now who's being sarcastic?"

They both looked at each other and started to laugh. She threw her arms around his neck and kissed him, "No really, it is great to see you, John."

"It's good to see you too, Lucy."

"What are you doing here?"

"Lucy, I'm in trouble, and I came here to ask for your help."

"John, do you need money?"

"No, of course not. We have never done more business. I understand your business is booming. Fashion, right?"

"Yes, now tell me what kind of trouble you're in."

Lucy was in total disbelief as John started to tell her the story.

"Stop, John, I have to sit down for this. Let's go to my flat."

Lucy drove and they did not say a word until they were in Lucy's apartment.

"John, what the hell did you get yourself involved in? How did you let yourself get into this mess?"

"Lucy, I've actually enjoyed it, but now we're coming down to the wire, and if we don't pull it off right we're dead, literally."

"I presume *we* means you and the little honey that got you involved with."

"Please, don't call her that, the woman is a lawyer and a cop who stumbled across the wrong information."

Lucy stared at him and said, "You're in love with her, aren't you? You have some set of balls to ask me to help you and your girlfriend out of a mess."

"Lucy, don't even start, remember what you and your little boy toy were up to. Please, Lucy, this is a life and death situation and I don't want to fight over what happened a long time ago."

"All right, but what can I do for you," Lucy said annoyed.

John looked at her and pleaded, "Just make an introduction. Peter told me you were dating a guy who controlled the Australian media."

Lucy laughed out loud.

"Wait a minute. You want me to ask my boyfriend to help your girlfriend? Well isn't this civilized?"

Lucy thought for a moment and then bent over and picked up an ashtray and flung it at John. She went into a rage, "Are you nuts? You screwed me in the divorce, abandoned me, humiliated me—"

John stopped her in mid sentence.

"You were the one having an affair and plotting to take my business away from me." John was calm and did not raise his voice, his speech was deliberate and cold, and Lucy realized he was right, but at the same time she was hurt and disarmed by his coldness.

"Lucy, I know we had our differences, but I always thought I could count on you as a friend; we did have a lot of good years together."

"Oh John, you're right it was my fault and of course I'll help you any way I can. I still can't control my temper and seeing you here and now has my emotions in high gear." He hugged her, pulling her in close and holding tight, she wept and just said, "I'm so sorry, I'm so sorry." She pulled away trying to compose herself and said where are my manners. "Would you like a drink?"

"Scotch," he said, "neat." They sat together on the couch looking out at the view of Sydney harbor. John broke the silence. "You have a beautiful place here. "You must be doing well."

Lucy smiled and said, "Let me give you the grand tour and took him by the hand and led him on a room-by-room tour. The flat was beautiful, twelve rooms in all and a veranda with a garden. "You have a lovely home here, you must be very happy."

Lucy said, "Yes, but the truth was she was extremely unhappy. "She was a captive of her business and her boyfriend was convenient and some comfort, but he would never compare with John. No man ever would in her eyes."

They went back to the couch and John told Lucy some of the events leading up to today, she sat there quietly in both amazement and horror but growing more and more envious of Rebecca. John sensed this and thought to himself, *It would be better for everyone if these two never meet.*

When he was finished, Lucy asked again, "John, how can I help you?"

"Well, I figure we are only in danger as long as we have that information, so we are going to disseminate it world wide but I need media coverage to make us familiar, if we become known and the information is out there we should be safe. I got the idea from the presidential scandals, even though Linda Jones and the Swipp woman were threatened, they were protected by popularity, if anything did happen to them it would have gone right back to the president. I'm counting on the same thing, timing is everything, and we will e-mail the information to all the news services as soon as I can get a media blitz here. It should be a coup for the news agency that breaks the story. What's your boyfriend's name?"

Lucy replied, "Niles Kent, he owns two of the largest media companies in Australia. His companies own major pieces of TV, radio, and print. He's an interesting man, no one seems to know where he made his money and I don't even know where he was born or grew up, he's very secretive but he's very powerful."

"Lucy, can you arrange a meeting?"

"Right away," she said as she reached for the phone. "Hello, Niles, it's Lucy, can you come to my flat right now? Yes it's really important. Okay then I'll see you in an hour." She hung up the phone.

"That's done, John. It really is so good to see you. Do you consider this a big favor?" John looked at her strangely and she said, "Just yes or no?"

"Yes it is a big favor; you are truly saving my life."

"Good, then I want something from you." John was about to say, *I knew it here it comes*, when Lucy said, "Just promise me you won't stay away this long ever again." John leaned over and kissed her. It stirred a lot in both of them but they both let it go. The doorbell rang.

"Here's Niles!"

John looked at him closely trying to get some handle on this guy. "John this is Niles Kent and this is John Moore."

They shook hands, both men trying to size up the other. "I've heard a lot about you, John. Lucy has always spoken highly of you."

"I've heard a lot about you too," John lied.

"What is so urgent, Lucy?"

"John has a proposal for you, he wants you to break a big story. Go ahead John, and tell him."

After an hour or so Niles got up and said, "All this is interesting to say the least. I'll check with my editorial staff and see how far we can take this. Where can I contact you?"

"Through Lucy. I just arrived and haven't got a place to stay yet."

"All right, but please make yourself available tomorrow around lunch. I'll call Lucy before noon."

"Great." Niles leaned over and kissed Lucy in a way to show John that he had territorial rights over her now.

John got back to Port Stevens about four o'clock. He walked into the suite and stopped dead. Rebecca wasn't there and things were thrown all over the room. His heart stopped. He carefully searched the place and on closer examination he noticed nothing was broken but everything was eschewed. Just then Rebecca walked through the door; he ran to her and hugged her tight. "What happened? Are you all right?"

"I'm sorry, John, I had a fit and threw all this around, and I went for a walk to calm down."

"I'm just happy you're all right." John looked at her closely and for the first time she was showing signs of wear from all of this. The youthful appearance of her face was waning and her hair was a little dull. That shine he loved so much was fading, but the most significant thing was her eyes, they were starting to get the dull dead look of a shark, they were loosing their glint; she was emotionally dieing from the inside out.

"Listen, I have some great news. It's almost over. I have a meeting tomorrow with Niles Kent. He owns a big chunk of the media here in Australia. When we're ready to pull the trigger he will blitz the story, giving us legitimacy and worldwide recognition."

"John, it's really going to be over!"

"Yes, now let's get this place cleaned up we have a lot of work to do before it's all over."

John called Lucy at 11:00 a.m. sharp. "Hello, John, Niles wants you to meet him at a restaurant called Tequila Down Under. Its Tex-Mex Australian style, it's quite good."

"Okay, what time should I pick you up?"

"I'm sorry, John, I can't make it, but I would love to have

dinner this evening. A red flag went up in John's head. "Are you sure you can't make it for lunch?"

Lucy hesitated. "No, I am sorry, Niles wanted me there too but I have a meeting that was arranged months ago and the people I am meeting with have just flown in from the States. The restaurant is on Queen Elizabeth Ave. two blocks from my flat, do you need directions?"

"No I'll find it. I'll call you after lunch." John felt better after she told him Niles had invited her to.

John walked into the restaurant at 1 p.m. and asked the host for Niles table. As they approached he saw Niles was not alone. "John, I would like to introduce you to one of my partners, Ascot Chen."

CHAPTER 55
Green Island, Hong Kong

"Sir, I have some news from Vancouver."

Ian jumped up. "What is it, Lieutenant? Did Bradshaw get them?"

"No, sir, he missed them."

"Are you kidding me?" Ian scowled.

"No, sir, it appears they have left Vancouver but Bradshaw did find out that they are holding Canadian passports under the name of Mc Kenzie."

"Where did they get them?" Ian said angrily.

"I don't know, sir?"

Ian, now disgusted, said, "Okay, get maps and data in the briefing room now."

"Already done, sir."

"Good I'll meet you in there in five minutes."

The lieutenant left and Ian sat back in his chair. He was thinking to himself that he wanted this Yank dead. He had made a fool out of him, and although the worldwide Intelligence community is after this bastard every failure is being brought back to him personally. Ian knew that when he was made case coordinator he was the fall guy. If the Op was successful he would make general, but if it failed his career was ruined and the latter looked like the way it was going. He got up and headed for the briefing room.

Upon his arrival all five men stood up. "At ease," he quipped.

By his speech and demeanor everyone in the room knew he was angry and they all had the same feeling, they did not want to get in his sights. "All right, then, what do we have?"

"Well sir, Bradshaw reported that they sailed in a private yacht from Vancouver the day before he arrived. We have run computer scenarios and here's what we got. They could have sailed north to uninhabited parts of Canada or Alaska or South to Seattle, San Francisco or further south to LA or Mexico. All indications are they left in a hurry so they probably did not have provisions, which means they had to stop somewhere. We are checking with all the Harbormasters and ship chandlers on every possible route. We are also checking on all airports, private and commercial on the entire coast of North America, under the names of Moore and McKenzie."

"All right, let me know when you find them."

"Yes, sir."

Ian turned and as if almost an after thought he told the lieutenant to do another in-depth profile on John Moore. "I'll be in my quarters. Let me know the minute you hear anything and this time I' m going myself. Make all the arrangements and have everything ready on stand-by for me."

"Yes, sir."

Ian went back to his quarters and was trying to get a mental handle on this guy. He came out of no where, he seemed to be able to counter anything they threw at him, and he was better at evasion and hiding than anyone he'd ever seen.

Ian thought to himself, *Am I being set up? Is this guy CIA? He seems to have unlimited resources, where did he get those passports? Why have I been put in charge of this OP? Something stinks.* Just then, the lieutenant came knocked on the door. Ian yelled, "Enter!"

"Sir, we got them, they flew from Seattle to Sydney Australia using German passports four days ago. They switched passports with a German couple who fit their general description, but when the real German couple presented their passports they were arrested under the names John and Mary McKenzie It took a couple of days to straighten it out."

Ian jumped up and started to move. "Get me there now. You can brief me on the way."

CHAPTER 56
Sydney, Australia

John ran into the suite. "Rebecca," he called in a panic.

"What?" she replied. "John, what's wrong?"

He tried to compose himself. "Lucy's boyfriend is one of the people looking for us."

"What?" she said.

Rebecca was frozen in panic; she went into an almost catatonic state. John screamed, "Rebecca, snap out of it we have to move and quickly." Rebecca changed color and she fell forward, limp. He tried to collect his thoughts as he picked her up and put her on the bed. He looked around the room and found a map they had gotten when they checked in. They were staying outside of Port Stephens. As John studied the maps Rebecca started to stir.

"Are you all right?" John asked.

"I think so," she said in a slurred voice. She sat up and the color started to come back to her face. "Oh! John this will never be over," she said and started to cry.

"Get a hold of yourself," John said calmly, "we are going to get out of this and it will be some story to tell our grandchildren."

Rebecca smiled got up shakily and started to collect their things. John said calmly, "Just essentials, we're going kayaking."

He put everything he thought they would need in a heavy plastic waterproof bag including the laptop with all the names and e-mail addresses they had compiled over the last couple of days. As they were walking out he said, "Wait a minute, they know where we are now anyway." He picked up the phone and dialed. "Hello, Chung."

"Yeah, boss, what are you doing calling me here, are you crazy?"

"No, Chung, they know where we are so it doesn't really matter. Do you know anyone you can trust in the Chinese media?"

Chong hesitated for a moment, "Yeah, the guy from Yen Sun the Chinese paper run by their Public Security Bureau."

"Great. Do you have his e-mail address?"

"Yes I do, hold a moment; it's ykpoa@yensun.prc."

"Great, thanks, Chong. I'll call you at that special number at 11:00 a.m. sharp in three days."

"Okay I'll follow up with my friend to make sure he gets the e-mail and see what suggestions he might have."

"Okay, Chong, but be careful."

"Don't worry about me, boss, you're the one who has to be careful. Don't forget I have relatives here."

John laughed as he hung up. He turned to Rebecca. "Okay, walk down the beach in that direction and I'll meet you in about an hour."

"John, where are you going?" Rebecca asked.

"John, don't leave me alone."

"Don't worry," John replied. "I'm just going to get us a ride."

He watched Rebecca walk down the beach for a moment and then walked over to the hotel office and looked for the young guy who checked them in. "Hi!" John said to the young man. "Do you have an ocean-going Kayak that I can buy from you?"

The young man seemed to go deep into thought. "I have a tandem I use to teach people," he replied, "but I need that for work."

John pulled out five one hundred American dollars from his pocket and said, "Will this cover it?"

The young man took the money, "Sure, and then some."

"Okay," John said. He then reached back into his pocket and pulled out five more hundreds and held them out in front of the kid. "You don't remember me or the girl or the kayak, right."

The kid smiled and took the money from John's hand and said, "What girl, what kayak, and who are you?"

He pulled the kayak to the water and noticed a waterproof lock box built right in to a compartment in front of the front seat. He deposited his plastic bag and pushed into the water. As he rounded the point of the bay, he saw Rebecca in the distance. It took about fifteen more minutes to catch up to her. Rebecca looked at the kayak and said, "John, what the hell is this? How far are we going to get in this thing?"

"Far enough, my dear, now get in."

She got in and was surprised to see how comfortable it was and within minutes exhaustion and fear caught up to her and she fell dead asleep. John looked back and was happy she was sleeping; he couldn't deal with another situation with her passing out. He thought she was pretty tough, but everyone has a breaking point, and she had reached hers. He better get somewhere safe soon and finish this thing.

CHAPTER 57
Hong Kong

"Hello, Yao this is Chong. Did you get an e-mail from my boss?"

"Yeah! What the hell is this?"

Not wanting to discuss this on the phone, Chong said, "Let's get together and I'll fill you in."

Yao asked, "OK, when and where?"

"I'm going to be followed, so do you remember the place we used to go swimming when we were kids?"

"You mean behind—"

"Yes, that's the place. In one hour and make sure you're not followed."

"Mao wen ti, no problem." Chong wasn't worried; Yao was one of the best operatives China had in Hong Kong. Chong told his son to go over to his Uncle Pang and tell him to meet Chong at the tunnel entrance with a police car; he figured if the cops were looking for him it would be the best way to go. He left his flat and went to the roof. He looked around and it seemed everyone watching him was on the street. He walked over the rooftops and went out of a building around the corner and at the far end of his road. He walked to the curbside and immediately got into a cab. He stayed in the taxi until he saw his wife's brother in the police car and paid the driver and jumped out.

"Pang, did anyone see my son contact you?"

"No," he replied, "where are we going?"

Chong instructed him, "Go through the tunnel and let's make sure we're not being followed."

They pulled up and stopped first on Nathan Road and circled a few times and than stopped again on Jordan Road. "No one is following," Pang said.

"Okay, go to Ky Yu Mon right behind the Green Island Cement Company."

Pang asked, "What the hell are you doing there?"

"Don't ask, the less you know the better."

Pang was silent for the rest of the trip. Chong told him to stop a block before the cement factory and got out. The area was relatively deserted and he stepped into a doorway and watched for several minutes until he was certain he wasn't being followed. When he got out to the old pier Yao was already there.

"Chong, good to see you."

"You too, Yao, it's been a long time. How's everything going with the communists?" They both laughed.

"Chong is this is for real?" Yao asked.

"Yeah, and my boss is right in the middle of it. He's a good man, Yao, what can we do for him?"

"If this is for real, we can pull him in."

"Yao, your government is probably in this as well." Yao had a curious look on his face. "Good, if we go public first we can point fingers and it won't come back to us." They laughed again. "I'm going to have to get clearance from Beijing for something like this, but it shouldn't take to long."

Chong told him, "Okay, but be careful; everyone and his brother are trying to get this info."

"I will. How can I contact you?"

"You can't. I'll have to contact you tomorrow at 10:00 a.m. I'll call you at the desk of the Peninsula."

Yao said, "Okay, good choice. I'll talk to you then." He turned and walked away. Chong took a taxi to Saikung in the New Territories and visited an old friend who had a fishing boat there. He couldn't sleep even with the two bottles of Moitai he consumed.

CHAPTER 58
Beijing, The People's Republic of China

"Minister, I have some information we should review right away." Minister Ma looked up at the general. She was an ugly woman by any standard, built like a brick, but she was the head of the PSB, and when she was upset it was serious.

"All right, will everyone excuse us please?" She watched the small group get up and leave immediately, and when the door closed behind the last one she said, "Minister, this just came in from Hong Kong and it is proof that corruption reaches the highest levels of our government."

The minister gasped. "What?"

"This is a list of all the activities for the past year with the Liddo group and our officials, you included, sir."

The minister went pale. "Let me see it." As he went over the information on the disc, he asked, "Has anyone else seen this."

"Just the man who sent it and me," she replied.

The minister simply said, "Good."

She replied, "Our man in Hong Kong, the one who sent it, had a good idea."

The minister seemed impatient. "Well, what was it?"

"If we go public with this and point the finger at all the western countries, it gives us a free out."

The minister looked at her and said, "Yes, this could be the answer." He thought to himself, *Why not we have already gotten the missile technology from the US and politically it would be very good timing to put the US on the defensive and have them stop this human rights BS.*

He looked at the general again and said, "Let's proceed, but keep Liddo's name out of it. We need them from time to time."

CHAPTER 59
Hong Kong

Chong called at exactly 10:00 a.m., and Yao was at the reception desk to answer. Yao said, "Lets bring them in. Where are they?"

"In Australia," was Chong's response.

"Where? Australia?"

"Yes, now what should they do?"

Yao hesitated and then said, "Have them contact a Mr. Li Fan Quai at our consulate in Brisbane; they will make all arrangements there."

Chong replied, "Okay, but can you put me up until this is over I have to have the ability to move around and they have a heavy net out for me."

"Sure you can use one of our safe houses in Kowloon."

CHAPTER 60
Sydney, Australia

John had been paddling for almost four hours due south along the coast. He turned to Rebecca and said, "We'll pull in when it starts to get dark." Rebecca asked if he wanted her to paddle for a while but John said no he had a rhythm going and he did not want to break it. John was surprised how fast they were moving; he estimated they had already traveled about a hundred kilometers, and that meant they were going at a good fifteen knots. He knew he had lost some time, as they had to go out away from the shoreline from time to time due to heavy surf.

I would like to come back here after everything settles down. He had paddled for about nine hours when he saw a small fishing town and decided to pull in for the night. He pulled into a small beach about 500 yards from the edge of town and covered the kayak with some branches and debris he found on the beach.

They were both tired and were glad to see a sign, which read "The prettiest cottages in Kiama." The sign didn't lie. They were shown a nice cottage right on the beach with a beautiful view. "This is great," John said to the pleasant woman who showed them the cottage. "We'll take it."

"Americans, are ya?" she asked.

"Yes," John said, "and we've been traveling all day and we're tired and hungry. Is there somewhere to get something to eat?"

"What would you like?" she asked.

"Anything hot, and a lot of it," John answered.

The woman said, "Yanks," as she shook her head and laughed. "I'll bring you some dinner and there are drinks in the mini-fridge."

Rebecca was giving John a rub down when the woman arrived with the food. "This looks fantastic," John said, "what do I owe you?"

"Twenty dollars Australian," the woman said. John paid and as soon as she left they both dove for the food.

"I'm famished," said Rebecca, pushing the food in her mouth. John didn't say a word; he just ate. After dinner he collapsed on the bed. He was feeling muscles he didn't even know he had, and within minutes he was asleep.

He was wakened by the sound of Rebecca in the shower. He shook the sleep out of his head and walked over to the window. It was beautiful. Rebecca walked out of the bathroom drying herself with a towel and John thought she was more beautiful than the scenery.

After John took a hot shower they went out for a walk and found a little café where they had a big breakfast. In the center of town was a fisherman's wharf, and John found a shop where he could buy some charts. They looked around town for a little while and went back to the cottage. John studied the charts and decided to go to Bateman Bay at the mouth of the Clyde River. They could paddle up the Clyde to Nelligen, a town so far out of the way they should be safe for a while. They said their goodbyes to the woman who owned the cottage and walked back to the kayak. John figured tonight he should make Bawley Point. He was happy with their progress. He had found a tidal stream, which was about a half a mile from shore, and it allowed him to travel at about 25 knots.

They pulled into Bawley point at 8:15 in the evening, a full two hours ahead of schedule. It took them no time to find a place to stay, and the desk clerk suggested a restaurant right across the road. After a good meal, they went back to the room and rested. It started out by Rebecca giving him a rub down but ended up in them making love through most of the night.

It was after ten in the morning when they woke up and John immediately checked the charts as Rebecca showered. When she came out of the shower John told her they had to leave shortly as he arranged to call Chong today at 11:00 a.m., which was in twelve minutes. John was sore and figured he would stop today in Duras just north of Batemans Bay.

He dialed the number at precisely 11:00 a.m. As he dialed, he realized that he had forgotten about the time change, but just as he was about to panic Chong answered. "Boss, I have great news for you: the Chinese have offered you protection and they are going to release the news."

John was ecstatic "That's great news, Chong. What do we have to do."

"You have to get to Mr. Li Fan Quai at the Chinese Consulate in Brisbane, here is the number."

John wrote the number down and thanked Chong for everything.

"No matter, boss. I'll see you soon."

John called the number and it seemed as if Mr. Li was waiting for his call. "Mr. Moore, it is so good to hear your voice. With all the people who are after you I was afraid you were not going to make it. Where are you now?"

"I'm safe," John replied. "How can I get to you?"

"Are you in Brisbane?" Mr. Li asked.

"No" John answered.

"Can you fly here?" Yes was the answer. "Take a private plane to Brisbane airport we will have a car waiting for you on the tarmac. How long will it take you to get here?"

"We can be there at mid-night tonight," John answered.

"Fine. I will arrange everything. Mr. Moore, one more thing. I will be there next to the car, and I'll be wearing a cap. If it's blue, everything is fine, but if it is red don't get off the plane."

"Understood," John said. He hung up and went to the hotel. He told Rebecca they would be safe soon.

They would kayak to Batemans Bay and take a plane to Brisbane, where the Chinese would give them asylum. It was ten past midnight when the plane landed and John could see the Chinese consul's limo from the window. He told the pilot to taxi over to it as close as he could. Before opening the door he looked out again and there was Mr. Li wearing a blue baseball hat. An enormous relief came over him. They were safe.

CHAPTER 61
Sydney, Australia

Just as his plane landed, Ian got a call on his emergency line. "Ian Grant here," he answered. His face became contorted. "What do you mean stand down? I almost have them…Yes, sir." Ian hung up and threw the phone into the bulkhead of the plane. He snarled at his aide, "We're going back to Hong Kong now. Make arrangements for me to go to London when we get back." Ian spent the rest of the flight anticipating the worst.

CHAPTER 62
Beijing, The People's Republic of China

John and Rebecca sat in the living room of a government guesthouse on the grounds of the Forbidden City. They were intently watching CNN on the TV. The announcer began by saying that "China announced today that it has uncovered corruption on an international scale so unprecedented that it has the implications of bringing down several Western governments, including the US. The scope of the corruption seems to cover police, intelligence agencies and high-level government officials from several governments. The American and a Hong Kong policewoman who handed over the information are now under the protection of the Peoples Republic. A summit meeting is already being planned in Beijing where sources say China will meet representatives from each nation to brief them individually on the information as not to disrupt the world economy, more to follow as it unfolds. On the US front John Wimple died today of a heart attack in his cell in the Federal Prison at Arlington. Mr. Wimple was serving an undefined term for refusing to answer questions relating to the ongoing investigation of the president. While he was in prison he had been paid $400,000 in consulting fees from the Liddo Group of Memphis, Tennessee, that is now being looked into by the office of the special prosecutor and as such no details of the investigation are forthcoming."

John looked over at Rebecca and smiled. "It's over; we can go home," said Rebecca.

"Not just yet," John replied. "It will take a while to sort this out, and Minister Ma told me today that our safety was going to be a negotiating point in their upcoming talks with the West. We are going to be here for a while, and I was hoping to go up and visit Father Paul."

Rebecca lit up, "John, that would be brilliant. I would like to thank him for all his kindness."

"All right then. Minister Ma asked if we would stay put until after the summit. He said it would be easier to protect us if we stayed here until then."

During the next week John and Rebecca relaxed and really enjoyed themselves. After dinner on Saturday night they walked through the garden in the residence area of the Forbidden City. John asked Rebecca to sit down on a bench positioned off the walk so it was very private.

He proposed.

Rebecca jumped up and threw her arms around him and said, "John, you have not only saved my life, you have made me the happiest woman in the world. Yes I'll marry you."

They returned to their quarters and made love well into the morning. It was the last day of the summit and John and Rebecca flipped back and forth from CNN to BBC. Arrests were being made all over the world and they were astonished to see the face of Ian Grant. The commentator was saying that Ian, while being stationed in Hong Kong, fell in with the triads and was the ringleader of an entire group of police inspectors and government officials. Six inspectors were being recalled to London including the head of the ICAC. Ian Grant had pleaded guilty to all counts including murder; he waved his right to trial and was to be hanged the next day in an undisclosed military base outside of London.

Back on CNN, the report was that a national investigation was under way and already over three hundred indictments had been handed down. The Speaker of the House had resigned after it was made public that he had a long-time affair. It was not clear if he was involved with any of the corruption that had been uncovered. The man went on to say, "He's at it again, the president has just received summonses from three women, all whom are claiming to have had sexual relations with that man." He continued with what almost seemed as an after thought.

"He's something else, isn't he?"

John looked at Rebecca and said, "It's over. Where do you want to go on your honeymoon?"

Rebecca said quickly, "Home to Hong Kong."

John held out his hands to embrace her, and as she leaned over to kiss him there was a crashing sound.

The bullet went through her head covering John with blood and bone fragments. John fell off the couch and kneeled at her lifeless side. He screamed a long horrifying silent scream.

After her body was removed from the room and all of the Chinese police and military people had left John sat alone, more alone than he had ever been before, when suddenly the phone rang. Still in shock he involuntarily picked up the phone.

Before he could say hello the voice on the other end said, "It's over. She paid for what she did to us. It was a minor annoyance actually. You are to forget everything that has happened. You are free to go."

He stared into the phone and slowly began to understand. He was so outraged by this that the phone broke apart in his hand. He stood there motionless for a long time, then collapsed on the floor. The man on the other end of the phone made a mental note to call his subsidiary in China and have them order another twenty boats; this had actually turned into a very profitable business.

"John, John," he heard the voice say. He opened his eyes, and there was Chong. John wept uncontrollably and Chong held him in his arms like a child. Chong whispered to him, "It's over. You can go home."

John thought that was the last thing he had said to Rebecca.